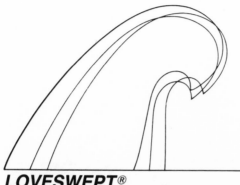

LOVESWEPT®

Virginia Lynn

Cutter's Woman

DOUBLEDAY

NEW YORK • LONDON • TORONTO • SYDNEY • AUCKLAND

L OVESWEPT ®

PUBLISHED BY DOUBLEDAY
a division of Bantam Doubleday Dell Publishing Group, Inc.
666 Fifth Avenue, New York, New York 10103

DOUBLEDAY and the portrayal of an anchor with a dolphin,
and the word LOVESWEPT and the portrayal of the wave device
are trademarks of Doubleday, a division of
Bantam Doubleday Dell Publishing Group, Inc.

Library of Congress Cataloging-in-Publication Data
Lynn, Virginia.
   Cutter's woman / Virginia Lynn.
      p.   cm.
   I. Title.
PS3562.Y44483C88   1991
813'.54—dc20   90-20348
                                              CIP

ISBN 0-385-41819-1

Dedicated to JoAnn Harding—neighbor, friend, confidante, and encouraging fan. I hope you know how much your friendship has meant to me. . . .

Cutter's Woman

One

Tombstone, Arizona Territory
April 28, 1881

Walking briskly down Tombstone's wooden sidewalk, J. Whitney Bradford became aware of sidelong glances as well as a few souls rude enough to gawk. Whitney knew the attention was neither for J. Whitney Bradford the author, whose sensational novels sold to a public avid for tales of the Wild West, nor for J. Whitney Bradford, pampered only daughter of prominent New York newspaper editor Morgan Bradford. No, the stares were all for J. Whitney Bradford the woman, whose low-cut scarlet gown with its short puffed sleeves and scant petticoats was the latest Paris fashion but woefully out of place in Arizona, where the norm was plain cotton dresses with necklines up to the chin despite the searing heat.

Tossing her silver-blond hair and carrying her tall, lush body—shown to perfection by the dress—proudly, Whitney marched purposefully toward the Russ House, casting a glacial look from her amber cat's eyes on any man impertinent enough to whistle or call out to her. She reached the hotel at last, unmolested, but secretly nettled that these western ruffians failed to recognize her gentility. In her native New York City, Whitney was welcome in the very best society, and many an estimable bachelor had sought her hand; but the marriage her well-meaning father had arranged for her when she was eighteen had proved such a disaster that when Whitney found herself suddenly widowed two years later, she had resumed her maiden name as if Mrs. Nathan Truesdale had never existed. She had vowed then never to remarry, and at twenty-four, she held fast to that vow.

And a good thing she hadn't wed again, thought Whitney, crossing the rather dingy lobby of the hotel, for no husband would have assented to his wife's traveling to the untamed territory of Arizona accompanied only by a lady's maid, and then proceeding unescorted to an interview with a half-Apache renegade outlaw in his hotel room. Indeed, her father had in vain exhorted the daughter he'd raised alone after her mother died in childbirth to defer her journey for a few months till he could accompany her. Morgan Bradford was unswayed by her argument that she needed to commit Cutter's story to paper before he should engage in one shootout too many, for he was the prototype of the larger-than-life hero she hoped would elevate her fiction from dimestore novels, like the fourteen she had already written, to literary epics that might be compared by the critics to Fenimore Cooper's Leatherstocking Tales.

Her determination to interview Cutter, who had agreed by telegram to meet with her for the offered remuneration of one thousand dollars, had not been deflected by her father's rumblings, or by the qualms of her maid, Mary Walton, when Whitney had insisted on leaving Mary in their own hotel a few blocks away and keeping her appointment with the outlaw alone. Her one concession to the risks she was taking was to pack a small derringer in her reticule, but she very much doubted she would have occasion to use it.

"So you're the . . . party . . . Cutter's been expectin'?" the desk clerk asked when she explained she had an appointment with Mr. Cutter and asked his room number. "That'll be Room 203, top of the steps and all the way to the left." Whitney was puzzled when he muttered, "They're bringin' in a better class now," but she didn't linger to clarify what he'd meant.

Ascending the stairs to the second floor, she lifted her skirts so they wouldn't drag across the floor and grow soiled. Her footsteps were padded by a well-worn carpet as she traversed the hallway lit by a faintly flickering gas lamp at the far end. It was shadowed and dim, and she felt a moment's uneasiness that she quickly dispelled with the reminder that she was a writer intent on breaking new ground.

Inhaling deeply as she arrived at the door bearing the numbers two and zero, Whitney paused. The last number was missing. But the door next to it was 201, so she must have had the right room. She rapped sharply with a gloved hand. The door immediately swung open; then she was pulled into the room by a firm hand, and the door slammed shut behind her.

It took an instant for Whitney to register that she had been unceremoniously yanked into a room by a total stranger. Then, chin lifted indignantly, she glared at the man who still held her by one arm. She was struck with the disturbing thought that the man had an extremely handsome face with clearly defined and unmistakably virile features. She had a brief impression of towering height, hair so black as to be almost blue, and sensually lidded eyes that were gazing back at her with impudent green lights. His voice was lazy and deep as he told her, "You're late and the water's cold."

Whitney's first impulse was to make an angry denial. But then, uncharacteristically, she could not utter a word. Her legs grew weak, and she drew in her breath in a short gasp.

The man gazing at her with an ironically lifted brow was completely, totally, magnificently . . . naked.

She swallowed hard and emitted a strangled gasp. She tried again. Another unintelligible sound, and now the man was cocking his dark, wet head to one side and staring at her with thoughtful, narrowed eyes, a most unsettling gaze that made her feel as if *she* were the one as naked as the day she'd been born. Clearly, she'd blundered into the wrong room, yet she stood mesmerized, as if rooted to the spot.

Whitney was vaguely aware that a high-backed tub sat in one corner of the room, and that wet footprints led from tub to door, explaining the man's startling state of undress. But a towel would have done a lot to hide the more private areas of his body, she thought dimly, and wondered why he had not thought of it. Instead, he stood in a sort of proud, pagan nudity that was startling and fascinating at the same time. He seemed completely unselfconscious about his mode of dress—or undress. And he was frowning at her as though it were *she* who had committed some social folly!

As if drawn by a powerful magnet, her gaze lowered, and she found herself staring at him in morbid fascination, gazing at the interesting planes of his broad chest and the hard ridges of muscle on his flat stomach. His skin was dark, almost a copper tint, she noticed with detachment, as if he spent a great deal of time in the sun. And she couldn't help but notice that the wide expanse of lean, rippling flesh on his body flowed smoothly in a unique blend of sinew and bone that was intimidating without being Herculean. His long legs were superbly made, muscled without being knotty.

Inexorably, almost against her will, her gaze focused, and Whitney felt a burning sensation begin to build up in her chest. Her lungs expanded, and expanded some more, and her face felt as if it were on fire, but her eyes still lingered on that shadowy, intimate area that was intriguing and forbidden.

"Like what you see?" the suggestive, amused voice drawled, whipping her back to reality in an instant.

Realizing that she had been staring at the more personal attributes of his hard-muscled body, she jerked her eyes up when he spoke, her flawless complexion pink with humiliation.

"Well?" the naked man asked peremptorily in a tone that immediately set Whitney's teeth on edge. His damp fingers tightened ever so slightly on her arm, and she glanced down at his hand, still unable to force out a single syllable. Hearing his soft laughter, Whitney dragged her eyes back to his face. Deep grooves bracketed the erotically curved lips; high cheekbones slashed down at harsh, rugged angles, and a fine, thin nose flared slightly, as if he were a wild beast finding easy prey. Whitney shuddered at the unbidden simile, and his next words showed that he must have mistaken her reaction.

"This is better than I expected," the cool, remotely amused voice said in answer to his own question. "A woman who doesn't talk." His movements were so slow as to be almost languid, yet filled with a firm purpose. Distractedly noting that the mobile lips were slanted in a sensual smile, Whitney had no time to recoil before he was bringing her close to him, her lax body forcibly pressed against his hard frame. Then his searing mouth descended upon her half-parted lips, preventing her from saying anything.

Something in her rebelled at his easy assumption she could be handled, summoning a latent response that had been smothered—first by shock, then by an emotion she couldn't pause to define—and Whitney opened her mouth to protest. That was a definite mistake.

Immediately, his tongue slipped between the unguarded barrier of her lips, exploring, plundering, burning into her senses with a jolt that ripped down the length of her spine. Unaccountably Whitney found her body incapable of obeying her mental command. Instead, she vibrated with a physical, sensual response, something so foreign as to remove any effort at thinking. All she could do was feel. His demanding tongue banished her weak attempt at resistance as he took command of her mouth, and Whitney was much too aware of the man's corded arms pressing her body tightly against his. The searing force of his kiss was tilting her head back at an awkward angle, and she felt his arms coil like steel bands around her back to pull her even harder against him.

When his mouth moved in rhythmic brushes against her stunned lips, then against the tip of her nose, trailing a damp path of fire over her parched, burning skin, Whitney made a strangled noise in the back of her throat that he chose to ignore. This was insane! Why was she allowing this naked stranger to maul her? She had to force him away from her, had to force his hard male body away from her strangely aching curves.

But—shockingly—his naked embrace had sparked something inside her, some unfamiliar yearning that made her relax into him instead of push him away, lean so close she could feel the imprint of his body against hers through the thin material of her skirts. It was maddening, it was frightening, it was . . . intriguing.

No one had ever kissed her like this man was doing, ruthlessly, almost savagely, heedless of her faint, weak protest or the laxness of her muscles. Didn't he realize—or care—that she wasn't willing?

Staring at him through the quivering line of her lashes, Whitney could see that his eyes were closed, and instinctively, she closed hers again, shutting out the sight of his face. His broad palms were splayed across the small of her back, and she could feel the strong, steady thud of his heart against her breast.

Whitney felt as if she had been plunged into a lake of fire. And for the very life of her, she could not imagine why she was not struggling and kicking and screaming and firing her tiny derringer at this bold seducer.

Something clicked in the back of her brain, a tiny part of her whispered that she had never experienced such a raw, intense visceral reaction in an embrace. And it was true. Her pulses were racing, and her breath was coming in short, labored gasps as her heart pumped madly to keep up with the fevered impulses racking her body. Had she been affected by the heat in this wretched territory? By all rights, she should have put a neat round hole in this impudent devil by now, yet she still hung loosely in his arms, allowing him liberties not even Nathan had enjoyed. . . .

Jerking free at the memory of her late husband, Whitney took a step back, pressing her quivering body against the closed door of the small hotel room. She stared at her attacker with wide, tawny eyes, poised between fury and the unsettling emotions pounding through her.

The man she now mentally referred to as the Seducer gazed back at her with calm detachment. He rested his hands on the blunt angle of his hips, and she resisted the urge to allow her gaze to follow. Every corpuscle of her being shrieked danger, and she took a deep, steadying breath before demanding: "What do you think you are doing?"

The Seducer allowed her words to hang unanswered for a moment, gazing at her steadily with an uplifted brow, mocking lights dancing in his wicked green eyes, and instead of castigating him further, Whitney had the distracted thought that his eyelashes were ridiculously long to belong to a man. Then he gave a casual shrug of his broad shoulders and said, "Doing what feels good, I guess. Why?"

Why? The single word danced about in a brain remarkably empty of an appropriate reply. Why indeed? *Why* stop him when she hadn't wanted to? *Why* didn't she want that dizzying, dangerous feeling to stop at all? It occurred to her that it was an interesting puzzle, and her inquisitive writer's nature began to assert itself, leaving the anger behind.

"It does feel good, doesn't it?" she said in a slow, thoughtful tone. "How curious. I'd never expected it to at all. It explains a great deal that has been puzzling me for some time."

The Seducer looked at her through narrowed eyes. "I'm thrilled to hear it," he said finally, though he didn't sound the least bit thrilled. More cynically amused than thrilled, she thought, and shrugged as a novel idea struck her.

"Kiss me again," she blurted out. She felt a faint tremor of shock at her bold request, but reminded herself she was doing this for her art, to be able to write of passion convincingly for a change.

The Seducer didn't move, just gazed at her for a long moment, and Whitney couldn't read his reaction. Then he smiled, a brief quirk of his lips in a sardonic slant that simultaneously conveyed amusement and insult.

His insolent gaze pricked at her, but she had gone too far to back down now, so she repeated more sharply, "Kiss me again! The way you did before. It was interesting."

Reaching around her, the Seducer curled his hand over the doorknob and gave it a quick twist, grabbing her by the arm as he did so.

In a flat tone that held no hint of his former amusement, he said, "*I* sent for *you*, and it wasn't to play games. Sex, straight and simple, that's all. No coy chatter. And I certainly didn't expect some female with a whiplash in her voice to come up here and start ordering me around. Not unless you're paying better than I am, and I doubt that."

More embarrassed than shocked by his blunt language, Whitney used her coldest, most imperious tone. "Sir, I doubt seriously if you know to whom you are speaking, or—"

That was as far as she got. The Seducer gave her a polite smile, yanked open the door, and thrust her outside into the dim hallway. "Tell Nellie I'm taking my business elsewhere," he said before he slammed the door shut in her face. Whitney blinked in shock. *Nellie?*

It took a few minutes for everything to register. She stood in the hallway for a long moment, gripping her reticule in one hand and trying to recover her former composure. The combination of the unusual, devastating heat and exhaustion had caused her to go insane. Had she really just asked a man—a naked stranger—to kiss her again? She had, and as the full impact of what she had done hit her, she prayed sincerely that she never had to face him again. It would be too humiliating. Hopefully he was just a nameless drifter passing through Tombstone, and would be on his way the next day.

"Well!" she muttered, gathering up the shreds of her composure. "That was a very interesting confrontation, if a bit unnerving." What would she do now? She was obviously in no condition to meet the outlaw Cutter and conduct an interview, not after stumbling into the wrong room and discovering more about herself than she ever wanted to know. No, she would retreat to her hotel, put up her feet, and have Mary bring her a cool drink. And she would never, *ever* tell anyone how low she had sunk this day.

But she would most certainly inform the hotel management about their shoddy appointments, and insist that they place the proper numbers on each door in their establishment. It was a disgrace to neglect the upkeep of a public lodging!

Straightening her spine and rearranging her slightly damp, wrinkled skirts, Whitney marched firmly down the hall, her composure restored. She was already on her way to pushing what had just happened to the very recesses of her mind.

Tomorrow this incident would not even be a vague memory.

Two

"Will there be anything else, Miss Whitney?" Mary stared down at her mistress with a slight frown. The usually unflappable Whitney had come back from her short interview inexplicably flustered and tersely requested something to drink, preferably something quite *strong*. Now she waved one hand in dismissal.

"No, I am quite all right now. Brandy was just the thing. I prefer solitude for the remainder of the evening, please. You did send that message to his hotel?"

Mary nodded. "Yes, I did. It's a shame you missed Mr. Cutter today. But I sent a telegram, so he'll expect you tomorrow in the lobby. If it weren't convenient, I'm sure he'd have sent a reply."

Whitney nodded vaguely. "Tomorrow morning will be a better time anyway," she murmured. "I'll be fresh then."

Shifting position, she let her head lie back on the high curve of her chair and rearranged the folds of the light blanket spread over her legs. The mellow brandy had immediately warmed her stomach, but had taken several minutes to relax the tense muscles in her body.

Whitney didn't hear Mary slip out the door to go to her adjoining room. She sat mulling over the things she would say to Cutter when she finally met him. If he was cooperative, so much the better; but she was fully prepared to deal with an uncooperative subject. She'd done so before, and knew a few tricks that would coax out the information she sought.

Tapping a well-manicured fingernail against her small, rounded chin, Whitney's gold eyes narrowed in thought. What angle could she use to make this novel transcend the genre of potboiler? Her protagonist's dual loyalties, with one foot in the white man's world and one in the Indian's, would supply a natural conflict. She hoped to draw Cutter as an American Childe Harold, with elements of Cooper's Natty Bumppo and Chingachgook as well. But she needed another angle. After all, hadn't there been a few novels written that were sympathetic to the Indian cause? Yet those had been largely rejected by the critics because of the violent conflicts still raging in the territories. She would have to find some other hook for her new work.

Well, she decided after several minutes of thought, an idea would probably come to her once she was in a discussion with Cutter.

"If he's able to express himself intelligibly," she muttered. What if he wasn't? What if he was inarticulate, a true savage, hardly able to convey his thoughts, much less discuss abstract ideas?

"Don't project problems," she scolded herself firmly, and settled back into the plump cushions of the lounge. After all, he had read her telegrams, so he wasn't illiterate. He need only supply her with the facts of his life; she would supply the eloquence and color herself.

Cutter looked at his friend Téjas with his brows arched in disbelief. "You did *what*?"

The slender Mexican gave a half shrug and placating smile, sliding a glance around the crowded bar as he did. "I did it for you, amigo."

"The hell you did! You did it for the money!"

Another shrug and a weak grin. "*Sí*, maybe I thought of that too—*muy poco!*"

"Very little, my ass," Cutter said coldly. "You knew I would never agree to something like this. It's an invasion of my privacy. And besides, these dime novelists are interested only in extorting spurious emotions to sell their books. And I'm not about to cooperate, Téjas. Count me out."

As he stood up, his lean frame towering over the much shorter Mexican, Téjas stood up, too, his voice urgent. "But it is so much money, *compadre*! A thousand dollars! And only for a few minutes talk. You can say what you want to say and leave out what you don't want to say—it sounds too easy to be true! This *Norteamericano* must be loco, heh?"

"No, you're the one who's loco." Cutter faced Téjas with hard, glittering eyes. "There's no such thing as easy money. You ought to know that."

Grasping at a feeble straw, Téjas protested. "But look here, at the telegram. All this foolish man wants is information so he can write a story and permission to use your name. The newspapers freely use your name all the time, and you get not one single peso! Think of it—one thousand dollars, buying acres of land to belong to the Apache, land no one can take away. . . ."

Cutter's glance was sardonic. "The Apache have that now, remember? The San Carlos Reservation."

"*Sí*, and you know how well they live." Téjas shrugged. "Maybe you could change that a little, no?"

"You know the reason we came to Tombstone. We already have a plan to change the conditions at San Carlos."

"And a thousand dollars would not help?"

Shaking his dark head, Cutter sat back down in his chair, then looked at Téjas with a slight smile. "You've been working hard on this, haven't you?"

"Maybe I'm nervous about the other, amigo. I do not like the thought of looking over my shoulder the rest of my life, not when we can accomplish the same thing by talking a little to some city man with more money than sense."

Tilting the chair on its back two legs, Cutter nodded slowly. "I admit it would simplify things, but Lone Wolf would be very disappointed. He enjoys irritating the army."

"He will find other ways to do that," Téjas said, and they both laughed.

A faint smile lingered on Cutter's mouth. "I'll think about it" was all he said, but Téjas took it as a yes, and grinned widely.

"Excellent! I knew you would see the wisdom in my plan, amigo, and now that you have—"

"Téjas—I said I'd think about it. That's all. I haven't even met this New York gentleman who wants to give me a lot of money for making up lies, so don't count on anything yet."

"Ah, you will do it." Téjas grinned again. "I know you will. One thousand dollars is *mucho dinero!*"

"Right now, ten dollars is *mucho dinero,*" Cutter countered.

"Not for the famous—or should I say infamous?—gunman known as Cutter! No, amigo, no one would believe that you did not have much money in your pockets from the banks you surely robbed, or—"

"Or the stagecoaches I held up at gunpoint?" Cutter gave a wry shake of his head and tossed a few coins on the tabletop. "There are times I almost wish I were as bad as my reputation, Téjas. Maybe then I'd have enough money to leave Arizona Territory."

Téjas gave him a shrewd glance. "But you would not leave even if you had more money than Jay Gould, amigo."

Shrugging slightly, Cutter rose and walked across the sawdust-covered floor, pushed through the double doors, and stepped out into the dark, dusty street. All up and down the main street of Tombstone, dark shadows wavered in eerie patterns, light thrown through the windows by gas lamps and lanterns. The air was thick with shrill laughter, tinny tunes, and an occasional shout. A normal night in the brawling town of Tombstone.

Cutter struck a match to light his thin cigarillo, and the brief flare illuminated his face for an instant. The familiar restlessness was etched into his features, the forces driving him suddenly strong. He swore softly, but when Téjas came up behind him, Cutter's face wore its customary impassivity.

"You are not angry, amigo?" the Mexican asked, and Cutter shook his head.

"Why should I be? You're just trying to make us some money, no matter how stupidly you go about it."

"Ah, just what I like to hear, amigo—compliments!"

"If you want compliments, you'd better meet your lady friend down at the Bird Cage" was Cutter's dry response.

Téjas laughed, and his dark eyes twinkled slyly. "And there is a lady there who always asks about you. . . ."

"Not tonight, Téjas. Not interested. Especially not after the . . . lady . . . I just threw out of my room."

Putting a companionable arm around Cutter's shoulders, Téjas steered him toward the other end of town, his voice faintly incredulous. "You threw out a woman? She must have been very ugly indeed!"

"Actually," Cutter said with a wide grin, "she was probably the best-looking female I've seen in a long time."

Téjas brows flew up in surprise. "*Ay di mi! Por favor*, amigo, tell me about this beauty you were foolish enough to throw away. We can console ourselves with a little beer. And then we can remind ourselves that woman troubles are so petty. . . ."

But the following morning when J. Whitney Bradford strolled regally into the Russ House lobby to meet the infamous Cutter,

Téjas was to amend his hasty observation. Perhaps woman troubles could be a bit more inconvenient than he had first considered.

At exactly nine A.M. Cutter slouched lazily in a high-backed chair, one leg propped across his knee, his fingers drumming on the wooden arm as he waited impatiently for the man Téjas claimed would pay them a thousand dollars for light conversation and tall tales. He wasn't comfortable about being there, and shifted position, recrossing his long legs.

It was the talking that made him nervous, the peeling away of the layers of protection he'd built year after year. He didn't want any chink in that wall he'd carefully erected around himself—his fierce reputation stalled many a too-hasty youth from drawing on him, and allowed him to avoid confrontations. The bad side of that coin was knowing that there were those who sought out men with such a name in an effort to magnify their own. Not Cutter. He was willing to leave well enough alone, and not enlarge his already exaggerated notoriety.

Cutter's dark face and well-defined features betrayed none of his impatience as he glanced casually toward the hotel doors. He didn't consider for one moment that the offer was as good as it sounded.

Fighting his restlessness, Cutter gazed at the rather stark interior of the hotel, then flicked a glance to Téjas, who was watching the entrance. A novelist. Above all inclinations to the contrary, he had agreed to be interviewed by a New York novelist who'd probably never seen a cow unless it was already sliced and on a plate. And now he sat here at nine o'clock in the morning waiting for some fancily dressed man in spats and patent-leather shoes, feeling like ten different kinds of a fool.

Cutter slumped a little lower in the uncomfortable horsehide and oak chair. He'd seen the way certain novelists portrayed the characters in their books, drawing crude, overblown word-portraits that caricatured a man, making him more—or less—that what he was. Take Billy Bonney. The eastern writers had had a field day with him, glamorizing the exploits of a young man who had rarely actually faced an opponent in a duel. Bonney preferred shooting from behind cover, or hitting a man in the back, yet the papers and novellas made him sound like a daring outlaw who could outshoot a dozen men and emerge unscathed. Cutter's mouth curled. Billy the Kid was dead on his feet and didn't know it. Too many men were gunning for him, and it was just a matter of time.

Now he was volunteering to let his life be distorted too, Cutter thought with another flash of irritation. He must be crazy to have let Téjas talk him into meeting Bradford.

Cutter looked up at Téjas, who was pacing between him and the lobby desk. "Bradford is late."

Téjas paused, frowning down at Cutter. "His message said nine o'clock, and there is still a minute to go—aha! That must be Bradford now. . . ."

The double doors to the hotel lobby swung open, and a portly man with a leather satchel stood briefly outlined against the bright morning light. He was holding open one of the doors for a woman to pass through. Téjas had his eyes on the man in the tight-fitting suit, while Cutter was staring narrowly at the woman attired in a stylish dress and a hat bristling with expensive feathers.

Cutter didn't move. He watched as Téjas approached the man, but his attention was on the woman. It was the same female who had come to his room, the chatty whore who had so irritated him with her imperious manner. What was a woman like that doing up so early? he mused, then answered his own question. Lack of business, probably.

When the woman approached the front desk, still not having noticed Cutter slouched in the lobby chair, he smiled to himself. Even from the back she looked good, her slender waist bracketed by curves in all the right places. Too bad she gave herself airs. A notebook of sorts was cradled under one arm, and she carried it as if it were important. Her hair was much lighter than he remembered, pulled back from her face and tucked beneath the curved brim of her hat. It was a style few could wear becomingly, but seemed to suit her. As she conversed with the desk clerk, Cutter tugged the brim of his hat lower over his eyes to shade his face. No sense in provoking another incident. He had enough on his mind.

While Cutter tried to avoid being noticed, J. Whitney Bradford was asking the desk clerk to point him out to her. The clerk pointed an obliging finger, Whitney turned, saw Cutter, and froze. Her normally reserved features dissolved into astonishment and dismay before she managed to calm her face back into a carefully blank mask.

The Seducer! Oh, no! was all she could think. She was momentarily at a loss. All her wits fled her, and she was paralyzed as the sharp memory of the previous day flooded back with blinding clarity—his broad chest, the smooth knotting of his muscles, the dark, supple skin, the hard, naked angles and planes . . .

Whitney hesitated, gazing at Cutter as if he were a specimen beneath an entomologist's glass, wondering if she should pursue the interview. As quickly as that thought flicked through her mind came another—why not? Just because he had been rude, crude, and supercilious did not mean that she could not get a decent interview. She had not come all this way simply to be put off by a man she had been unfortunate enough to meet when he was entirely nude.

Lifting her chin in a gesture Morgan Bradford would have recognized with some disquiet, Whitney strode purposefully forward just as Téjas approached his partner.

"Mr. Cutter . . ."

"Amigo—"

Téjas and Whitney, who had spoken simultaneously, paused and exchanged glances. Téjas gave way to her with a graceful bow and half-amused lift of one brow. "Señorita, I yield to beauty. . . ."

Ignoring his gallantry, Whitney turned back to Cutter, who had risen warily from his chair and was staring at her relentlessly.

"Mr. Cutter, I believe we have an interview scheduled for this morning, so let's not waste too much time on amenities. Since we have already met—in a fashion—I suggest we go right into the question phase of the interview, if you don't mind." She shifted a sheaf of paper to an angle on her arm and poised a pencil over it, fixing Cutter with a steady gaze as she asked, "When did you kill your first victim?"

There was a long, awkward pause, in which Téjas managed a sort of wheezing gasp and Cutter's features settled into a stony mask.

"You?" Téjas finally gasped into the silence. "*You* are J. Whitney Bradford?"

Whitney afforded him a brief glance. "Of course. Who did you think I was?" Then she answered her own question with an amused "Oh. Of course. I see now. You thought that fat tonsorial salesman in the ill-fitting suit was the famed J. Whitney Bradford. How laughable. And how grossly incorrect. I am J. Whitney Bradford, and I am here to conduct an interview. Now, if you gentlemen will please be seated, I will . . ."

"No."

The word dropped quietly into the growing tension, a word that Whitney was not accustomed to hearing. Not applied to herself, at any rate, and she stared stupidly at the man who had said it.

Cutter stared back at her, his jade eyes obdurate.

"I beg your pardon?" Whitney finally said in a slow, disbelieving voice.

"No. There will be no interview."

This last was said over one shoulder as Cutter pivoted on his heel and walked a short distance away, leaving Téjas to offer an explanation. He did so, but very badly.

"Señorita, I . . . we . . . Cutter was not expecting a woman, you see, and he has never given an interview, and if you were a man . . ."

"Don't babble drivel at me!" Whitney snapped, jerking out of her shocked stupor to glare at Cutter's hapless friend. "I came all the way from New York to get an interview with this . . . this outlaw—an interview he agreed to—and now I expect him to keep his word!"

Téjas gave a half shrug and held out his arms in a gesture of surrender. "There is nothing I can do."

"Sir, I expect an interview with Mr. Cutter, and as you two seem to know each other, I will leave it to you to remind him of his obligations. I still have his correspondence, I might add, and it states his acceptance of my terms."

Téjas had the grace to look faintly embarrassed. "Ah, perhaps I should tell you, señorita, that Cutter knew nothing about those telegrams. I . . . uh . . . I handle his letters for him."

"Meaning, I suppose, that he can't read or write." Her voice was scornful, hiding the bite of disappointment and frustration she was feeling. "Very well, I suppose he can't be held completely responsible, but he'll have to prove it. I *will* have that interview!" With that she stormed from the lobby.

"Whew!" Téjas muttered, and swept off his sombrero to wipe beads of sweat from his forehead. "*Muy peligroso*, that one!"

Cutter did not agree.

"I don't see the least bit of danger in her, Téjas," he said in a mild tone. "You worry too much."

"*You* did not see the fire in her eyes, or listen to the bite in her words, amigo." Téjas shook his head at the memory. "I can see why you put her out of your room."

"At least now I understand why my second female visitor looked puzzled when I said at least Nellie sent replacements quick enough," Cutter mused aloud. "I guess I should apologize to Nellie."

Ignoring that, Téjas muttered, "This woman will give you much trouble, I believe."

"What trouble can a woman cause me?" Cutter asked with a smile. "She'll fuss and fume for a few days, stew over this like a wildcat with a hurt leg, then go back to New York to lick her wounds. After all, she can't force an interview from me."

Three

Cutter was to regret his assumption that J. Whitney Bradford would be so easily defeated.

Oh, she did go back to her hotel room, and she did fuss and fume, pacing the floor of her room until Mary Walton was quite at her wit's end. But then, with characteristic determination, Whitney set about forcing Cutter to accede to her demands.

"I'll show him that he can't go back on his word!" she stormed, seating herself at the small secretary against one wall and pulling forward a clean sheet of paper. Her pen poised over it for a moment, and then a wicked smile curved her mouth.

Mary shuddered. "Oh, now, Miss Whitney, surely you don't mean to do anything too terrible, do you? Shouldn't we go back to New York and let your father's legal advisers take care of this Mr. Cutter?"

"And admit to my father that he was right? That I should have waited until he could come with me? Not on your life!" she said determinedly. She chewed on the end of the pen for a moment, then added, "Though Papa can be useful by sending a few telegrams for me . . ."

Her first action was to post written notices, paying a boy three cents each to nail them on every empty wall in Tombstone. Whitney gazed with immense satisfaction at the handbills, and thought that they should certainly bring that arrogant gunman to her without delay.

ATTENTION ALL CONCERNED CITIZENS OF TOMBSTONE TIRED OF DANGEROUS MEN? WEARY OF DEAD BODIES FOR BREAKFAST EVERY MORNING? HELP ELIMINATE THESE EVILS. CONTACT J. W. BRADFORD AT THE COSMOPOLITAN HOTEL CONCERNING THE ACTIVITIES OF THE GUNMAN KNOWN AS CUTTER. WILL PAY TEN DOLLARS TO EACH VISITOR WITH INFORMATION.

The posters brought her more attention than she had supposed. In the following week and a half, Whitney interviewed a solid seventy-two of Tombstone's citizens, who swore to the man they had been eyewitnesses to shootings by the gunman.

"Seventy-two?" Whitney murmured ruefully when she surveyed her notes and depleted purse. "That would make him very active, indeed! Somehow, Mary," she said to her maid, "I think there is more myth than truth about this man."

"I wouldn't count on it all being lies," Mary said darkly. "You're going to make that outlaw pretty mad if you keep this up, and I hate to think what a man like that might do."

Whitney gave a derisive snort. "Mad? I can only hope he gets mad enough to come directly to this room and refute all the rumors about him."

None of the notoriety, however, succeeded in bringing the outlaw to her hotel, much to Whitney's frustration and chagrin. When the week had passed and he still had not responded to her clever ploy to smoke him out, she sent a terse note to his room stating that he could review and refute any sworn testaments she'd taken, provided he gave her the interview.

There was no reply, and no Cutter.

Not one to be stopped by minor—or major—setbacks, Whitney decided to make use of the contacts her influential father had given her. Morgan Bradford had—reluctantly, she was sure—wired her the names of two men who could help. One was an old friend who had a ranch thirty miles outside of Tombstone, and the other was the commanding officer of the nearest army post.

With characteristic determination, Whitney hired a rig and a driver to take her to Fort Buchanan. There she met Lieutenant Andrew West.

A tall, lean redhead, the lieutenant was young, and his blue eyes sparkled with interest. It had been a long time since he had met a polished city woman, and never had he met a woman like Whitney, with steel in her voice and fire in her eye.

"Ma'am," West began when she had finished speaking, "your father's telegram requesting the army's cooperation was passed down to me from the commanding officer here." West's smile was wry. "Your father's influence is far-reaching, I see, but I don't know that it's wise to pursue this."

"I'm not afraid of a little danger, Lieutenant, and besides, just what can this Cutter do to me? String me up by my thumbs?" Whitney peeled off her lace gloves in a dainty motion that fairly captivated the young officer. She was seated across from him, her skirts draped about her in an appealing fall of taffeta that rustled with her every movement.

"It's not that, ma'am." West paused and searched his brain for a way to explain that it would not be wise to tweak Cutter's nose and perhaps aggravate a situation already precarious. The posters nailed up around town had caused quite a stir, and it was certain that the half-breed gunman would be dangerously angry.

None of that made a nickel's worth of difference to Whitney, however. Though she might admit a certain nervousness to herself about the possible outcome of her actions, she fully intended to brazen it out to anyone else.

Never, Morgan Bradford had always been fond of saying, *never let your opponent think for an instant that you might waver in your course. It is death to the outcome.*

Whitney believed that. It had always worked for her father, hadn't it? And so far it had worked for her. If nothing else, she had learned that most people wilted before the force of sheer determination.

The only qualm she had was that she still recalled, however briefly, the feel of his compelling lips on hers, and his hard, naked body pressed alarmingly close to her. It had been unsettling then, and it was unsettling now. For some reason, she could not shake the memory from her mind. It clung tenaciously, returning when she slept or even when she was awake, startling her with its intensity, coming close to frightening her. But fear was not a trait associated with the Bradfords, and so she knew that she was allowing the memory to disturb her only because it was so alien. And perhaps because it reminded her of Nathan and—unpleasant things.

Whitney turned her attention and charm to Lieutenant West, who, she could see, was falling under the spell of her resolve.

"As to the other matter you mentioned, ma'am, I suppose you should have an escort. For safety's sake, of course."

"Of course, Lieutenant," Whitney returned sweetly, and favored him with a slight smile.

"There are still bands of renegade Apaches running around out there, you know. Not that I want to scare you, but they've been raiding isolated homesteads and even small settlements in this area."

Whitney lifted one delicately arched eyebrow. "And what does that have to do with me, Lieutenant? I'm not taking an excursion into their camp, only attending a fiesta in my honor. Mr. Tucker is an old friend of my father's, and he has sent me an invitation and a promise to help me gather the information I need. This Cutter used to work for him, you know."

"But Kermit Tucker's ranch is a good thirty miles from Tombstone, and the roads aren't exactly secure, if you understand what I mean."

"I understand perfectly, Lieutenant. You want me to be afraid." Whitney paused, then smiled an apology that clearly charmed the already-smitten young officer.

"You are mistaken," West lied in a calm voice. He leaned over his desk, fixing her with a steady stare. "Perhaps you haven't heard, but the conditions at the San Carlos reservation are tense right now. Some ridiculous medicine man has been stirring up the Apache, and Geronimo is looking restless. The men at Fort Bowie and the reservation officials are having their hands full trying to keep order and hold in those renegades who rebel." His smile was placating. "This is a very dangerous situation for you to ride into."

Whitney fixed her large amber eyes on the lieutenant's intent face. Her voice was low, husky, trusting. "But Lieutenant West, if *you* are my escort, then I know I will be perfectly safe."

West's rigid military posture wilted, and the hard lines in his face softened. He almost smiled foolishly as he looked down at her.

"It is true," he said after a slight pause, "that I am known for my skills at inflicting damage upon the enemy. And if you are to go, you should be well guarded." Whitney remained silent, gazing up at him with expectant eyes. "All right. I'll gather up some of my best men, and we'll escort you to Mr. Tucker's ranch Thursday. I can complete two tasks with one trip, I suppose, but—I won't bore you with my business."

A beatific smile spread over Whitney's face as she rose from her chair and extended a soft, pale hand to the officer. "Thank you,

Lieutenant. I cannot tell you how very grateful I am, and how safe I feel now."

"My pleasure, Miss Bradford. I shall arrange for an escort back to town for you now . . ."

It was all Whitney could do not to kick up her heels and shout a triumphant "whoopee" before she left him.

The buggy ride back to Tombstone was hot and dusty, and Whitney was not in the best mood when the driver helped her down across from her hotel. "Driver, where may I find a gunsmith?" she inquired after a glance up the busy thoroughfare did not readily show her one. There were too many signs, all competing for eye space.

Taking the money she pressed in his hand, the driver said, "Spangenberg's, ma'am. On Fourth Street near Brown's Hotel, a block down that way." He pointed.

She was hot and thirsty and certainly didn't feel like walking a block, so Whitney decided to send Mary. The small derringer she carried—and had not had the presence of mind to use—needed to be looked over by a gunsmith, but it could wait. No, she needed a bath more than anything at the moment.

Stepping across the uneven boards of the sidewalk, Whitney picked her way toward the Cosmopolitan Hotel with precise, dainty steps. The glare from the sun hurt her eyes, and even the brim of her stylish hat did not offer enough shade.

"How can human beings live where it is so wretchedly hot?" she muttered to herself, lifting the hem of her gown as she stepped into the dusty street. She wasn't aware she'd spoken loud enough for anyone to hear until a hard male voice drawled close to her ear, "Just as easily as human beings live in New York, where it's so damnably crowded."

Whitney whirled around, and found herself staring up at Cutter. His hard, jeweled eyes met hers with a polite courtesy that did nothing to still the quick lurch of her heart. It leapt even harder when he put a hand on her elbow to steer her slightly to the right.

"Wagon coming," he said when she made a slight protest, and Whitney put one hand atop her feathered hat to keep it from slipping as she glared up at him suspiciously.

"How kind of you. Now, if you will step aside and let me pass, I prefer not to stand in the heat a moment longer." She turned away from him and began walking.

Cutter fell into step beside her, much to Whitney's annoyance.

She stopped short. "Can't you take a subtle hint that you're not wanted, Mr. Cutter?"

His smile was lazy and politely amused. "I kinda had the impression that all those posters you put up, and the note that you sent me, meant you wanted to talk to me, Miss Bradford."

Piqued by his attitude and previous refusals, Whitney stilled the quick surge of triumph she felt and decided to make him squirm a bit before she pretended to reluctantly give in and do an interview. She shrugged airily.

"Well, that was then! The time for negotiation is past, and I fully intend to proceed with my story without your assistance, thank you. Now, if you will move aside . . . ?"

Cutter stepped deftly in front of her, resting both hands on lean hips, the polite smile still curling lips that seemed unaccustomed to such courtesies. "I think you might want to listen for a minute. It'd be to your advantage."

Whitney ignored the rapid pounding of her heart and tilted her chin higher. "I hardly see how."

"Let me show you. . . ."

Before she could protest too loudly, Cutter had taken her by the elbow and steered her to the shade of an overhanging porch. "Now, listen," he said in a suddenly hard tone that halted her angry protest in mid-sentence, "and listen carefully—I don't like those posters, and I'm tired of your curiosity. Drop your meddling before you get in serious trouble."

Whitney's irritation soared. She glared at the man with all the scorn she could express, hoping he recognized how little she thought of him. It was too much that a man with his reputation for violence and crime should dare to criticize her for delving into his past—especially after he had agreed to an interview . . . or at least had allowed a friend to commit him.

"If I were a man, Mr. Cutter, you would have given me an interview and taken my money," she began calmly. "But the moment you discovered I was a woman, you decided not to keep your word. Is your word good only when given to other men?"

"My . . . word . . . was given under false pretenses, Miss Bradford, as I'm sure you meant it to be." Cutter stared at her without expression. "Most people would assume J. Whitney Bradford was a man unless told otherwise. You never said you were female."

"And you, Mr. Cutter," Whitney said with rising temper, "never said you were an illiterate, insufferable, provincial scoundrel! I'm afraid we've both been misled!"

A faint smile flickered briefly on Cutter's face. "That is beside the point. I strongly suggest that you stop your meddling, or you may not like the result."

"Oh? And what will you do—add another name to your long list of victims?"

For a brief instant Whitney thought she had gone too far. She recognized in the sudden opacity of his eyes a flash of fury that he was too well controlled to let show on his face, and felt her heart plummet. She took an involuntary step back, and her voice came out in a quavering squeak.

"My father is Morgan Bradford, and if you dare to harm one hair on my head . . ."

"Miss Bradford, I could send your father your entire scalp, and he couldn't do a thing about it," Cutter informed her in a pleasant, silky tone. "Keep that in mind."

Keep that in mind? It was difficult to try to keep anything *else* in mind at the moment, except the urgent need to flee.

Wheeling, Whitney strode away on trembling legs, not daring to look back at him. She felt suddenly as if she had been standing in a steam bath. Her dress was wet with perspiration, and moisture pooled on her face, sliding warmly down her neck to dampen her bodice. Without knowing quite how, she somehow made her way back to the security of her hotel room and Mary's cool, comforting care.

Perhaps it wasn't such a good idea to provoke Cutter, she mused later, soaking in a tub of perfumed water that came up to her shoulders. Her long hair lay in damp ropes against her neck and shoulder, water-dark against her pale skin. She leaned back against the high rim of the tub and closed her eyes, inhaling the rich, sweet scent of honey and almond bubbles that clustered around her body.

A Chinese screen angled around the curved edges of the tub, providing a barrier against the rest of the large room, and Whitney could hear a muted voice. She didn't open her eyes, but called out, "Mary? Is that you? Please bring me a glass of chilled wine at once."

Singing a light air from an Italian opera, Whitney scooted lower in the tub, until just her head was above the water and bubbles. Light poufs of perfumed water tickled her chin, and her bent knees made small ivory islands amid the bubbles. Some of the earlier tension of the day faded away, and she resolved not to allow anything to ruffle her so badly again. That wicked half-breed gunman with his bronzed skin, jade eyes, and veiled threats would not find her such an easy mark the next time!

Muffled footsteps padded across the thick carpet of the room, and

Whitney held out a hand for the wine Mary was bringing. "It's well chilled, I hope? This dreadful heat is maddening, Mary, and I wish this were over and I was back in New York."

"You're not the only one," drawled a deep voice, making Whitney's eyes snap open. Instinctively sitting up, she let out a shrill scream.

Cutter stood there, his eyes raking her with casual—and, worst of all, indifferent—interest. He held out her wine and asked politely, "Will there be anything else before we continue our earlier conversation?"

"Yes!" she found the voice to say, and abruptly sank down into the tub so that only her head was above water level. "Get out!" She prayed the bubbles would not evaporate, and made an involuntary movement to hide her body with her arms.

"Don't bother. I'm not at all interested. And I've seen much better," he added with another insulting glance.

Whitney's arm lashed out, fumbling for a towel, but instead knocked the wine from Cutter's hand to the floor. Her efforts only succeeded in making the concealing bubbles swirl dangerously away, however, and with a tiny snarl of frustration she sank deeper into the high-backed tub again.

"Get out of here! Mary! Mary!"

"No one answered my knock, so I took the liberty of coming in. I suppose Mary will be back soon enough. And while she's gone, Miss Bradford, I intend for us to have a nice, quiet chat."

"You're out of your mind!"

"Probably, but it looks like you've got little choice in the matter." Cutter snagged a chair with one hand and dragged it close to the tub, straddling it and giving Whitney a calm stare.

Near tears with anger, embarrassment, and frustration, Whitney smacked the water futilely, sending up water spouts that drenched her and missed Cutter. He grinned, and she choked back a pithy comment.

"What is it you want?" she grated out between clenched teeth that had an alarming tendency to chatter. "Money? My father will give you all you want. . . ."

"Ah, it's that easy for you, isn't it? All you have to do is call on Daddy, and you've got whatever it is your little heart desires."

Cutter's eyes were narrowed, and Whitney couldn't tell if he was angry or just annoyed. Either way, it seemed dangerous at the moment, with her in such a vulnerable position. How could Mary have left her in an unlocked room for any ruffian to abuse?

Daring to lift her chin a notch—and keeping her arms carefully over her chest—Whitney met Cutter's remote gaze calmly. "I don't need my father to tell me that a man like you is a black-hearted villain, Mr. Cutter. Or to advise me on how best to deal with such a man!"

Cutter seemed amused. "Really?" He scooted the chair a little bit closer, and his faintly ironic gaze seemed to pierce the bubbles clinging to her. "And how would you deal with a man like me, Miss Bradford?"

"Hanging is too speedy—I think something slow and drawn out would do nicely!" she snapped.

She regretted her quick retort immediately as Cutter began to helpfully suggest in great detail various tortures preferred by the Apache. Whitney felt a surge of nausea when he described a particularly inventive—and gruesome—method of dealing pain to enemies.

"Please, enough! I can't listen to any more!" She put her hands over her ears, careless of bubbles or exposed skin, and squeezed her eyes shut again. "No more!"

"Ready to bargain, Miss Bradford?"

Her eyes snapped open again, and she quickly moved her arms when she saw where his gaze was resting. Did he have to be so . . . so *male*? Why did she have this odd, burning, breathless feeling inside? And why did it seem as if he knew it? She looked at him warily.

"Bargain for what, Mr. Cutter?"

"For the end to your ridiculous pursuit of information concerning me. You can't be finding out anything useful."

"That's all you know! There are plenty of citizens in Tombstone ready and willing to talk to me about your past—and present—activities!"

"Accurately?"

"Probably."

"Ah. You sound so certain. Truth and journalism are not comfortable bedfellows, I take it."

Whitney wanted to scream at him in frustration, but deep down she knew he was telling the truth. Hadn't she had the same maddening thought? And why did he have to sit there so confidently, with his denim-clad legs straddling the chair and his arms resting lazily across the back of it, making the graceful lines of the chair seem ludicrous just by the sheer force of his masculinity? His jet-black hair was long in the back, brushing his wide shoulders, and she had a sudden picture of how he must look in a beaded headband and breech clout. His sun-bronzed features had an almost regal cast to them, and he probably looked more at home in Apache garb than in the clothes of a cowhand, she mused. Her gaze flicked over him almost speculatively, noting that his rawhide boots were worn and dusty, and the gun belts slung carelessly from his lean hips jutted out at awkward angles, and looked quite lethal. How many people had he killed with them? she wondered, and looked up to meet his clear gaze.

Cutter almost laughed. The haughty Miss Bradford's face was so unguarded at the moment, revealing her every emotion, and she was totally unaware of how young and vulnerable she looked. To his surprise, he felt a brief pang of sympathy for her. After all, it wasn't all her fault she was spoiled and accustomed to having everyone jump at her slightest wish. She must have been brought up that way, being Morgan Bradford's only child and heir. But when he might have relented in his intimidation of her, Whitney made the mistake of speaking her mind.

"You're little more than a savage playing dress-up, aren't you, Mr. Cutter?"

Cutter's inclination to compassion vanished, and he stood up in a smooth, lithe motion like the uncoiling of a rope, reaching for her at the same time. He ignored her startled, breathless squeak of dismay, hauling her up out of the tub and yanking her close to his body, his fingers tight around her upper arms.

For a moment he was too angry to do more than glare at her, but then the soft feel of her skin beneath his hands made him want to touch her more intimately. His gaze dropped to the ripe fullness of her breasts pushing against him, and he was much too aware of how good she felt in his arms. It was a cruel irony that a woman who had such luscious curves, delicate features, and smooth ivory skin should have been brought up to be as blunt as a man. Women were supposed to be soft and yielding, welcoming a man instead of taunting and berating him.

Cutter's hold altered subtly, and he could feel the rapid thunder of her heart beating against him. It didn't ease his anger to realize that he had succeeded, at last, in frightening her. Her slender thighs trembled next to his, damp and warm through the denim over his legs, and he felt his involuntary physical response to her nudity and beauty.

She'd be a challenge to seduce, he thought. He'd enjoy wreaking havoc with that supercilious composure of hers, hearing that aristocratic voice reduced to a low moan as she begged him for more of the pleasure he knew so well how to give. . . .

Whitney barely felt the punishing pressure of his hands on her. She was too aware of her nudity and the green fire in his eyes.

Tremors racked her body, and she quailed at the silky menace in his voice as he bit off his words.

"I've warned you for the last time, Miss Bradford. I don't intend to warn you again. And if you assume I can be a savage—you're right."

As if to prove his point, Cutter slid one hand to the ridge of her spine, pressing her naked, quivering breasts so hard against him, she felt the prick of his shirt buttons into her bare flesh. She moaned softly, and then the world began to spin with alarming rapidity as she felt his hands move lower, cupping her buttocks and bringing her up even closer, so that his belt buckle bit into the soft round of her belly.

Forcing her lips apart, Cutter kissed her ruthlessly, expertly, until her knees buckled and she hung helplessly in his embrace. It was an utter invasion, an assault on her senses that should have disgusted her. But to her utter horror, Whitney felt a slow response curl up inside her, making her lean into him, surrendering to his touch and the burning line of kisses he trailed over her damp, perfumed skin. She didn't know what was happening to her, except that she had never felt such sensations before meeting this man, and that they were somehow terrifying and wonderful at the same time.

Whitney couldn't know that her reactions were a thing called desire, the normal reaction of a woman being played with skillful eroticism. The lubricious sensations slowly licking through her inflamed body were like a fever, hot and consuming. In spite of her resolve not to reveal her frailty, Whitney whimpered, a small sound deep in the back of her throat.

Cutter heard it with a ripple of satisfaction. So the frosty and outwardly unapproachable Miss Whitney Bradford still had the soul of a woman!

He ran his palm lightly over her curves, reveling in the smooth feel of her skin, as soft as satin and fragrant as a flower. The women he knew weren't like Whitney. Fate hadn't given them soft skins and perfumed bodies, or a wealth of silver-blond hair that fell in rivulets over her slender shoulders. None of them had amber eyes fringed with thick, dark lashes, huge and luminous and hazy with bewildered emotion. Whitney's facial features—the short, straight nose, high, chiseled cheekbones, and voluptuous mouth—were not the most perfect he'd ever seen, but were still arranged in a package so enticing that he could easily visualize a host of men falling at her feet. Of course, inside that aristocratic head of hers was a calculating brain that could be intimidating to most men. She was as unexpected as a desert cactus—all prickly and barren on the outside, but soft and vulnerable on the inside.

She moved against him, a weak struggle, her body soft and trembling. Cutter felt the surge of a desire so strong it surprised him. His arms flexed to lift her, then he stopped.

Whatever messages her body might be sending him, he knew that if he took advantage of the moment, there would be hell to pay later. And this woman, he knew instinctively, could summon more hell than most, in spite of her momentary surrender.

Whitney was moaning softly against the material of his red chambray shirt. "Don't! Don't you dare!"

She hung limply in his embrace, her forehead resting on his shoulder in the pose of a child, but her entire body was quivering.

Pushing her away with a pang of regret, Cutter knew that he wouldn't follow his urgent inclinations. It would complicate things too badly.

Whitney swayed slightly, gazing up at Cutter with an expression of bewilderment, her lips swollen and bruised from his rough, demanding kisses. Her senses were drowning under the assault of unfamiliar emotions as well as physical reactions, and she still reeled from them, confused and terrified at the same time.

Sucking in a steadying breath as he released her arms and gave her a considering stare, Whitney looked back at him for a long moment. Her presence of mind was slowly returning, and with it came anger.

She flushed, her ivory skin staining a bright shade of rose that made her eyes glow a brighter gold, and felt her body begin to tremble again, this time with rage.

"Depraved murderer! Get out before I have you arrested!" she ordered Cutter. "Now!"

Ignoring her command, Cutter asked in a reasonable tone, "Arrested, Miss Bradford? For what?"

His knowing gaze traveled slowly over her body, and Whitney promptly snatched up a thick white towel from the rack near the tub, trying to hide herself as she sputtered angrily:

"You know for what!"

"Yes, but do you?" Cutter returned smoothly. He took a step away, then paused and looked at her. "You've had the last warning you'll get from me. If I were you, I'd get on the next stage out of Tombstone. It's too dangerous in Arizona for a woman like you, Miss Bradford."

Arranging the towel so that it hid part of her body—why hadn't she asked for bigger towels?—Whitney retorted, "But you're not me!"

Cutter's lips smiled, but his eyes were cold and indifferent. "No, I'm not." He gave her a last sweeping glance, then disappeared around the Chinese screen.

When Whitney heard the door close behind him, she abruptly sank back into the now-cold water of the tub, the towel sill clutched in front of her. She tried to still her quivering nerves and shaking body, and to her horror burst into tears. What was the matter with her? A Bradford never cried, never showed weakness! Yet she had allowed that wild ruffian to touch her, to hold her in his arms and kiss her—and worst of all, she had kissed him back.

"I'll get even with you, Cutter," she muttered fiercely, glaring at the empty chair. "I'll show you what it means to cross a Bradford!"

Four

Lieutenant West cupped Whitney's elbow in one palm, gently guiding her through the door and out of the theater. "This has certainly been the best week I've spent since arriving in Arizona, Miss Bradford," he said into her ear, bending his head close so that his lips almost grazed her cheek.

Whitney acknowledged West's comment with a distracted nod of her head as they ambled slowly down rough wooden sidewalks. Tombstone had a much livelier night life than she would have supposed. It was probably because of the silver strikes so close by, she mused. All manner of people had arrived in the boom town, from best to worst. She had been surprised at the easy integration of social groups.

When Lieutenant West had invited her to the Bird Cage Theater for a production of *Pinafore*, Whitney had been dubious. But she was pleasantly surprised by the performance, though it wasn't up to New York City standards. Still, Tombstone was showing enterprise for a town that was only a little over two years old. She was vaguely surprised to find she didn't dislike the place now as she had just a few days before.

Of course, that might be because she hadn't been faced with

Cutter again, but now had Lieutenant West as her constant companion—a welcome change, she told herself as she allowed him to steer her toward an ice cream parlor, his hand protectively on her arm as they strolled down the erratic sidewalk. Tombstone might affect an outward air of propriety, but just down Allen Street, and on the dark back streets, frequent gunshots and bawdy laughter could still be heard.

"Why doesn't the sheriff do anything about that?" Whitney wondered aloud, and West laughed shortly.

"John Behan? You must be joking! That lazy son—rascal—is too greedy and worthless to put himself out just to maintain law and order." He gave a snort of disgust that quickly altered to a polite cough when Whitney frowned at him. "Excuse me—I didn't mean to speak so plainly, Miss Bradford."

"Why not? If that's how matters are, why shouldn't I be told? After all, I tried to enlist Sheriff Behan's help when I first arrived, and as you have just said, found him very uncooperative."

"If it wasn't for Marshal Earp, matters would be a lot worse, I suppose."

"Earp? Isn't that the gentleman you introduced to me yesterday? The one with the droopy mustache?"

West laughed. "I've never heard him described that way, but yes, that's Virgil Earp. His brother Wyatt intends to run against Behan in the next election. I sure hope Wyatt wins. At least he'll get things done in Tombstone, where Behan just sits on his . . . hands."

Whitney hid a smile at the lieutenant's obvious efforts to temper his language. She should probably tell him that she'd heard much worse in the newsrooms of her father's paper. "Didn't you tell me that Wyatt Earp was part owner of a gambling establishment down the street? The Oriental Saloon?" she asked, tilting her head to look up at West. "Why on earth would anyone elect him sheriff when it would be such an obvious conflict of interest?"

"Tombstone needs a strong-willed man, a man who isn't afraid to buck both factions here."

"You mean the ranchers versus townsmen, I presume."

West's smile deepened, and his gaze flicked over Whitney's large amber eyes and the perfect oval of her face with growing respect as he said, "Yes. You hit on it."

"I've noticed from the papers that there seems to be a bit of friction between the townsfolk and the surrounding ranchers. And Mr. Tucker—whom you're escorting me to visit tomorrow—made veiled references to 'rank newcomers and nuisances' in his letter."

Pausing to escort Whitney around a group of rowdier citizens,

West jerked his thumb toward them when they'd passed without incident. "See those men? They're cowhands from spreads outside Tombstone. At times the army has to be called in to smooth over trouble with men like that."

Whitney slid them a backward glance. True, the men were all wearing guns, and they were boisterous and bold, staring at her as if she were the only woman they'd ever seen, but they'd been polite enough to tip their hats when she'd passed.

"I don't see the full extent of the problem."

Lieutenant West's mouth tightened slightly, and his voice was uncharacteristically hard. "Let me elucidate with a little story. Six army mules disappeared not long ago. Virgil Earp, as a deputized U.S. marshal, has authority to recover stolen federal property. Virgil, Wyatt, their brother Morgan, and a detail of soldiers I led rode out and found the animals on the McLaury ranch. We got there just as the McLaurys were changing the brands on the mules. Virgil made them promise to surrender the mules to me on the following day." West's voice grew even harder. "The next day McLaury claimed that 'rustlers' stole the mules, making me look like a fool and successfully getting rid of the evidence and any hope of prosecution by the army."

"Why didn't you take the mules with you?"

"Because Virgil assured me the McLaurys would bring them all in. Without challenging his authority, I had little choice." West smiled ruefully. "I've learned not to be so trusting since then, of course."

Whitney was quiet for a moment, then said, "I suppose a lot of that goes on. Kermit Tucker is a prospering rancher in this area, so I'm counting on the fact that he must know many similar stories about Cutter's shady dealings."

"I imagine he does." Lieutenant West slid a protective arm around Whitney's slender waist to assist her over a large gap in the wooden sidewalks that bridged deep ruts between street and shops. "After Behan's appointment to sheriff this past February, the McLaurys and the Clantons have been able to do pretty much what they want to do," he said when they were safely on the other side.

Whitney immediately grasped what he wasn't saying. "Ah. Then that is why Behan is so eager to keep the cowboys' affections! He depends on them to vote him in as sheriff in the next election."

"Right." West gave her a long look. "You're pretty smart for a woman."

"Is that a compliment?" she asked tartly, pausing in the light of a store window to glare up at him. "Are women thought to be inherently stupid, Lieutenant West?"

"No, no," he hastened to assure her. "It's just that you're the first woman I've ever known to grasp the situation at once. Except maybe Nellie Cashman, and she's not at all like you."

Nellie. The name brought to mind Cutter, and his dry comment that he would complain to someone named Nellie about her that first night, the night she had interrupted his bath. He must have been expecting a woman—Nellie?

"Who is Nellie Cashman?" Whitney asked abruptly.

"She operates the Russ House down the street. Perhaps you've seen it?"

Seen it? Oh, yes, she'd seen it! She'd visited Room 203 and seen much more than she'd wanted to see!

But before she could make a lame comment, West was continuing. "The Russ House serves the best meals in town, and Nellie has the reputation for being an angel of mercy. She used to prospect for ore herself, you know, and has a soft spot for all the miners here. She's always taking up collections and sponsoring benefits for prospectors who are in trouble." West's voice was admiring. "She has friends everywhere, even Black Jack—"

He stopped short, and Whitney looked up at him curiously. "Who is Black Jack?"

West's normally florid complexion was even redder, and he looked down at the uneven boards of the sidewalk as he mumbled, "Black Jack is queen of the . . . uh . . . back streets, you know."

"Back streets? Are you by any chance referring to those houses with the red lamps in the windows?" Whitney asked wryly, and West nodded miserably.

"Yes, and I'm sorry to have mentioned such a subject to a lady like you, Miss Bradford."

"Really, Lieutenant! Do you seriously think I have never heard of such—occupations? I'm not exactly naive, though I've no wish to continue to discuss the subject." Her knuckles were white around the gold-beaded evening bag she carried, and she wished furiously that she had never been so unfortunate as to go to the Russ House. To have been mistaken for a . . . a lady of the night was bad enough, but to have a man like Cutter complain about *her* to the proprietor of the hotel was the worst insult yet!

Her voice was calm when she added, "I suppose Miss Cashman has interests in that kind of business?"

West seemed startled. "Not that I know of. She just befriends everyone in town."

Even worse, Whitney thought glumly. Now, instead of the woman being a procurer, she was an angel of mercy. And Cutter had complained about the inadequacy of his *guest* to her!

"Why would a woman of Miss Cashman's stature allow herself to consort with such riffraff?" she wondered, not realizing she'd spoken aloud until West answered.

"Why?" West obviously fumbled for a reply. "I guess because she likes most people. She has friends all over the United States, from what I understand."

Whitney, whose previous experience with friends had been limited to men of her father's acquaintance, still did not understand. She'd never had a friend, not a true friend, other than her father. The girls at her school had never seemed inclined to be friendly, and to tell the truth, she had considered them a bit silly and insipid anyway, always giggling and whispering about young men and new gowns when there were more important things to talk about.

When she had first married Nathan, she'd thought she might understand the whisperings of other young married women, but she hadn't. Marriage and the marriage bed had been a shock, an unpleasant shock. She'd seen nothing to whisper or smile about either in performing her "wifely duty," or giving up her independence and being Mrs. Nathan Truesdale instead of Julia Whitney Truesdale. Why must a woman change her name? she'd argued, but even her father had been adamant in his agreement with Nathan. She'd forgiven him that, finally, but had never quite forgiven his calm assumption that marriage would make her happy. It had made her more miserable than she'd ever been in her life, and when Nathan had died, she'd found it difficult to pretend a grief she did not feel.

Until two weeks before, when that blasted half-breed gunman had held her against his naked body, Whitney had not considered it possible that intimacy could be enjoyed instead of endured. Cutter had awakened her curiosity with his touch, and it was strangely disconcerting.

Whitney was so lost in thought and disturbing memories that she was barely aware they had stopped in front of the crowded ice cream parlor.

When she would have stepped inside, she looked up and saw Cutter watching her from several yards away. He was leaning coolly against a porch post, long legs crossed, arms folded casually across his chest, his posture lazy and relaxed, and somehow dangerous at the same time. Her heart skipped a beat and her throat tightened, and she wondered if he knew what she planned to do, knew that she intended to interview a man who had once been his friend.

Kermit Tucker freely admitted to befriending Cutter years earlier, before he'd earned a reputation as a gunman who had few scruples about killing.

She glanced quickly up at West, and saw that he had not noticed Cutter. Feigning a headache, she asked the lieutenant to escort her back to the hotel immediately, and though puzzled, he complied.

"Thank you for the pleasantest evening I've had since I've been in Tombstone, Lieutenant," she said graciously at the door to her room. "I'm feeling a bit better now, and I'm sure a good night's sleep will clear up my headache completely. What time do we leave in the morning?"

"Five o'clock. If you and your maid will be in front of the hotel at that time, my troop will escort you out to Mr. Tucker's before it grows too hot."

"Mary and I will be ready," Whitney promised. "Do you think we can ride the entire thirty miles before it grows too warm?"

"Some of the way," West returned with a grin. "But it gets hot early in Arizona."

"So I've discovered. Good night, Lieutenant."

"Please call me Andrew. And may I call you Whitney?"

"Of course," she told him pleasantly.

He grasped her hand and pressed a fervent kiss on her knuckles. "Good night, Whitney."

Upon entering her room, Whitney told Mary she would undress herself and bade the maid good night. All she wanted to do was go to bed and spend a deep, dreamless night of rest. After she interviewed Kermit Tucker, she intended to take the stage to Benson, and there catch the next train back to New York. She hoped that Cutter didn't think it was because of him, but would know how she detested Arizona. Besides, she had a book to write, and that certainly couldn't be done here.

No, she couldn't concentrate in brawling Tombstone, the town where silver was king and human lives worthless. Not here, not where the bodies of nameless drifters and cowhands lined the alleys on Sunday mornings, shot down in cold blood, their killers ignored and unpunished, if the *Tombstone Nugget* was to be believed. "Is there no justice for the nameless?" she'd written in her journal.

Yawning, Whitney slid between the cool, scented sheets of her bed and blew out the lamp on the bedside table. Mary had left the windows open to invite in cooling breezes, and they filtered lightly in through the half-open shutters. Whitney lay back and stared up at the shadowed ceiling. She hoped for sleep to claim her, but too many thoughts and impressions kept her awake.

Could she really write the kind of novel she wanted to? One that would give her critical acclaim and earn her the respect of her father's peers? It wasn't her own peers she wanted to impress, but her father's. Though much younger than they, she'd always socialized with her father's set, without, however, feeling fully accepted by them. She wanted to belong at last, to fit into a niche where she could be comfortable with herself and others. For even though Morgan Bradford indulged her, petted her, spoke proudly of her accomplishments, he still considered her a female, and as such, not quite as good as a male.

There were times when resentment burned hotly in Whitney about the way men regarded women. Couldn't they be equals in important matters? Why did men consider themselves to be stronger and more superior in *every*thing? It wasn't right, and more important—it wasn't true. Oh, in physical strength, yes, but that wasn't everything. And there were times when a woman could even beat a man at that.

A faint smile curved her mouth, and she wondered what the arrogant Mr. Cutter would have done if she had had presence of mind enough to use one of the tricks Chin had shown her. Chin Yu was an old friend of her father's, and after a narrow escape on a New York street—where Morgan had declared she had no business being—Chin had offered to show her a few moves that required no strength to catch an attacker off guard. Even though Morgan had blustered and fumed about his daughter dressing in trousers and learning how to toss men over her shoulder, Whitney had been eager to learn. Chin had declared her an apt pupil, but she had never thought of using the moves he'd taught her against Cutter.

She certainly should have! she thought fiercely. The arrogant gunman needed to be shown he couldn't bully everyone. Too bad she had been so rattled she'd not even thought of Chin's instructions. But if ever an opportunity arose to redeem herself, she would do so gladly!

She was still visualizing the astonishment on Cutter's face at her expertise when she drifted into a slumber peopled with arrogant gunmen and naked Indians with bronzed bodies as magnificently sculpted as Michelangelo's *David*.

Five

"I had no idea Mr. Tucker's ranch was so far out," Mary complained to Whitney.

Whitney, as hot and uncomfortable as her maid, had little sympathy to share. The barren land seemed to stretch forever, and the sun appeared to sear right through the protective top of the big, lumbering wagon West had insisted they use.

"It's better on those roads than a smaller gig," he had explained when she'd objected. "It may not be as comfortable as a padded brougham or gig, but it will make the trip without losing a wheel," he'd added, and Whitney had reluctantly yielded. Now she was miserable.

"Complaining will hardly lessen our discomfort," Whitney said irritably, and waved her fan more vigorously in the futile hope of stirring up a cooling breeze. Thank heaven she had shown sense enough not to wear a multitude of heavy petticoats in spite of Mary's insistence that true ladies never went out without them. But now Whitney was beginning to wish she had yielded to her first inclination to wear a riding outfit and leave Mary alone in the wagon. Perhaps she wouldn't be shaded, but she could at least ride along at a decent pace instead of choking on dust stirred up by the vehicle's wheels.

"Comfortable?" Lieutenant West reined his horse close to ask, and Whitney couldn't help the blistering glance she shot him.

"Not hardly! Just how far *is* Mr. Tucker's ranch? It has to be close by now!"

West's smile was apologetic. "No, it's still a good ten miles away. Would you like to stop just ahead? There's a bit of shade and some hills by a small creek."

"No trees, I'll bet," Whitney muttered, wiping at a thin line of perspiration trickling down her face. "Are there none in Arizona?"

It was a rhetorical question, but West chose to reply. "There are plenty of trees in the higher elevations. In the Dragoon Mountains to the north," he said with a wave of one arm, "there are vast stands of pine and fir, but not nearly as large as in other mountainous areas."

Intercepting Whitney's incredulous gaze, West laughed. "I guess you're not really interested in that."

"No, Andrew, I admit I am not. I am much more interested in getting to some shade, where I don't have to breathe in dust with every lungful of air."

Her irritability only made Lieutenant West more determined to please her, and he nudged his mount as close to the wagon as he could get, keeping up a steady stream of conversation that made Whitney want to scream. What did she care where Cochise had made his stronghold? Though she vaguely recognized the name as that of an Apache chief, at the moment it was not important. Cochise was dead anyway, and the rest of the Apaches were penned up on a reservation. Or, rather, most of them were. A few had escaped, to loot and pillage, West had told her that first day. But they stayed in Mexico all the time, and Mexico was far south. Wasn't it?

Lieutenant West was glad to answer that question for her, too, and pointed south. "No, only about twenty miles, I'd say. Not far at all. But don't worry." West laughed and indicated his squad of heavily-armed soldiers with a jerk of his thumb. "These men are seasoned in warfare, Whitney. I picked only the best for your escort today. We have to rendezvous with another troop from Fort Bowie, but I intend to be back to dance with you at the fiesta tonight." He smiled widely. "Duty will not delay my pleasure, and besides, my troop could use some recreation too. They've had to drill almost every day lately."

Whitney concentrated on the road winding ahead of them, an almost trackless ribbon of dirt snaking through red dunes and hills and scrub. Perspiration dotted her face, and she could feel her dress growing damp.

When Lieutenant West called a halt beside a narrow stream working across the ridged land, Whitney was so grateful she almost laughed aloud. The jolting roll of the wagon was growing more uncomfortable with each passing mile, and she wanted to get down and relieve her cramped leg muscles.

Possessively placing Whitney's hand on his forearm, West walked her toward the small muddy stream gurgling through deep cuts in the ground. The thirsty cavalry horses were already crowding forward, heads lowered as they thrust dusty muzzles deep into the water to slake their thirst. It made slight currents in the stream, eddies that swirled in concentric patterns, like watery pinwheels.

"How odd," Whitney murmured, seating herself on a large flat rock beneath an overhang to gaze with appreciation at the water. She opened her paper fan and waved it gently, enjoying the respite from the heat. Shadows thrown by towering rocks provided relief from the burning sunlight, making odd distorted patterns on the ground. "Arizona has the most unusual geography I've ever seen," she observed, slanting a smile up at West. "How can you stand living here year round?"

"It's not so bad. Actually, I've gotten used to it, though I could never live as the Apaches do."

"What do you mean?"

West waved an expansive arm. "They literally live out in the open, sleeping under cactus or trees or brush, getting food from seemingly nowhere. I've never seen anything like it. An Apache can be only a few feet from a man, and remain hidden in an area you'd swear could hide nothing. Flat, barren land and rocks seem to be paradise for the Indian."

Whitney gazed dubiously around her, at the endless stretch of land broken only by the jagged edges of hills clawing at the far horizon. The world seemed to be composed of brown and red, with the blue of the sky the only pleasant color. She looked back at the brown water tumbling through shallow cuts in the ground.

"Paradise is what one is accustomed to, I suppose," she murmured.

The deep overhang provided a shallow cave of shade and privacy, and Whitney stretched lazily, smiling distractedly up at West when he begged to sit beside her. Raking her hat from her head, she pulled one hand through the tangled braid she'd taken loose, finger-combing her hair into a more orderly style. Her attention centered on the sluggishly moving water through ridges of rock, and she wondered how anything survived in this hostile land. West had assured her that there was a great deal of plant and animal life, but she had seen nothing to support his claim. Only a few hawks that soared so high in the sky they were just dark specks against a brilliant blue background gave credibility to the certainty of some kind of animal life.

"Well," she said, "I am certainly going to have a great many details to include in my book. If I had not seen all this for myself, I would never have believed it possible."

West smiled uncertainly. "You mean the remoteness of the area?"

"Oh, that and the fact that people actually choose to live out here. I can see why the West breeds such renegades and outlaws. The severity of the living conditions must be a large factor."

A faint frown etched Lieutenant West's brow, and he shrugged. "I agree that conditions here are not as civilized as in more settled areas, but I think there is a raw beauty to this land that you're missing."

Whitney turned and looked at the lieutenant. "You really appreciate this land, don't you?" she asked in some surprise. "I just assumed that you felt as I do." Her interest was piqued, and she listened attentively as West began to describe the sunrises over bluish mountain peaks, and the surprise of a sudden summer storm that made barren rocks sprout with green plants in a matter of minutes.

"It's like magic," he said softly. "Where a few minutes before there was only dry, dead rock, all of a sudden green plants spring to life, and tiny creatures swim in puddles that were cracked fissures in the ground before the rain. It . . . it's almost like Creation." He shrugged somewhat self-consciously. "Of course, not everyone feels the way I do, but I find it impressive."

"Yes, yes, I can see that you do." Whitney gazed at him thoughtfully, seeing his sensitivity for the first time. "And I can see that I've missed important details. I should have been listening more intently instead of just asking questions. All of this"—she waved an arm to indicate the rocks and desert—"should be described more fully. The land helps to explain the man, I think."

"Why Cutter?" West asked suddenly, startling her. "Why not someone else? Why did you choose him as a subject?"

After a moment of thought Whitney said slowly, "I don't quite know. I was reading through the Pinkerton reports I'd commissioned on Tombstone and was intrigued by him, by his mixed heritage. I saw a conflict that might shape a man's destiny. There's Cutter—a dangerous gunman traveling a fine line between white man and Indian—a man burdened with the conflict of races. How does he cope? Would he have chosen to be a killer if he were all white or all Indian? It seemed a fascinating subject to explore."

"Do you still think so, after having met him?"

"More so now. I think Cutter is an enigma to himself. After all, a man who is intimidated by a woman is quite insecure. And his stubborn refusal to give in only proves my belief."

Perching on the rock beside her, West pressed his thigh against hers. His voice was low, intimate, as he said, "I hate to think of you being anywhere near a man like that. You're too . . . innocent."

Whitney turned to stare at him, and her face was only inches away. West *did* look concerned, and there was an odd light in his eyes as he gazed at her. "Well," she murmured, wondering why he made her feel so uncomfortable, "we don't have to worry about that now, do we?"

"No." West took one of her hands between his, his blunt fingertips stroking the palm lightly. "Whitney, you make me feel as if I could do anything for you." His blue eyes were earnest as he added in a rush, "I *would* do anything for you! I'd die for you if I had to, I swear I would!"

Nonplussed by his fervor, Whitney just stared at him, and West took that as an indication that she was deeply affected by his words. He quickly drew her close to him, and Whitney had no time to escape before he was kissing her.

The pressure of his mouth on her lips brought only a feeling of distaste, and she put her hands between them and gently pushed him away. "Lieutenant, please! You're far too bold, and . . . and everyone is watching . . . please do not do that again!"

West caught both her hands. "Whitney, you're so lovely," he said. "And if my men see us, they will certainly understand my impetuosity."

She stood up and said tartly, "I'm glad to hear it, because I must admit that I do not! It's growing late, and the shadows are getting shorter. I insist that we continue our journey now."

Retrieving her reticule from the ground where it had fallen when she stood, Whitney straightened and looked at West. He was standing stock-still, his eyes wide and his mouth slightly open. She frowned. Had the heat affected him, or was this some lingering effect of his ardor?

Then she heard it, knew even before Lieutenant West said the one awful word what had transfixed him. The high, shrill, undulating screams echoed from the rocks and ground and sky, reverberating to the very core of her being as she slowly turned around. Apaches.

Not just one or two—swarms of them, streaming over a crest just across the muddy creek, riding as if part of their horses, their painted faces a blur as they rode down on the heat-drowsy soldiers. Whitney was vaguely aware that West was beside her, that he was shoving her roughly toward the back of the shallow rock depression and telling her to get down. Her attention was trained on the painted men hurtling toward them as if spawned from hell, their copper-colored bodies curiously graceful as they fired weapons from atop their swiftly racing mounts.

West was a well-trained soldier, and under different circumstances would not have hesitated to shoot from the protection of the rock shelter. But he had the first responsibility to the safety of the women with him. He didn't dare draw enemy fire then, and there was another woman still out by the wagon. Pulling his service revolver, he told Whitney to stay, and cursed himself for not posting lookouts. But he'd been so enamored of Whitney and her pale beauty that he'd thought only of getting her to himself for a little while. Now he had endangered his entire mission. . . .

Scrambling out of the cave, West ran in a crouching zigzag toward where his men had taken cover behind rocks and the wagon. "Keep that wagon covered!" he shouted, all soldier now, his movements swift and automatic.

Whitney felt a distracted admiration for his presence of mind in the face of danger, but her primary emotion was cold, stark terror. She was frozen, unable to move, but remained in a crouch where West had shoved her, watching and waiting as if the events taking place in front of her were on celluloid. She could hear Mary's high-pitched, terrified scream, the shouts of the soldiers, and the shrill neighs of the horses, but it was as if it were happening to someone else. Shots rang out, punctuated with screams—human or animal? They sounded alike, the terrified screams of the horses blending with the screams of Apaches and soldiers.

The wagon had been overturned, and soldiers were using it as a barrier. Arrows jutted from the wood sides and bench where she had sat such a short time earlier, and the horses had been cut free, whether by design or accident, Whitney did not know.

Guttural shouts mingled with barely recognizable English, and somehow that frightened Whitney more than the arrows and bullets. Those half-naked men were so alien, so different, so terrifying, and what would she do if she had to face one of them?

Shuddering, Whitney crouched lower behind the flat rock she'd been sitting on only a few minutes before. Her mouth was dry and her knees were shaking, and the thunderous beat of her heart almost drowned out the shouts and cries. She squeezed her eyes tightly shut and put her hands over her ears, praying that it would end soon, that the terrible savages would just go away and leave them in peace.

Minutes later her waiting ended.

A soft scrape of foot on rock announced someone's approach—soldier or Apache? She felt rather than saw the shadow at the opening to the rocky cleft, and tried to make herself invisible. Then, recalling the tiny derringer she had dropped into her reticule, she fumbled hastily for it, curling her fingers around it and feeling a little safer with it in her palm. An urgent desire to run made her entire body quiver, but Whitney forced herself to remain still in the hope that if it was the enemy, he would not see her.

Her hopes were dashed when she heard a harsh, raucous voice exclaim in triumph. Whitney opened her eyes to see a dark, leering face beneath a dirty headband and coarse black hair. He wore only a breech clout and moccasins, and had a rifle in one hand. A long knife protruded from the leather thong around his waist. Other than that, he was bare to the elements. Paint streaked his face and chest, vivid against his bronzed skin, making him look even more frightening as he stared at her. A scream froze in her throat, and her eyes locked with the Apache's. He was grinning.

Bringing up the derringer with a shaking arm, Whitney held it in front of her, letting the Apache see it, hoping he would flee. He did not. He only laughed harshly and took several steps closer. Squeezing the trigger, she closed her eyes. The tiny pistol clicked harmlessly. Her eyes jerked open.

But this was no time to regret she hadn't had the gun checked. She glanced from the gun back to the Apache.

When he took two quick steps toward her, she gamely squeezed the trigger once again.

To her surprise—and delight—it fired. Unfortunately, her aim left much to be desired for accuracy.

With a howl of fury the painted warrior grabbed his arm where the bullet had grazed the skin, and glared at her so fiercely she knew she was doomed.

"Dear God," Whitney whispered as the Apache reached for her, jerking her from her hiding place. She half stumbled beside him as he dragged her into the open, calling out to more Apaches on the crest just beyond the creek. One of them called back in the same guttural language, and her captor gave her a shove forward.

Whitney became aware that her hat was gone, and didn't remember taking it off. Her hair was loose, falling around her face in untidy tangles and obscuring her vision, and she gave her head a quick shake. If she was to die, then it would be with her head up, as befitted a Bradford.

"Let me go!" she said tartly, jerking her arm away from the Apache. "I won't run away."

As if he understood what she was saying, the Apache gave a grunt and a shrug, but ignored her. His hand clasped cruelly around her wrist as he dragged her with him. The heel to one of her shoes caught on a rock and she half fell, but the Apache did not slow his pace, nor did he slow so that she might regain her balance. Stumbling, Whitney shouted at him to stop, but he never looked down at her. One knee dragged in the dust, and her arm felt as if it were being wrenched from the socket.

Grinding her teeth together, Whitney managed to pull herself to her feet to escape the indignity of being dragged facedown over rocks and dirt. The Apache seemed not to notice or care. He simply ignored her existence as if he dragged female captives at his side every day. Maybe he did, Whitney thought with a shudder. Wasn't that the chief profession of marauding Indians? And now she was their captive. Had anyone else survived the attack?

Brushing tangled strands of hair from her eyes, Whitney forced a glance toward the wagon, steeling herself against the worst. Several uniformed men lay still on the ground, but she did not see Lieutenant West. Nor did she see Mary. Her gaze swung back to her captor. His eyes were riveted on the wagon being torn apart by his companions. It did not occur to Whitney to wonder why.

"Where's Mary?" she asked in a trembling voice, and hated it because she was showing fear. The Apache's fierce gaze flicked toward her, then away, and Whitney followed his glance. Sitting in a disheveled heap only a few yards away, Mary Walton had her face pressed into her hands, but she was alive. Whitney's immediate attention focused on her maid. "Let me go to her," she said in a stronger voice, but the Apache ignored her again.

"Whitney," a hoarse voice croaked, and she whipped around to see Lieutenant West on the ground only a few feet away. She hadn't recognized him. His hat was gone, his face dirty and bloody. "Whitney," he said again, and she felt her heart lurch.

"Andrew," she whispered, his name coming out in a broken voice. "Oh, Andrew, you poor brave man! Are you all right?"

When West would have replied, an Apache clubbed him with the butt of a rifle, knocking him senseless. Whitney reacted with hysterical fury.

"Damn you! You had no right—there was no reason to do that!" She jerked away from the man who held her and ran to West, kneeling on the ground beside him, taking his face between her palms.

Her voice was tight with anxiety and pain. "Andrew, can you hear me? Oh, do speak to me, Andrew!" she said. He looked so pale and still, the light spray of freckles on his face standing out like ink blots on paper. He was still breathing, but shallowly and with difficulty, and she saw the blood on his right shoulder where he'd been wounded.

She had no time to help him. Her captor leapt after her, and jerked her from the ground by her hair. Whitney turned on him like a cornered animal, her lips drawn back from her teeth and her eyes wide and wild. The Apache held one end of her long hair in his fist, and his black eyes were cruel slits, but Whitney was past caring. Spurred by fury and near hysteria, she launched herself at him, gouging at his eyes and taking him by surprise.

With a grunt the Apache fended off her nails while his companions doubled over with laughter. Goaded by his companions' laughter, the Apache threw her roughly to the ground and straddled her, a knife in one hand and anger glittering in his dark eyes.

Gasping for breath, Whitney was certain she was about to die, or, at best, be scalped, when another Apache—apparently the leader— shouted something at her captor. It made him pause, and with a snarl he leapt to his feet, his legs still straddling her prone body.

Rocks dug into her back, and she could feel the bite of sand against her palms as she levered her body to a sitting position. Her skirts had been tossed up around her knees, and were torn from her struggles, but she didn't give them a glance. Her attention was riveted on the Apache leader, who had vaulted lightly down from the bare back of his horse and was approaching.

Whitney's throat closed with fear. He looked even more menacing than the warrior who wanted to scalp her. He was tall, much taller than the others, and he wore the same breech clout and knee-high moccasins. Belts of ammunition were looped over a wide shoulder and across his bare chest, and jagged streaks of paint decorated his cheeks, forehead, and jaw. A narrow cloth band held the thick dark hair from his eyes, eyes that found and held hers.

A shock rippled through her as Whitney saw that the Apache's eyes were green, and that his mouth was crooked in a familiar mocking smile.

"Cutter!" she gasped out, her eyes growing wider. "Oh, you wouldn't!"

Then her gaze flicked to the wounded soldiers and the lieutenant lying on the ground and groaning with pain, and she knew that he not only would—he had. Her head whipped back to face him, and her voice came out in a puzzled whisper. "Why?"

Cutter stopped beside her and reached down to curl his hand around her wrist, jerking her to her feet. He did not release her, but held her arm tightly, keeping her close.

"Why? Because your *Andrew* there made the mistake of taking you along on a payroll run."

What was he talking about? "I don't know anything about a payroll run. I . . . I'm going to a fiesta," she said lamely.

Cutter laughed, and his companions joined in. To Whitney it all sounded as if it came from a great distance away, and she turned slowly to look at the chaotic scene—the destroyed wagon with the boards that made up the bed ripped out and splintered, and the small canvas sacks lined up in neat rows on the ground. Printed on the sacks were the initials U.S., with smaller writing beneath that she could not see. PAYROLL. U.S. ARMY PAYROLL, and it had been hidden in the bed of the wagon carrying her and Mary to Mr. Tucker's.

"That . . . that is the reason we were attacked?" Whitney asked. It sounded as if her voice were coming from a great distance away.

"One of them" was the hard reply. Cutter flexed his arm and jerked her closer, his other arm scooping her legs from under her as he threw her over his shoulder. There was the brief feeling of weightlessness, then Whitney's breath left her lungs in a rush as she slammed into him. The loops of ammunition belts dug painfully into her chest, and her head dangled down his back so that all she could see was the ground. "You're the other reason, Miss Bradford. . . ."

Six

The next few hours were a blur of random images that Whitney found painful to recall later—the pained, dazed expression on Mary's face as she'd helplessly watched a screaming, struggling Whitney thrown atop a bareback pony with her hands tied in front of her; Andrew West's unconscious form and the prone bodies of several soldiers; the hard, jolting rhythm of the horse as Whitney and her captor rode swiftly over ridged hills and flat, burning sands.

Cutter's arm held Whitney tightly against him, and the cold inflection of his voice in her ear warned her not to fight him. "It will only make it harder on you, and it annoys the hell out of me," he said when she tried to throw herself from the horse to the ground.

"I hope you are annoyed!" Whitney hurled at him. "I hope you're caught and hung!" When Lieutenant West catches up with us, I'll have the last laugh!"

"If the entire United States Cavalry can't catch a handful of Apache warriors, do you really think the few men we just left behind will be able to rescue you?" Cutter returned coolly. "A little more realistic thinking might save you some disappointment, Miss Bradford."

His arm tightened around her midriff when she struggled against him, cutting off her wind and making her gasp for breath. Whitney quickly realized that to continue fighting him would only make it harder on herself. She decided to switch tactics.

The hot sun beat down with a vengeance as they rode over a vast treeless plain, and she tried to ignore the searing heat against her pale skin as she leaned back into Cutter. If she was his captive, she'd better learn to use her wits. Brute strength was on his side, but she had her intellect. Intellect and femininity, and she recalled suddenly the night he'd held her against him, and his obvious desire. It stood to reason he wanted her still, and perhaps she could use that weapon to gain the upper hand.

"Cutter," she said softly when they slowed to a walk in the shade of towering buttes, "are you still angry with me about the interview?"

"The one we didn't have?" he asked in that dangerous voice that made her breath lock in lungs remarkably empty of air. "How could I be angry because you bought and badgered every citizen in Tombstone into saying whatever you wanted to hear? Would I be unreasonable enough to resent your blatant bribery?"

"All right, all right," she said with a gulp. "I realize how annoyed you must be, and how wrong I was." She tried to half turn to see his face, but his arm around her was too tight, and the wind whipped her hair into her eyes.

"Be still!" he warned when she tried to hold her hair back and twist to see him, and Whitney swallowed the hasty retort on the tip of her tongue.

Forcing a placating smile, she murmured, "Sorry. I was just trying to . . ."

"Don't bother. I know what you're trying to do, and it won't work." The silky voice was flat, deflating any hopes she had as he continued. "Don't you think if I wanted you, I could take you whether you wanted me to or not?"

Whitney's throat grew tight, and she felt an icy chill ripple down her spine in spite of the heat. It had not previously occurred to her that Cutter would truly be dangerous to her. She had underestimated him, given him credit for being more civilized than he was. How utterly foolish! This Cutter was not the man who had traded quips with her. This Cutter was every bit as violent as the men he rode with, the hard-eyed warriors who had probably murdered dozens of innocent people without a single qualm. She couldn't help a moan of despair.

"Singing again, Miss Bradford?" came the irritating taunt in her ear, and Whitney ground her teeth together at the awful reminder of his appearance at her bathtub.

"Funeral hymns!" she snapped in spite of her chills of apprehension, and even Cutter's laugh was cloaked with menace.

"Don't die yet. I'm not through with you."

"I had *your* death in mind, if you must know!"

"That would leave you in a fine fix," Cutter pointed out reasonably, tightening his arm under her breast. "At best, you would be left with my companions, none of whom are as pleasant as I am. At worst, you would be left alone out here, with the coyotes and rattlesnakes for company."

"Preferable to yours!" she said much more convincingly than she felt at the moment. He made sense. What would she do if he abandoned her? Only one of the men riding in the V-shaped line behind them looked even remotely friendly or presentable, and there was always the man she had shot. He had looked distinctly *un*friendly at last sight. Squirming against the pressure of his arm under the weight of her breast, Whitney said, "You could let me go" in so hopeful a tone, Cutter almost smiled. Almost.

"Why would I do that? I went to a lot of trouble to get you."

"Won't you tell me why?" She felt the prick of tears at the back of her throat, and was horrified that he might sense her weakness. "I can't be of any use to you," she said firmly, convincingly, but he wasn't buying.

"If you weren't of any use, Miss Bradford, I can assure you that I would have thought of several methods of disposing of you by now." He nudged his horse into a rocking lope. "You're already more trouble than I had anticipated, and I'm beginning to regret taking you."

Seizing on the word *regret* with wild hope, Whitney tried to turn and look at him again, but the motion of the horse threw her back and forth, so that she only managed to bump heads with him, making him swear softly and threaten to tie her over the horse like a sack of meal if she didn't stay still.

It was galling to think that she had come to this! Whitney fumed silently. Ordered around by a half-breed gunman in a startling state of undress, his bare arms shoved up under her breasts in much too close a manner to be decent or comfortable, his bare thighs lean and hard under her legs. And no woman in a skirt should ever attempt to ride astride, she thought distractedly, noting that the dirty, torn folds of material were bunched up around her knees and showing a shocking amount of stocking-clad leg.

She tried not to notice the leers in her direction, or the hot eyes she felt on her. She would get away from this horrible nightmare, she just had to! The pressure of Cutter behind her was nerve-racking, and she tried not to think of his hands on her, or the way he would casually allow his fingers to brush against her breast in a lingering touch that she decided to ignore. She needed to concentrate on escape, on seizing the first opportunity to get away from this nightmare.

By the time night fell, she had ceased thinking of escape. Though she'd tried at first to watch the route they were taking, that had ceased to matter too. All that mattered was the aching, numbing weariness that invaded her entire body, and the tight leather strips around her wrists. They had ridden at a steady pace all day, and were now somewhere in the mountains, what mountains she had no idea. Cutter and the others seemed to know exactly where they were going, but all that concerned Whitney was rest.

When they stopped at last, she clung weakly to the damp neck of the horse, her fingers tangled in its mane as she held on to keep from falling to the ground. Cutter had dismounted easily, and stood by the horse's head, talking to the others in that strange, growling language they used. She didn't bother looking at him when he stepped back to her side, but kept her bound hands fastened to the horse like a lifeline.

"Miss Bradford." Cutter's voice wasn't as hard as earlier, and if she hadn't been so tired that she was almost hallucinating, Whitney would have thought there was a note of sympathy in his tone. "Miss Bradford, if you'll let go of the horse, I'll swing you down and you can rest."

His words finally penetrated her haze of exhaustion, and Whitney peered blearily up at him, through a tangle of pale hair in her eyes. "Rest? Yes, I'd like that. . . ."

When he stood her on the ground, Whitney's legs buckled beneath her and she fell to her knees. She heard the tear of her skirts, but was too weary to care. It wasn't until Cutter lifted her to her feet that she realized one side of her dress was ripped from hip to hem.

"Oh," she said, fingering the frayed edges of the rip and staring stupidly at the ruffled hem of her pantalettes. She'd forgotten that she hadn't worn petticoats beneath the dress. "My dress . . ."

"It's ruined," Cutter said, "but I'm sure your father will buy you another Paris original."

His mockery escaped Whitney, and she nodded blindly. "Yes, I'm sure he will," she murmured. "He likes to see me in pretty clothes."

Cutter made a disgusted sound and propelled her toward a flat rock a few feet away. "Sit down," he ordered curtly. "Téjas will build a fire and give you something to eat. And don't get any ideas about flattering him, either. Right now you aren't exactly looking your best."

Until that moment Whitney had not considered the idea that she might be able to enlist one of the other men's aid, and when she looked up and saw the vaguely familiar face staring at her with something like sympathy, she felt a little bit of hope.

The man looked at her and smiled, gesturing for her to sit on a small rock at his feet. Of medium build, with a dark complexion, he had straight black hair trimmed neatly over the ears. Had he not ridden with the others? She vaguely recalled being joined by a solitary rider sometime after riding away from where she had been abducted. He was the only man who wasn't dressed in breech clout and moccasins. Not that it mattered. Even in trousers and shirt, he wore guns and guilt like a giant banner. He was, after all, the enemy. And subject to gentle persuasion.

"I didn't catch your name," she said when Cutter walked away. "We were never introduced."

Téjas grinned widely as he struck flint to dry sticks for a fire. "No, señorita, we weren't. If I remember, you were a bit too angry to ask for an introduction when we first met."

Whitney managed a thin smile. "Yes, I was, wasn't I? Somehow, that doesn't seem to matter now."

"I can see it wouldn't." Téjas slid a glance toward Cutter, where he knelt and talked with the others. "You should have taken his advice, Señorita Bradford. It would have saved a lot of trouble."

Her glance followed his, and she counted eighteen men. All renegades? Her gaze returned to the slender Mexican across from her. A small tongue of flame caught from the sparks he made with the flint, and it lit his face with a flickering light.

"What did Cutter call you?" she asked, making her voice friendly but not too friendly. After all, he must have heard Cutter's caustic comment, and she couldn't be too obvious. A tremulous smile curved her lips as she pushed awkwardly at the stray curls of hair falling, featherlike, into her eyes, tickling her nose. When it resisted her tired efforts, she blew upward, her bottom lip thrusting out to direct the current of breath at the offensive hair.

"Téjas." He reached out and tucked the strand of pale hair behind her ear. "It's Spanish for Texas."

"Tay-cass?"

"No, Tay*hass*," he corrected her, and when Whitney repeated it correctly, he smiled. "Right."

"Well, Téjas, I think I'm in trouble," she said with an attempt at humor. Téjas's dark liquid gaze was solemn.

"Sí, señorita, I think you are too."

It was worse than she'd thought. She said around the sudden lump in her throat, "So what do I do? Throw myself on his mercy? Appeal to his conscience?"

Téjas flicked another glance toward Cutter, then shook his head. "I do not think it would help."

A cold weight settled in the region of her stomach, lying like a gigantic stone. "What do you mean?"

Shrugging, Téjas blew the tiny flame into a tidy blaze, then sat back on his heels and looked at her for a long moment. "It's too late for that. When it is discovered that the army payroll has been taken, and that you have been captured, every soldier in Arizona will be looking for us. The matter is out of your hands."

"Not if I get word to my father," Whitney put in quickly, and lowered her voice. "I could do that, you know. And once I was returned safely, he would use his influence to smooth things over."

Téjas shook his head, and his eyes were filled with pity. "Señorita, I think you believe what you are saying, but you do not know how matters really are. There will be no *smoothing things over* once the army captures any of us. We knew that at the beginning, and do not expect it."

"Nonsense!" Whitney insisted. "My father . . ."

"Is in New York, and can't do a damn thing," Cutter said shortly, coming up behind her and putting a hard hand on her shoulder to keep her from rising. Just his touch made Whitney stiffen, and the breath catch in her throat. His hand tangled in her hair, slowly winding it around his fist and pulling it so tight she was drawn up toward him. He gazed thoughtfully at the thick curls nestled in his palm as he continued in a tone that was softly menacing. "Don't you remember what I said about sending him your scalp, Miss Bradford? I can still do it, and no one will lift a hand to stop me."

Whitney felt the wings of fear flutter in her breast, and stared up at Cutter's dark, implacable face with wide eyes. He stared back at her, his eyes hooded and unreadable and vaguely terrifying. This wasn't going well. Did he mean he would really . . . really scalp her?

Reading the uncertainty in her eyes, and her struggle in the tremble of her lips, Cutter smiled. "You might think about that," he advised her when it seemed as if she would argue, "whenever you're tempted to open your mouth unwisely. I'm not known for my patience."

"Or your morals," she muttered, then winced as his hands tightened almost imperceptibly, but enough to make her scalp tingle with splinters of pain. Swallowing the hasty comments that sprang to mind, Whitney had the swift, inescapable conviction that she would like to keep her scalp in a reasonably good condition— such as still on her head. And even though part of her refused to believe that he would actually kill her, Whitney decided there were times when judicious silence was the best defense. She pressed mutinous lips tightly together.

"It's about time you shut up," Cutter observed when it became apparent she didn't intend to let him provoke her. He unwound the silky lengths of her hair from around his hand, taking his time, letting his fingers brush against her cheek and the vulnerable nape of her neck, noting her shiver. Weighing the bright, lambent strands of hair in his palm, Cutter slowly drew the blunt tip of one finger across that peculiarly soft patch of skin below Whitney's ear. Hearing her quickly indrawn breath, he smiled. Idly, almost casually, he gently explored the whorls of her ear with the same maddening fingertip.

What is he doing? she thought vaguely through the heated haze that was stealing into her weary body. *Why doesn't he just leave me alone?*

She shuddered, then cast an imploring glance toward Téjas as Cutter threaded her hair through the web of his fingers again, but found no help there. Téjas deliberately looked away, as if unable to watch the silent seduction of her senses, the leisurely lulling of her resistance. Steeling herself, Whitney heard her voice, as if from far away, tell Cutter to stop.

To her relief, his hands stilled, and instead of being angry, he only laughed, softly, but unthreaded her hair from his fingers and let it fall heavily against her back. She refused to look at him but kept her eyes trained on the tiny licking flames of the fire. It was less dangerous than looking at Cutter, and she knew, suddenly, how the ancient Greeks of legend must have felt upon facing Medusa. If she allowed herself to look at Cutter, at his dark, mocking face and riveting gaze, she would turn, irrevocably, to stone.

But then he was talking to Téjas again, using that harsh language that sounded to Whitney like two tomcats in a fight, and Téjas answered in kind. She felt Cutter move away, and gave a slight turn of her head to watch him go.

His stride was fluid, curiously graceful, though she would not have thought of applying that term to a man before now, and the light from a full moon made his ebony hair gleam like a raven's wing. When he motioned for the others to join him, he squatted Indian-style, jackknifing his long legs as the men spread out and counted the small cloth bags that had so recently belonged to the U.S. Army.

When she turned her head again, Téjas was watching her, his dark eyes shadowed with thought. Obviously, he had been appointed as her guard, Whitney reflected, and wondered if he would be lenient. Maybe by himself, yes, she decided, but his loyalty lay with Cutter, who had no tendencies to mercy.

Huddled by the fire, Whitney watched quietly as the men divided up the payroll bags and put them in leather packs. None of them looked very savory, but all had the same harsh look as Cutter had. Téjas appeared to be the only man who was not Apache, but even he spoke the language with proficiency. Whitney recalled Cutter's vivid descriptions of Apache tortures. Surely, he wouldn't—but then, she'd never thought he would abduct her, either.

Why? What did he hope to gain? Her abduction would only complicate things for the renegades, wouldn't it?

It was Téjas, his accented voice kind and sympathetic, who explained Cutter's reasoning. "You are . . . insurance against the soldiers who follow us. With you as our captive, they will not dare attack for fear of your life."

Whitney felt her hopes for a bargain fade away. "But if you release me," she tried weakly, "then they will not be after you."

"The stolen payroll," Téjas reminded her, and she bowed her head in momentary defeat.

There had to be a way out—she couldn't let these men get away with abducting her . . . or worse. She barely looked up when Téjas put something in her hand and told her to eat. The disturbing thoughts haunting her left her with little appetite, but she managed to chew listlessly on a flat, dried cake of some kind. It almost choked her, and she asked Téjas for some water.

She stared at the leather pouch he gave her. "Am I supposed to drink from the same pouch everyone else has used?"

"If you're thirsty," Téjas said. Wordlessly, Whitney handed it back to him. "Tell me if you change your mind."

Whitney shook her head. "I doubt I will," she said. Warmed by the fire, she grew sleepy, and found herself actually nodding. Jerking up her head, she tried to stay awake, but it felt as if grains of sand were pricking at her eyes.

When she nodded for what must have been the tenth time, Téjas appeared with a blanket for her, and murmured that she could lie down by the fire, where she would be warm. "No one will bother you tonight," he comforted her, and it did not occur to Whitney to look for a hidden meaning in his words. She accepted gratefully, and made herself as comfortable as possible. Wriggling, twisting, her bottom lip caught between her teeth, Whitney tried to arrange the folds of blanket over her with her still-bound hands, until Téjas took it from her and told her to be still as he draped it gently over her.

"I'm a lot of trouble, aren't I?" she said with a glance up at him. "It must bother you a great deal to be put in the position of having to console an unhappy, defenseless woman."

He smiled. "Not really. I'm used to comforting Cutter's women."

Did Cutter make a habit of abducting unwilling females? Whitney wondered uneasily. She certainly hoped not. If Téjas was inured to that sort of thing, she might not be able to play on his decency.

She fell asleep almost instantly, and did not wake until Cutter shook her roughly at first light.

"Get up. If you want to eat or take care of any private needs, you'd better do it now. There won't be time later."

Whitney glared angrily up at him as he stood with legs spread and stared back at her with an uplifted brow. "Well?" he said in that cool, indifferent tone that made her hackles rise. Whitney got clumsily to her knees.

"It's not easy to do anything when my hands are tied so tightly!" she snapped, holding up her bound wrists. "Are you afraid I might hurt you?"

"No. You're just easier to control this way." He gave her a rough shove toward Téjas. "Take care of her for me. I don't have time to argue."

A furious retort died on her lips as she caught the quick shake of Téjas's dark head behind Cutter, and Whitney pressed her lips tightly together. She walked with as much dignity as she could muster toward the clump of bushes Téjas indicated, wishing she could disappear. It was bad enough being a hostage, but to be so publicly humiliated was maddening!

Téjas was waiting for her when she emerged from the bushes, and she gave him a defiant glare. "I find this situation intolerable!"

"A captive cannot always choose situations," Téjas said smoothly. "Are you ready?"

Whitney glanced at his horse. "I'm to ride with you?"

"Sí. I hope you do not find my company intolerable as well?"

"No, I find your company vastly preferable to my former companion's!" she shot back, her chin lifting as she strode to the horse's side and waited for Téjas to help her up.

The Mexican was not much taller than Whitney, but he lifted her effortlessly, swinging her atop the horse and vaulting up behind her. He reached around her to grasp the reins, and whispered softly, "Señorita, it might be wise to arrange your skirts more modestly. Not all our companions are immune to your charms."

Glancing down, Whitney saw that her ripped skirt had parted and revealed a slender thigh in thin pantalettes. She saw the steady stares from two of the painted warriors, and quickly covered her leg with as much of the skirt as possible.

"I'm sorry I'm not attired more modestly!" she snapped, and heard Cutter laugh. "Seeing that my baggage was left behind, there's nothing I can do about it!"

"What makes you think I want you wearing anything at all?" Cutter asked, then said something in Apache to those with him. They all laughed, but she noticed that two of the men still stared at her avidly. It made her uncomfortable and apprehensive, and when she heard Téjas say something sharp in their language, she knew that he did not like it either.

She felt safer with Téjas than with Cutter, though she knew that he would do whatever Cutter ordered him to do. She shrank back against the Mexican, and avoided looking at any of the Apaches, including their leader. Whitney wondered uneasily what Cutter had in mind for her, and sensed that some of the conversation between him and Téjas concerned her. She saw Téjas shrug, and they started off at a fast pace.

They ate as they rode, munching on the flat round cakes Téjas said were made of corn meal, then washing them down with water.

"It has the consistency of a cow chip," Whitney muttered with distaste, struggling to swallow the dry cake.

"But it's better than nothing," Téjas pointed out, and she agreed sullenly.

"Yes, but probably not as good as the cow chip."

She felt Téjas shake with laughter, and that irritated her even more. "Really! I suppose I'm the main source of entertainment now?" she asked sarcastically, and Téjas sobered instantly.

"I hope not, señorita."

Whitney tried to look over her shoulder at him, but with the wind and her long, loose hair, could catch only a glimpse of his face. "There's something you're not telling me," she accused him, and he didn't answer. "Téjas? What is it?"

His voice was harder than she'd ever heard it. "Cutter was right. You ask too many questions. Console yourself, señorita, that all will be well in the end."

For the next several hours Whitney was silent, wondering with dread what would happen when they stopped again. Somehow, she knew that there had been argument concerning her, and recalled the hot, avid stares from the two Apaches. One of them was the man who had dragged her from the cave where West had hidden her, the one she had shot. She shuddered thinking of him, and was suddenly glad that Cutter was the leader. At least he only *talked* about scalping her, whereas she felt the others would have done so immediately.

Whitney lost track of time and direction, and was barely aware when they rode from the mountains onto the hot, flat plains again. The terrain passed in a blur of endless riding, with the sear of the wind on her face and the blistering heat of the sun beating down. The Apaches never seemed to mind the heat or the sun, and if Téjas had not thought to give her a battered hat, she would probably have looked as red as the proverbial beet. The wide brim of the hat helped to keep some of the sun from her face, and held the hair from her eyes.

The brief stops were only to water the horses and refill the leather pouch. When would they reach their destination? Whitney thought wearily. And what was their destination? She was so tired that she almost didn't care, but longed only for an end to the constant riding.

They were back in the mountains again when they stopped for the night, making camp on a small plateau choked with stands of pine and evergreens Whitney could not identify. She sat stiffly on a rock near the fire Téjas built.

Numb from the unaccustomed riding and depressed and apprehensive at her situation, her gaze was blank, the irises of her amber eyes mirroring the weariness of body and soul instead of the vast wildness around her; she didn't even see the desolation of the red and purple ridges, and the stark beauty of the thick, towering trees. A cool wind blew, making her shiver. In the distance she could hear the wail of an animal, a coyote, Téjas had told her earlier. Its howl hung in the air for a long moment, seeming to drift on the wind, wavering and haunting and lonely. For some reason, sudden tears pricked her eyelids, and Whitney looked up at Téjas with drowning eyes.

"Nothing will ever be the same again," she whispered in a choked voice, and the Mexican gazed at her for a moment.

"Things always change. Life is nothing but change," he said in a matter-of-fact voice, and knelt beside her to untie her bonds.

With the return of circulation came pain, and Whitney flinched as

Téjas rubbed her bruised wrists in a gentle, chafing motion. "Change does not have to be bad," he continued. "And there are those who can take the worst and make good out of it." He looked up at her with dark, thoughtful eyes. "I think you are a woman who could do so if she chose."

"What are you trying to tell me?"

Shrugging, he said, "Nothing, only—don't surrender your soul."

Whitney frowned. What did that mean? She was so tired, and wished he wouldn't talk in riddles. Especially since Cutter was approaching with long, purposeful strides, and he wore an expression on his face that did not bode well.

"Aren't you the careful little nursemaid?" Cutter said to Téjas, who shrugged and ignored him. "I didn't expect you to treat her as if she were made of glass, you know."

Pausing, Téjas sat back on his heels and gazed steadily up at his companion. He said something in a dialect Whitney did not understand, his tone sharp, and Cutter stiffened. His reply was equally sharp, and Téjas stood and wheeled around, walking away. Whitney stared after him with some apprehension.

Her gaze shifted to Cutter, to his dark face beneath the Indian headband. The beautiful jade eyes were narrowed and cold, fixed on her so steadily that she felt like running after Téjas. She tried to swallow the lump in her throat, but it would not budge.

"What do you want?" she managed to ask tartly, keeping her chin lifted in a gesture of defiance.

Cutter said something in Apache, and the men behind him burst into raucous laughter again, making Whitney even more apprehensive. Kneeling in front of her, Cutter jerked his head toward the Apaches behind him. "It seems that you're a bone of contention, Miss Bradford. Any suggestions?"

"I don't know what you're talking about!" Her gaze flicked from Cutter's unrelenting expression to the half-clad men behind him, and she felt the prick of fear bite at her deeply.

"Don't you?" Cutter cocked his head to one side, and his tone was quietly mocking. "Somehow, I think you do."

Whitney stood up. "Look, if you and the rest of this primitive collection of aborigines want to play games, *fine*, but leave me out of it!"

When she would have walked past him, blindly headed toward the only source of comfort she'd encountered among them, Cutter stopped her, one hand snaring her arm and jerking her around to face him. His voice was silky, but his eyes betrayed him, glittering at her like splinters of emerald ice.

"Leave Téjas alone. It won't work. I've watched you play your own little game, Miss Bradford, and you're not that good at it!"

"As usual, you don't know what you're talking about," Whitney shot back at him, trying—unsuccessfully—to hide her fear with desperate bravado. Her glance shifted from Cutter to the other Apaches, then to where Téjas stood quietly watching and listening. She realized with a sinking heart that he would not come to her defense. She was quite literally on her own.

Switching from anger back to a cold implacability, Cutter shrugged. "It doesn't matter." His fingers coiled more tightly around her wrist, and he pulled her forward.

"It seems," Cutter said in a pleasant tone, jerking her head up with immediate suspicion, "that there is some disagreement about who you belong to, Miss Bradford."

Her voice came out in a croak. "What?"

He indicated one of the Apaches with a wave of his arm. "Lone Wolf says that you belong to him since he was the first to reach you, and that if I—their leader—do not take you, you will be his woman."

"Take me where?"

Cutter blinked, his dark pupils widening slightly in surprise, then smiled faintly. "*Take* you, Miss Bradford—as a man takes a woman."

"That's the most ridiculous—" Her protest halted as she saw from Cutter's sardonic gaze and Téjas's tight frown that it was not ridiculous at all.

"Ridiculous or not," Cutter continued in a disinterested tone, "Lone Wolf says that it has been many months since he has had a white woman, and that even though you are too pale, you have good teeth and strong legs. He has even—very generously, I might add—offered to share you with his cousin, Buffalo Horn."

A wave of fury washed over Whitney, battling with the last shreds of fear. Fury won. Her voice rose to almost a shriek.

"You tell Lazy Wolf and Buffalo Butt—"

"Lone Wolf and Buffalo Horn," Cutter corrected her, "and be careful of what you say—Lone Wolf understands English."

"Then he should speak it!" Whitney snapped.

When Lone Wolf said something to Cutter, he translated for her, "He said English is too uncivilized a language, and he refuses to speak it. As his woman, you will learn to speak a civilized tongue. Or, even better, lose your tongue so that you can't speak at all. So—do you choose Lone Wolf and Buffalo Horn, Miss Bradford? They're fine, strong warriors and good hunters."

Cutter's gaze was faintly mocking, but his tone was serious, and Whitney stared at him for a long moment.

"Of all the absurd . . . surely you don't expect me to even consider what you're suggesting?"

"I don't see that you have much of a choice," Cutter said with a lift of one dark brow. He folded his arms over his sun-bronzed chest and smiled at her. "Unless I exercise my option to take you as my woman, you have to choose between us. Though I'm beginning to think I should just give you to Lone Wolf and be shed of you. . . ."

It felt as if a vise were slowly closing around her heart and lungs, and Whitney began to feel light-headed. In the fading sunlight she saw the glitter of anticipation in the eyes of the two Apache warriors, and the mockery in Cutter's face. As badly as she hated to give him the satisfaction, she heard herself say in a weak voice, "It's like choosing between a boil and a wart, but I suppose I choose you. . . ."

"Flattery, Miss Bradford, will get you nowhere," Cutter said, and took several steps forward. Whitney had a blurred glimpse of Téjas's face as Cutter grabbed her, and that was her only warning.

With a swift twist of his wrist, Cutter ripped away the rest of her dress, leaving her in her chemise and lace-trimmed pantalettes. Whitney screamed with shock, grabbing at her torn garments. When Cutter tossed them carelessly aside and reached for her again, she managed to step deftly out of his reach.

"Don't you dare . . . *dare* touch me!"

"Going back on your word, Miss Bradford? Tsk, tsk. And I thought you were so zealous about that sort of thing."

His soft voice did not ease her fears the least bit. She could see the menace and determination in his eyes, and it launched her into a frenzy of resistance.

Did he mean to take her there, in front of everyone? Her mind buzzed, and she was only vaguely aware that Cutter was trying to calm her as she backed away, coming to a halt against the inflexible wall of a rock. Each time he reached for her, she lashed out at him, kicking and screaming defiantly.

Dimly, through the whirl of her spinning hair and the pinwheel of her arms, she could hear Téjas say in a faintly admonishing voice, "She fights for her virtue like a tiger, amigo."

"Tigers aren't known for their virtue," said Cutter with a grim set of his mouth, ducking the wild swings aimed in his direction. "And any tiger can be tamed with a little judicious handling."

Breathlessly, through the stinging silk of hair in her eyes and mouth, Whitney panted. Slowly she said, "I . . . won't . . . be . . . handled!"

Her brave statement was for naught, however, as Cutter proceeded to do just that, much to her dismay.

"Whitney! Whitney—calm down," he demanded, succeeding at last in grabbing her arms and holding her. She writhed and kicked, half sobbing, driven across the line into hysteria. As if she had needed anything else to propel her into losing control; his obvious intention was more than enough. He'd have to kill her first, she decided grimly, and renewed her efforts to break free. Death would be preferable to the fate he had in mind. . . .

Cutter's mouth set in a harsh line as he tried to keep her from breaking away from him. "Dammit, Whitney, it's not what you think," he said close to her ear, but she was past hearing. Summoning all the strength in her body, she fought Cutter like a wildcat, twisting and squirming.

"Will you be still, dammit? I'm not going to hurt you! Did you hear me?"

His words finally penetrated her frenzied mind, and Whitney slowly grew still. Cutter whirled her around to face him, his eyes raking her tear-streaked, dirty face.

"Stop fighting me—I have to make a good show of this."

Then he turned with her in front of him, facing the amused Apaches. Whitney froze as Cutter put one hand on her breast, and her eyes glazed with panic. She could hear him talking in that deep, guttural tongue again, and saw the leering grins on the faces of the men watching. Her gaze sought and found Téjas, and she tried to read his hard, set features. His dark eyes were wide and sympathetic, and she could see his concern, but knew he could not—would not—help her.

When Cutter caught her even closer, running his hand intimately over her body, Whitney closed her eyes. He'd lied to her, and now she faced the worst. She could hear the laughter of the Apaches, and felt Cutter lift her in his arms.

"You lied again," she said dully without looking at him, and his grip tightened.

Cutter's voice was flat as he held Whitney hard against him and said in English so she could understand, "I claim the white captive as my woman. She is not for any other man to take."

His words fell on Whitney's ears like blows, and her apathy fell away. How dare he treat her like a chattel, like a prize he had taken! Rebellion flared in her eyes, and Cutter felt her stiffen.

Unleashing a torrent of angry curses that would have done any reporter in her father's newsroom proud, Whitney blistered Cutter's ears with every denouncement she could think of. Her fingers curled into claws that raked at his face.

Cutter could hear Téjas's laugh behind him, and the Mexican's opinion that maybe he had, indeed, caught himself a tiger he couldn't tame, and wasn't it a novelty to have a woman fight him so hard? Irritation battled with a certain amount of detached admiration for her courage and strength of purpose, but her resistance was making matters damned inconvenient. Damn her, didn't she have any sense at all? Couldn't she see what he was trying to do?

With deliberate deft movements Cutter trapped Whitney in the vise of his arms until she sagged weakly against him, gasping, her eyes still defiant. Then he picked her up and flung her over his shoulder, snatching up a blanket from the ground, stalked up the slope behind their camp and into the privacy of the rocks and brush.

Téjas watched, his mouth set, his eyes shadowed. The Apaches waited, listening, and in a few minutes they all heard Whitney screaming. Téjas looked down at the ground and shook his head. It was the only solution, and it had been unavoidable, but he still didn't have to like it. In spite of her struggles, Whitney was now Cutter's woman.

Seven

Cutter held both Whitney's wrists in one hand, jerking her arms up over her head. His hard-muscled body was slanted over hers, holding her down, his face only inches away.

"Can't you fight harder?" he taunted when she twisted beneath his weight. He was angry—angry at Whitney and angry at Téjas, and angry at Lone Wolf for forcing him into an explosive situation. And most of all, he was angry at himself. Why had he given in to the impulse to abduct her? He'd meant only to frighten her badly, so she would give up her ridiculous mission to pin him down to that damned interview. Not normally given to this particular method of terrorizing, he'd changed his mind when he'd discovered that West intended to be her escort on his ill-fated payroll run. Why not? he'd thought. It might very well get two birds with one stone. Unfortunately, the bird he'd intended to just frighten had the bad judgment to nest cozily in the lieutenant's arms with her hair loose and flowing like ivory silk, her lips parted, and instead of remaining in the background as he'd intended, Cutter had allowed himself to be drawn into the situation.

Cutter could tell himself that he'd ridden into the fray because Lone Wolf had lost patience with Whitney's desperate struggles, but he knew better. Subduing female captives was a specialty of Lone Wolf's, and he'd been given orders not to really hurt her, just terrify her. But after she'd recognized him, the options were narrowed to one—a hostage had to be taken until the payroll gold was disposed of, and it had seemed only natural to take Whitney, as he'd told an obviously skeptical Téjas.

So, he mocked himself with more than a little irritation, *now that you've got her—what are you going to do with her?*

One option came to him in a rush of heated blood that wasn't getting any cooler with her soft body writhing under him. And it almost didn't matter that the object of his attentions was struggling like a landed trout. Cutter ran his hand over her body, slowly exploring her curves, his eyes coming to rest on her flushed, angry face. Silky hair tumbled into eyes of a molten gold, and the pale porcelain cheeks were stained a rosy pink that looked, in the glimmer of the crystalline moonlight, as if they had been delicately painted.

"Is that the best you can do?" he asked mildly when she tried to bring one knee up to catch him in the groin. "You're very bad at this, aren't you?"

Whitney screamed again, the sound bursting from a throat already raw. Cutter's heavy weight was pressing her against unyielding rocks on the hard ground, and her every movement was thwarted by his quick reactions. She was furious, but also terrified. Her screams had subsided to half sobs of frustration and fear, the sounds hoarse and almost unrecognizable, and still he had not done more than hold her down and subject her to his unwelcome touch.

But she knew what came next—she remembered Nathan and his cold, cruel hands—and she remembered the degrading acts that followed. Whitney was almost frantic with apprehension. She didn't know what was worse, the waiting or what was to come. She'd almost exhausted herself with her struggles, and Cutter wasn't even winded. He held her easily, almost contemptuously, with one hand, his lean body pressing into her so heavily that she could hardly breathe. She could feel the smooth musculature of his bare chest against her, the flexing of those long bands of muscle that looked so smooth and sinewy and could be so inflexible. His hips and thighs rubbed against her belly with her every movement, and she couldn't help but notice that he was becoming more aroused by her continuing struggle. The quick, unbidden memory of his body as she had first seen him came to mind, and she banished it before she lost her sanity from fear and the waves of chills that racked her.

It was no use. Through the thin breech clout he wore and the even thinner material of her pantalettes—oh, why hadn't she worn petticoats, *yards* of petticoats?—she could feel every detail of him, urgent and insinuating, pressing into her so hotly she began to lose the ability to breathe. And when she glanced up into his eyes with a glazed look of confusion and suffering, he had the cruelty to grind his body more closely into hers.

It was too much. Twisting her head so that she would not have to see his triumph and gloating, Whitney closed her eyes against Cutter. Her hair was caught beneath her so that she could avert her face only so far, and she could feel his gaze resting on her, almost speculatively, she thought, as if she were his next meal. And perhaps she was. She tried to remember some of the details of the torture he'd related to her, but, thankfully, she could not recall a single mention of cannibalism.

But then, she wasn't so certain, because he began to taste her, small tastes, almost experimental, and she went rigid in his tight embrace. Her lashes flew up, revealing eyes of a startling gold, with pupils unfocused and deep as the Arizona canyons.

"Whatever you're going to do," she managed to gasp out in a voice that was dismayingly weak and afraid instead of scornful and arrogant, "do it and get it over with!"

Cutter's smile was cold, a sensuous quirking of his lips that did not reach the unfathomable eyes, and his head bent, his dark hair catching the moonlight in its straight, gleaming fall, moving slowly to lavish searing kisses on the exposed thrust of her shrinking flesh.

Surrendering in theory and surrendering in reality, Whitney quickly discovered, were two entirely different propositions. One involved only the dissolving of resistance in the mind, and the other—oh, the other—that, she was finding out, involved so much more. When did Cutter change from roughly dominating her to this tantalizing coaxing of a response from her unwilling body? He had altered his method so subtly that it took her a moment to absorb it.

How could I have forgotten—even for a moment—the expert manipulation of his hands, the skilled caresses that could wring response from a turnip?

"What . . . are . . . you . . . doing?" she demanded in ragged breaths as the outlaw began slowly to untie the laces to her tattered chemise. It was such a pitiful scrap of clothing, but it lay between her and nudity, and she tried to press her spine into the ground, seeking escape from the swift, sure fingers that undid the laces as deftly as a lady's maid. Of course, he had probably had a great deal of experience in untying laces, Whitney thought dimly.

"You told me to hurry, love, and I hate to keep a lady waiting when she's so obviously hot and ready," Cutter said in an irritating purr that made Whitney stiffen even more.

Unhappily, she said, "But I'm not . . . hot!" And as if to prove her claim, she shivered, a long, undulating shudder that went from the tips of her white-blond hair down to her bare toes.

"There's a difference," said Cutter in a tone that was faintly mocking, "between hot, and—*hot.*"

"You're talking in riddles, and I don't know what you mean!"

Weaving his hands into her own tight-laced fingers, which she still held over her head, Cutter pulled them down so that her arms were between them, and he began to examine her smooth, manicured nails and the soft pink palms that had never seen a callus.

"Maybe you don't," he said thoughtfully, as if just realizing another possibility. "In fact, I'm beginning to think you really have no idea what I'm talking about."

Shifting slightly, pulling her hands lower between them so that her arms were neatly trapped, he deliberately put her hands on him, against the smooth, flat plane of his belly, nudging aside the edges of his buckskin covering, and Whitney tried to jerk away.

"Don't! Oh, don't! If you have to . . . to do what it is you're going to do, don't expect me to participate!"

"Participation is expected," Cutter said against the curl of her ear, his breath stirring pale strands of hair and making her shiver again. "In fact, darlin', participation is necessary. I can't . . . create . . . alone."

"Create what?" Her voice was miserable, but she thought that if she could keep him talking, she might delay what looked to be the inevitable.

"Create the stars, spread moondust and magic, that sort of thing. You know, the euphemisms for fornication that are found in those wonderful novels you females devour so avidly." His mouth crooked in a smile. "Except, of course, you don't read those, do you? It seems you prefer the more adventurous type of literature, tales of gunfighters and wild, painted savages. That's why you came out here, isn't it? To do research? Well, Miss Whitney Bradford, I intend to assist you in your research. We can't let any avenue go unexplored, can we? And you can always go back to New York, to your safe little padded nook where reality can't touch you, and write about the time you were kidnapped by Apaches, taken into the mountains and . . . ravished . . . until the sun came up in the morning."

His lips bent to her ear again, ignoring her soft sob, spreading his own brand of punishment with searing kisses, then moving to her lips to take them, gently at first, lulling her to immobility, then harsher, plundering her mouth and her soul with heated brutality clothed in the disguise of desire.

For Whitney, the past times Cutter had been so bold and hateful as to make her unwilling body respond to his touch were now simple moments of play. They had been nothing to the raging torment that he was awakening in her now, the licking flames of something new and different and urgent that began in the core of her being and radiated outward, like a meteorite spinning carelessly and heedlessly toward its own destruction.

This . . . this was cruelty at its worst, much worse than a simple, cold rape. That she could have borne with the soul-searing knowledge that she had been overpowered by a much stronger force. *What is done to one*, she reflected with sodden misery, *is not nearly as bad as what one does to oneself. . . .*

"You're not cooperating," Cutter said against the soft underside of her breast. His mouth sought, and found, the rapidly hardening peak, lips closing around it with erotic sensitivity, making Whitney gasp and arch unthinkingly into him. "That's a little better," he murmured when she began to ache in all the colors of a rainbow, and Whitney could almost hear the sound of her imminent surrender.

"I hate you," she said through the thick clouds of heated despair, but it sounded like a caress, and Cutter only continued his devoted attention to her breasts, cupping them in his palms, lavishing first one and then the other with consuming, moist kisses. She had to escape, had to rescue herself before the final humiliation of surrender overwhelmed her. . . .

From somewhere deep inside, the black memories that were always there, slumbering like a sharp-fanged beast, surged up to claw at her, and she recalled Nathan, his painful, clumsy caresses that had left her shaking and quaking with apprehension. It had been so awful, so cold and impersonal, as if she were a rag doll at his disposal, that she had learned to disassociate herself from him at those times. That had only served to make him crueler as he'd tried to wrest a response from her, tried to tear away the shrouds of restraint that emasculated him. Those long, horrible nights had taught her that she could retreat inside herself and be safe, that there were parts of her no one could reach, and with the return of that memory, Whitney descended into the velvet void of oblivion.

She was still awake, her eyes open, unblinking golden orbs that saw without seeing. But the integral part of her that was necessary for subjugation, for cooperation, had spirited away into a safe hiding place where it could not be reached.

In the silver wash of moonlight that spread like cool fire over the brush-studded mountains, Cutter saw that he'd lost her, and he didn't know how or why. Her flesh was still warm, still moist from his kisses, but her slender arms were limp and flaccid, unresistant. There was no response, no struggle, just a blank acceptance that was more daunting than screaming fury.

It had an extremely dampening effect on his ardor, and he mused somewhat wryly that he should have known better than to try to seduce a woman who had no scruples about raping the lives of others. People like J. Whitney Bradford, accustomed as they were to demanding and getting every wish fulfilled, reacted with complete shock when faced with objection and refusal. And especially coercion—though it might be their own style to use it freely.

It took several moments for his body to get the message that his mind had already absorbed, so Cutter's voice was tight with frustration when he shook her gently and said, "I think I've subdued you enough for the time being."

Dragging her attention back to him, she intuitively saw that he was momentarily defeated, though she wasn't certain as to the reason. Had it been something she'd said or done? Whatever it was, she was grateful, relief flooding through her in a return of strength as she said tartly, "What do you mean—time being? Surely you don't intend to force me to go through anything like this again!"

In spite of his frustration and the urgent need still pricking him, Cutter saw the mordant humor in the situation and said more calmly than he felt, "Just as soon as I think I'm willing to endure your prickly form of surrender again."

"I did not surrender!" she flashed, her pride stung, though she knew that he meant her sudden escape into the yawning pit of oblivion.

His grip tightened briefly, warningly, on her wrists as he said in that dangerous tone that made her shiver with a return of dread, "It's too bad you're such a shrew. Maybe I should change my mind and let Lone Wolf have you. He'd shut you up quickly enough, and maybe teach you a few manners in the process."

"Oh, you'd like that, wouldn't you?" Whitney ground out, trying to recapture her brief moment of victory back from the shadows where it had fled. Why couldn't she make him feel as weak and helpless as she felt at this moment? "I suppose the reason *you* can't teach anyone manners is because you have none yourself!"

Cutter laughed. "How would you know? Aren't you the same woman who demanded that I kiss you again because you were interested in seeing if it felt the same? What book of etiquette do you find that in?"

Whitney twisted, glaring up at him. "You would bring that up!"

"Ah, I see. Good manners are defined by who's making the rules at the moment, right?"

"Murderer! Half-breed killer!" she spat out, resorting to random insults to prick him. She immediately regretted it.

Even though his expression remained impassive, fine lines bracketed his mouth, and Cutter's eyes narrowed to cold slits. Whitney knew that she had succeeded in gouging a response from him, but feared that she would pay a heavy price for her success.

He looked at her for a long moment, as if contemplating some horrible revenge, but then shook his head. "How old are you?" he asked abruptly, startling a reply from her.

"Twenty-four. Why?"

"It's amazing that no man has killed you before this. I thought maybe you were younger than you look." Releasing her, Cutter swung to a sitting position, one arm still on each side of her prone body. He ignored her gasp of indignation and said, "Don't flatter yourself that I want you. I took you as my woman only because Lone Wolf has a distressing habit of killing the women he takes, and I didn't figure you'd do us as much good dead as you will alive."

Whitney could not think of anything to say that might not anger him again, so she pressed her lips tightly together and remained silent. The night air was cold on her bare breasts, but she didn't dare call attention to herself by trying to cover them. She lay quietly waiting, thinking for the first time since Cutter had carried her kicking and screaming up the hill, that he might not actually harm her. But right now the outlaw looked so fierce and unapproachable that it was impossible to ask him his intentions.

The silver blaze of moonlight reflected from the uncertain hope in Whitney's eyes, and Cutter said flatly, "Don't assume that because I haven't taken you yet, I won't. I don't need any trouble with Lone Wolf, and I don't owe you anything. It's your fault you're here in the first place."

Whitney asked carefully, "Why do you say it's my fault? I didn't ask to be abducted."

"Didn't you?" Cutter's eyes were dangerous. "I can remember

warning you several times that you were walking on shaky ground with your actions, but with your customary arrogance, you chose to ignore me. Or maybe you thought your father would be able to buy me off. It was your choice, and you chose unwisely."

Whitney hated herself for asking, but she couldn't help blurting out, "But you will let me go, won't you? I mean, you can't keep me forever."

Cutter's compelling gaze found and held hers for a long moment. "Can't I? Who's going to stop me? And don't bring up your father again, please. I've never met him, but I already hate him."

Feeling the distressing prick of tears begin to sting her lids, Whitney shut her eyes. Why did he torture her so? Why didn't he let her go?

As if reading her mind, Cutter leaned forward again so that his face was only inches from hers. His tone was casual, conversational, but it barely concealed the barb of his words. Her eyes flew open.

"Women like you who use old money and soft bodies to get what they want make me long for fresh air. Maybe I'll educate you—keep you around to show you how the rest of the world lives, Miss High-and-Mighty Bradford. It might open your eyes, but somehow I doubt it." His hand slid, softly menacing, to cup her chin in his palm. "You're so selfish that all you think about is what you want. You never stop to think about the other person's needs, do you? You probably don't even know that there are people who go to bed hungry every night of their lives. And if you knew, you probably wouldn't care. Right now you're more worried about that soft white body of yours than you are anything else, and you know what? You've got every reason to worry, because I'm not sure when I'll get tired of you and decide to take my chances with the U.S. Army."

Rising in a smooth motion, Cutter jerked Whitney up with him, giving her no chance to resist. His probing gaze was thorough and insulting, and she could feel the hot flush of embarrassment stain her face and neck, but she did not attempt to cover her bare breasts with her arms. She would not give him that satisfaction.

He seemed to recognize her rebellion, and a faint smile slanted the hard lines of his mouth.

"Take the blanket. I'll wake you up soon so that your ardent admirer doesn't begin to think I'm not doing you justice."

Whitney nodded silently, feeling relief and apprehension at the same time. When Cutter motioned for her to lie near him, she did so, rolling up in the blanket and thinking she would not be able to sleep a wink the entire night. She lay staring at the moon-drenched shapes of trees and bushes distorted by shadows.

She didn't understand Cutter at all. Just when she thought he was one way, he switched directions and changed her mind about him. He was still a killer, and now she knew he was also a thief, but she wasn't certain how *evil* he was. Were there degrees of evil? she wondered. She'd never considered that before. Evil was evil, plain and simple, black and white, no gray. But now she wasn't so sure. It would have been easy enough for Cutter to let Lone Wolf take her, or to take her himself, but he'd chosen not to. Was it possible he'd meant it when he said he didn't want her?

For some reason, that rankled, and Whitney felt a wave of irritation. Of course he wanted her. She'd felt his desire the first time she'd met him, and again when he'd come to her hotel room. But he hadn't acted on it. In some ways, she thought, Cutter was a great deal like her. When he wanted something, he took it. So why hadn't he wanted her?

Shifting, she glanced at him. He was only a few feet away, as if not quite trusting her to be too far, sitting on the ground with his long legs bent. He still wore the breech clout and knee-high moccasins, a costume so brief as to be almost nonexistent, and Whitney wondered if he was cold. If so, he didn't give any indication of it. He sat staring straight ahead, his face impassive. She gave a light shudder. Cutter was much more Apache than he was white, she thought drowsily. If not for his lucent green eyes, she would have sworn he was all Apache. . . .

Startled from sleep by a hand on her shoulder, Whitney gave a small scream before she recognized Cutter's dark face. Everything was in shadow, and she realized that the moon was hidden by a tall mountain peak. Cutter's teeth flashed briefly, and his voice was rich with laughter.

"Scream louder. I don't want Lone Wolf to think I'm not man enough to take you more than once."

Whitney glared at him. "Wasn't once enough? Do I have to put on a show?"

Cutter's response was to pull the blanket from her so quickly she couldn't grab it. He shoved her back when she tried to sit up, straddling her body, his hands raking over her bare, quivering breasts. Whitney immediately obliged him by screaming very loudly, the sound echoing through the night. Instead of stopping, Cutter continued to touch her, lightly, casually, as if only remotely interested.

Writhing beneath him, she panted, "All right! You've made your point! I'll scream as many times as you want me to, only—only stop!"

Hooking his fingers in the waist of her pantalettes, Cutter yanked downward with a swift movement, ripping them away, making Whitney scream again. "You can't wear them in the morning anyway, or they'll know I didn't take you," he said practically.

"What do you expect me to cover myself with now?" she snapped, near tears. How much more could she endure? The past two days were more than she could bear, and she wished this nightmare would end.

Shrugging, Cutter said, "I'll find something."

Whitney didn't know where to put her hands. She could not cover her breasts and her femininity at the same time, and she squirmed miserably. "Let me cover myself," she said more firmly than she felt, but Cutter shook his head.

"I might as well get *some* entertainment out of this," he pointed out. "After all, if I remember correctly, *you* weren't shy about staring that first day I met you."

She groaned at the memory. Would that day haunt her forever?

"I was too shocked to do anything but stare," she protested in a shaky voice.

"Ah, I don't quite believe that."

"And besides, you took advantage of me at my bath too! Don't you remember?"

"But I didn't look. I only touched." A thread of caustic laughter edged his voice, and Whitney looked at him sharply.

"This isn't funny!"

"No," he agreed, flipping the edges of the blanket back over her. "It isn't. The next time I tell you to scream, I suggest you oblige me more quickly."

Whitney loosed a shrill scream of frustration, catching Cutter by surprise. He recovered quickly, and grinned at her in the shadows.

"Not bad, but it sounds like I just cut your throat."

"If that's part of your lovemaking technique, I'm sure you're not very popular," Whitney said tartly.

"I've never considered including throat-cutting in my *technique*, as you call it, but since I've met you, it's crossed my mind several times," Cutter replied, his voice comfortably chatty.

"Then I assume that you've also considered making love instead of taking me by force," Whitney heard herself say before she could catch the comment. She flushed, hoping he'd let it pass. "I did not mean . . ."

"Like I said before, don't flatter yourself," Cutter broke in with that warmly inviting smile that covered acres of innuendos.

"I don't consider it flattery, but more of a threat!"

"Consider it any way you like." Cutter raked an impatient hand through his hair, pulling off the cloth band and holding it out of his eyes. He'd be glad when morning came and he could go back down the hill, dragging a subdued captive with him. Or at least that was what he'd planned earlier. Whitney did not seem in the least subdued, and without actually harming her, he was beginning to think he wouldn't be able to force her into pliant submission. Lone Wolf was no fool, and he wanted her. He'd take it as a personal insult if he thought Cutter had tricked him. How did he get that through to this hardheaded, imperious woman?

Cutter's eyes met, found, and held hers. "Look," he said pleasantly, his tone belying his cold eyes, "whether you want to or not, you'd better act the part of a well-ravished captive in the morning. Lone Wolf won't take it lightly if he thinks you're not my woman."

"Do you care what he thinks?"

"Normally, no. But this time it's different. We've got a job to do, and can't afford any complications."

"I'm a complication?" Whitney snapped.

"The worst kind. Sex and greed are two of the biggest motivations, and both are at stake here. I don't need you fouling things up."

Whitney was silent for a moment, wondering how she could use this information to her advantage. Cutter's next words banished that notion.

"If you don't cooperate, I'll have to ensure that Lone Wolf has no reason to think otherwise."

The meaning of his words quickly penetrated, and she gave a nod. "I'll cooperate," she said around the galling lump in her throat. "I think I can show my hatred for you easily enough."

To her surprise, Cutter laughed. "Well, I didn't expect you to give in gracefully, I suppose. Just remember not to give Lone Wolf any reason for suspicion, and I'll be satisfied."

It occurred to Whitney as she settled back beneath the blanket that Cutter was going to a great deal of trouble to avoid the easiest way out, and she wondered why. It couldn't be because he didn't want to take her against her will. He obviously didn't have any scruples about taking what he wanted. Somehow, it was faintly humiliating to find out that a renegade half-breed outlaw could so easily reject her, and she didn't know why.

* * *

Dawn came in a soft, pearly glow that preceded the sun. Pale golden light gilded treetops and boulders, and the air was sharp and crisp and invigorating. Whitney could not recall ever having been awake before the sun rose, unless, of course, she was just returning home from some party or ball. And then, she'd always been too tired to notice.

But she was awake now, watching silently as Cutter slashed a hole in the blanket she'd slept in. He gave it to her and told her to put her head through the hole, then tore off a strip of blanket to wrap around her slender waist, forming a crude dress that ended just below her knees.

"That'll get you down the hill," he stated calmly. "After that, I imagine Téjas will be quick enough to find you something to wear. I'm not sure what, but it will be better than the blanket."

Squirming inside the itchy wool, Whitney muttered, "I certainly hope so."

The smile he gave her was flavored with mockery. "Not quite like one of your expensive French gowns, is it?"

"May I ask what you find so offensive about my French garments, Mr. Cutter? You've made several references to them, and I wonder why."

"One—just one—of those dresses from Paris would feed an entire Apache family for a year," Cutter pointed out so reasonably that Whitney almost didn't hear the steel behind his words. "And I don't mean the spoiled beef and half-rotten grain the army passes off on those unfortunate enough to live on one of the reservations. I mean real food, and blankets, and medicine." He gave a shrug. "But that doesn't mean anything to you, does it?"

A faint frown creased her brow as Whitney stared at him. "Before a few days ago, no, it wouldn't have," she said slowly. "I had no idea there were people going hungry on government land."

"Did you ever think to investigate? Or were you interested only in gathering sensational anecdotes you could use to sell more books?"

"That's not fair!" Whitney flashed angrily. "How am I supposed to know about such things?"

Cutter's voice was flat when he said, "You do now," and she gave a start. He saw from her recoil that his words had struck a nerve. "Think about it," he added, then gestured to the slope leading down to the camp. "It's time you show how well you can act. And you might keep in mind that if you don't do it well enough, it won't be an act."

"That thought alone will motivate me to give a stellar performance!"

When she would have stalked down before him, he shoved her firmly to one side. "Remember—I'm the captor, you're the captive. Think you can remember that?"

"Don't you want to drag me down by my hair?" Whitney couldn't help asking, and Cutter grinned devilishly.

"I'm too tempted to trust myself with an answer."

Whitney soon found herself in the galling position of pretending to be a thoroughly subdued victim. It was easier than she thought it'd be—she just didn't look up at any of the men waiting to stare at her. Only Téjas approached, and the glance he gave Cutter made Whitney realize that even he didn't know the truth. She could feel the sympathy almost oozing from his finger pads as he took her arm, and wondered again if Téjas could be beguiled into helping her escape Cutter. It was something to think about.

Cutter thought she made a rather convincing victim. Her hair was tangled and matted with leaves, and she kept her gaze trained on the ground and her mouth shut. The last was a welcome relief, and made Téjas's cold stare much easier to understand. The voluble, verbal Miss Bradford was a stark contrast to the subdued, silent wraith that slunk convincingly behind him now.

Lone Wolf slyly jerked a thumb toward Whitney, and said that he had heard the sounds of their enjoyment long into the night. Cutter replied in English that once trained, the white captive might make a decent squaw.

Whitney's head jerked up, then she quickly lowered her eyes when she saw them watching, feeling the slow burn of anger. Damn him! Did he have to rub her nose in it?

"I'll get you something else to wear," Téjas offered, and pulled Whitney with him. He said nothing about the night before, no words of comfort or sorrow or criticism of his friend, but Whitney noticed the tight lines on each side of his mouth.

When he gave her a pair of *colzones*, loose trousers worn by Mexican peasants, and a *camisa*, or loose blouse, Whitney whispered her thanks.

"*De nada*," Téjas said with a shrug. "It is the least that can be done for what you have suffered."

Feeling slightly guilty, Whitney rationalized that she *had* suffered, even if not as much as everyone assumed. She could not look into Téjas's eyes, but kept her gaze on the ground, wondering if Cutter had overheard. It was very likely he would tell Téjas the truth, and she didn't want to overplay her hand.

"I'm all right, really I am," she assured him. "I'm not hurt, only . . . only embarrassed."

That much was true, she told herself. Still, it was harder to pretend to Téjas that Cutter had brutalized her than it was to continue the act for Lone Wolf. Maybe it was because Téjas was decent and seemed to care what happened to her, and that in itself was a startling thought. After all, he was in this just as deeply as Cutter was. They were all thieves and murderers.

Whitney tried to keep that in mind when Cutter pulled her atop his horse with him, his arm below her breasts and holding her tightly. She was much too aware of him, of the warm pressure of his body against hers, and his thighs resting beneath her legs as she rode astride. There was not a moment when she wasn't too aware of him, of the feel of his hands when he pulled her down from the horse or lifted her atop it; of the curved muscles of his chest against her back and the corded muscles in the arm that held her. And always there was the memory of how he had held her against him and kissed her so ruthlessly into surrender, creating a curious response that was both disturbing and frightening.

Even when she closed her eyes, she could see his face, the pitiless green eyes and hard, sun-browned features, a handsome covering for a ruthless savage. There were times when she thought she hated him more than she feared him, and times when she thought of Lieutenant West and Mary left out in the desert to die, and shivered with terror. Just because he hadn't taken her, he'd said, did not mean he wouldn't.

Eight

That night, when Cutter motioned for her to lie next to him in his blankets, Whitney was about to protest when Cutter anticipated her.

"And don't argue, or I'll have to prove to Lone Wolf that you're a tamed tiger by making you perform tricks," he said when he saw the fires of rebellion glowing in her tawny eyes.

Pursing her lips to argue, Whitney thought better of it. At least he wasn't dragging her off into the wilderness like the night before, and she could lie close to the fire. Giving a tight nod of her head, she lay carefully in the blankets Cutter had spread on the ground.

What she hadn't counted on was that he would lie so close to her, pressing her curves to his hard body in a tight embrace. Her back was to him, and she was startled when he pulled her up and into the angle of his belly and thighs, his lips brushing her ear as he warned with a tremor that was distressingly like laughter in his voice, "Shhh—they're listening."

Whitney could almost feel the watching gazes of the Apaches, and knew they were expecting Cutter to sleep with her. Fuming, she lay stiff and still, not daring to relax for fear Cutter would take it as surrender. When her taut muscles contracted beneath his hand, he laughed softly, the sound rich with genuine amusement. Shivering, Whitney felt his breath whisper over her cheek.

Lightly at first, like the soft padding of a kitten across her bare torso, his fingers explored the luscious curve beneath her breasts, stroking downward in a teasing caress that made her squirm and hiss, "Stop it!"

"Stop what? This?" The clever fingers found and held the rigid peak of a breast and made her body vibrate with reaction. "Or this?" His hand swooped like a hawk beneath the drawstring waist of her *colzones* to cup and hold the nest of tight curls between her thighs, and Whitney went rigid with shock.

"Why are you doing this?" she whispered miserably, and felt his shrug.

"Because it feels good, sweet Whitney. Don't you think so? Haven't you ever had a man do this to you?"

"No," said Whitney, because it was true. Nathan had never bothered with more than the briefest preliminaries, and then never cared if she responded. His had been the touch of a self-absorbed man, not like Cutter, who seemed determined to wrest shivering responses from her poor flesh.

His voice was thoughtful as his hand moved up to her rib cage, his touch somehow lighter and not as searing when he pulled her into him and said, "How interesting."

"Is there anything else you'd like to know?" she inquired in a frosty tone that almost left ice hanging. "Such as the intimate details of my personal habits, and an alphabetically arranged list of any sins I may have committed, mortal and venial?" A faint tinge of desperation laced her voice as she added, "Since we're inquiring into the most confidential areas of my life, suppose we investigate *your* past with a clear and keen eye. Do you like broccoli? How many women have you made love to, and do you prefer the missionary position, or are you more inventive?"

She'd meant to expose his question for what it was—out-and-out prying—but, unfortunately, Cutter chose—with some malice, she was certain—to take her literally.

There was no hint of amusement in his rich, warm tone, the one as beguiling as the sweetly scented blossom of the Venus's-flytrap, and his words gave all the appearance of complete sincerity.

"I don't particularly care for broccoli unless it is in a clever sauce, and I must admit—sorrowfully—that I have never counted the women who have been carried away by my charms in bed. As for the latter—ah, sweet Whitney, I am still finding new ways to reach for the stars. Would you care to help me?"

"I would not!" she said, and felt his body shake with laughter. Her cheeks flamed, and she wished she could just melt into the ground. He thought her amusing when she was trying to be condemning.

Though she wouldn't have thought it, Whitney did have the effect of flaying Cutter's never too active conscience with her words and actions. There was something oddly appealing about a woman who defended her virtue with such stubborn courage, especially when her body betrayed her at every turn.

Minutes slid past, and when he did not move the hand lying on the curve of her rib cage, she began to relax. Then his voice murmured into the whorls of her ear, "If you don't count the casual encounters, sixty-five."

"Excuse me?"

"Sixty-five women. That's only the ones I've made love to, not just used for convenience."

Convenience . . . "I suppose you mean, like the woman you had sent to your hotel room as if ordering fresh towels?"

"Something like that."

There it was again, the thread of amusement in his voice, infuriating and embarrassing at the same time. He must think her a fool or worse, to imagine that she might consider this sort of conversation anything close to witty or enjoyable!

"I hope, for your sake, that you are exaggerating," she ground out from between her teeth. "There are rampant diseases that can be quite debilitating!"

"How kind of you to be concerned. Or are you thinking of yourself?"

"*I* haven't been as free with my body as you have! I am fortunate enough to have better sense than to be so loose and immoral."

"And here I thought it was more than my imagination that you kissed me back," said Cutter in the beguiling tone that could strip away her pretensions in an instant. "Does this mean you prefer going to the edge of intimacy—and stopping? There are certain forms of contagious disease that can be caught that way too, you know."

"Shut up!" she almost shouted, and could hear the stir from the blanket-wrapped forms around the fire. "I can't stand talking to you like this anymore," she added more quietly, hating Cutter and the way he could so easily provoke her in spite of her best intentions.

To her immense relief, though she knew it was only because it was growing late and he had tired of baiting her, he said, "Then go to sleep, love. We'll continue this some other time."

It was a long time before she relaxed enough to fall into an exhausted sleep, and longer still before Cutter felt able to do the same. He lay looking up at the star-sprinkled night sky, wondering cynically why he didn't just follow his natural inclinations and complete her seduction. Maybe it had something to do with his newly discovered conscience, that long-dormant inner voice that could be so annoying to the hedonist. He'd become much more decadent than he'd ever considered, a fact that was faintly enlightening, vaguely puzzling. If he had degenerated into a man with so little regard for the state of his morals, why stop now? Why allow Whitney Bradford—by anyone's definition a spoiled and overweening young woman—to appeal to his better instincts? It came as rather a shock to him to find that underneath the numerous layers of protective covering, he still had feelings. And some shreds of decency. It was most inconvenient to discover that now, when he had happened upon a woman who stirred the slumbering chords of a desire untrammeled with some of the more dissipated forms of sensuality.

There was something about Whitney that made him stop short of taking her against her will. And in spite of the evident responses he was able to coax from her with his casual seduction, he knew that it would be a raping of her spirit to take her until she was ready.

A tightening in his body prompted him to the inescapable conclusion that he would have to rid himself of her as soon as possible, or he would be going against his own better judgment as well as Téjas's warnings.

"Amigo," Téjas had said, "if you keep her, it will cause a great deal of trouble, and not just a complication with Lone Wolf. I have this feeling that nothing will go as planned."

Which, of course was obvious. The unexpected addition of a female was trouble enough; Whitney's temper only compounded the problem—as did his damnable male urges that were so insistent, he found it hard not to give in to them. This, thought Cutter grimly, should be an excellent opportunity to test his resolve.

For the next few days Cutter managed to stay as far away from Whitney as he could, given their circumstances . . . until night fell and he was expected to lie beside her in his blankets, enduring her soft, trembling curves against him. He began to form a different vision of hell from the one he'd had before. . . .

Crouching on the ground before the fire Indian-style, Whitney had the dismaying thought that she now bore an appalling resemblance to an Apache squaw. In spite of the floppy hat Téjas had given her and the long-sleeved shirt and trousers, her pale skin had acquired the tint of a sun-ripened peach. Long tresses bleached even whiter by the sun were caught back from her eyes with a strip of cloth, falling in two thick braids down her back. And she'd even learned to understand a few words in Apache, words grunted impatiently at her by the men when she was too slow or confused.

Vees'án, or bread cooked in the ashes, was a common word directed at her. *Tú* was another, and the person speaking would indicate that she was to give him the water pouch. A word that sounded like "coo" meant fire.

Whitney had also learned *dah*, or no, and she used it to Cutter as often as she dared. He was somewhat amused by her rough grasp of a handful of Apache words, but not very impressed.

"As much as you hear it, you've learned only some very elementary words," he observed with a blistering smile that succeeded in taking her down a peg or two. "And those have to be repeated several times before you understand."

Flashing him a scowl, her voice was unconsciously haughty as she retorted, "I'm not at all accustomed to being spoken to as if I'm common! Nor do I see any reason why I must struggle to understand what those heathens mean, when they understand English and could save a lot of time by speaking it. . . ."

That was as far as she got before Cutter grabbed her arm and jerked her close. His expression was dangerous. "I suggest you watch not only what you say, but how you say it. I'm not as good-natured as Lone Wolf, and I may have some objections to being referred to as a heathen."

Flicking an uncertain glance toward the Apaches not far away, Whitney bit her bottom lip to still its sudden quiver. The strain she was under was slowly wearing her down, and she felt as though she was ready to explode with tension. It had been a week since she'd been abducted, and they were still riding—aimlessly, it seemed to her, though Téjas had said they had a destination in mind. She looked up into Cutter's hard green eyes.

"Why don't you let me go?" she asked sulkily. "You wouldn't have to listen to me then."

"I don't have to listen to you now." Cutter's smile was nasty. "I could do what any self-respecting Apache does to a woman who won't shut up."

"I know, I know! You'd beat me with a big stick! You have suggested it so many times, I'm surprised you haven't done just that."

Cutter's hand rose to grasp her jaw, squeezing so tightly, Whitney's eyes widened in apprehension. "Or," he said softly, "I could cut out your tongue. Your father may even thank me for it one day." He released her.

"My father has probably routed every soldier in the entire territory, and they're hot on your trail!" Whitney said much more bravely than she felt. There had been no sign of pursuit, no sign of soldiers or even another white man, and she was beginning to have a sinking feeling that she might not be rescued. Where was Morgan Bradford? Did he even know his only child had been kidnapped?

Morgan Bradford was agonizingly aware that Whitney had been taken. Upon receiving an urgent telegram from not only Kermit Tucker, but one from Lieutenant West as well as Mary Walton, he had taken the first train to Arizona Territory, and was now in Tombstone, discussing her rescue with the U.S. marshal.

Virgil Earp was a tall, quiet man with a thoughtful manner, and he was not in the least impressed by the angry demands of the New York tycoon.

"Mr. Bradford, when you calm down enough to listen instead of talk," Earp said quietly, "we can get on with our discussion."

Bradford sucked in a deep, angry breath, but realized that the marshal was right. "She's my only child," he said tersely, and Earp gave a polite nod.

"I understand that. My guess is, that band of renegade Apaches will keep her in as good health as possible. They're smart enough to know we'll be after them, and smart enough to know we won't take too many chances with her life."

"Then why haven't you gone after them?" Bradford demanded tightly.

Earp swiveled in his chair, his large frame making it creak ominously. "I explained our position to you. We did send out some men, but that's a pretty large area out there. Our best bet is to wait until they make their demand of us, and believe me—they will."

Bradford wiped a hand across his face and sank down into the wooden chair he'd been offered when he'd first stormed into Earp's office. "I'll pay anything they ask!" he said hoarsely.

"They're counting on that." Earp frowned. "They took a rather large payroll when they took your daughter, and the lieutenant in command said he recognized their leader. Does the name Cutter mean anything to you?"

Bradford's lips tightened. "Yes. That's the outlaw my daughter came out here—against my advice, you understand—to interview. I am at a loss, Marshal, to understand why a dangerous outlaw like Cutter could be running loose in the streets of Tombstone."

Earp gave an eloquent shrug. "He's never been convicted of any criminal charges."

Bradford stared in disbelief. "I've seen the thick folder my daughter compiled. News clippings listing his crimes in black and white!"

"Being charged and being convicted by a jury are two different things," the marshal explained softly. "The last fracas he was in, he got off because eyewitnesses testified that it was self-defense. I've got no liking for the man myself, but I have to say that he gave Smith every chance to back out, and even let him empty his first pistol before he was forced to shoot back." Earp shrugged again. "It's not always the fastest gun who survives—it's the man who can stay cool enough to take his time and aim."

Sagging back into his chair, Morgan Bradford shook his head. "I take it this Cutter keeps his head, then."

"Pretty much so." Earp looked at him shrewdly. "He ain't liable to make too many mistakes, if that's what you're thinking."

Bradford's pale eyes locked with the marshal's, and he said softly, "Oh, no, you're wrong, Marshal. Cutter has already made one huge mistake—he abducted my daughter!"

Cutter had come to the same conclusion. Taking Whitney had been a mistake from the beginning. Lone Wolf had accepted Cutter's taking of her, but he could not keep his eyes from following the tall, slender figure of the white captive he wanted, and Cutter knew it was only a matter of time before he brought up the subject again.

Slanting a glance toward Whitney, where she knelt close to Téjas by the fire and talked quietly, sometimes laughing at something he said, Cutter felt a twinge of impatience. In spite of her outward compliance, he had to force her to his blankets every night, force her to lie next to him, his arms around her as if she were really his woman, her curves pressed back against him. He was unable to stop his body's reaction to her, and he knew she was aware of it. If he didn't get rid of her fast, he'd have to either give in and take her or let Lone Wolf have her. His pressing need left him in a nasty temper most of the time, and even Téjas looked at him narrowly and stayed out of his way.

It was an explosive situation, and Whitney unwittingly sparked an eruption.

It had been two weeks since she'd bathed, and when they camped beside a clear running mountain stream, she begged Téjas to allow her a bath.

"Please! Oh, Téjas, I feel so dirty and unkempt, and I promise I won't be foolish. You can go with me, and turn your back while I bathe."

Hesitating, and not wanting to bring up the matter to Cutter, who acted like a gut-shot grizzly most of the time, Téjas allowed Whitney to talk him into it.

"It's against my better judgment, but I suppose it won't do any harm as long as I stand guard," he muttered at last. His smile was faintly weary. "You are a big responsibility, little one, and I admit I will be glad when you are allowed to go free."

Pushing at the opaline strands of hair that dangled in fetching curls over her eyes and small, straight nose, Whitney looked up at him with a sudden catch of her breath. There was no mistaking the golden lights in her eyes that caught and reflected a rushing surge of hope. "Oh, Téjas! Do you think that will be soon?"

"No," he admitted, hating to spoil her brightened mood but knowing it was better than to allow her unfounded hope. "But whenever it is, we will all be better off for it."

Whitney recovered quickly from her disappointment. They were too far into the wilderness for her to expect release soon, but it was still an ever-present thought in her mind.

"You're dying to be rid of me," she teased in spite of her disappointment, and Téjas grinned.

"Aren't you dying to go?"

"Right now I refuse to think further than the bath you promised me."

"You've grown wiser in the past two weeks," Téjas observed, smiling at her slow nod.

"Let's say—not as certain that I can make things go my way." She wore a faintly puzzled expression on her face, and Téjas hid a smile. "It's been very hard for me to realize that I can't force Cutter to do what I want him to do. Instead of telling him what I really think of him, I have to pretend to be meek, which is only a thought better than pretending that he . . . never mind."

Téjas narrowed his dark eyes. *So that was it.* He'd been wondering why Cutter was so edgy, and why he occasionally let his guard down enough to gaze at Whitney with brooding lights in his eyes. Now he knew. His former judgment of Cutter's good sense was restored, and Téjas was in better spirits than he had been for some time. It was one thing to take a captive, and another to force a woman. Cutter knew that, which had made his abduction of her even more puzzling to Téjas. But now he began to revise his earlier opinions into a thought too startling to be considered. He would have to think about it awhile. It didn't seem likely, not when they were so different, at opposite ends of logic and living from each other.

But as Téjas sat on a flat rock near the mountain stream with his rifle resting casually on his lap, the disturbing thought came to him that the situation was probably much worse that he'd imagined. How long would Cutter wait? If he had not taken her yet, it was only a matter of time before he acted on the desire even Téjas could read in his eyes. And Lone Wolf made no secret of the fact he wanted her. He'd tried to barter for her, but Cutter had flatly refused, saying he wasn't tired of her yet.

Rubbing his jaw, Téjas wished they would complete what they had set out to do so Whitney could be released. Unfortunately, they couldn't exchange the gold until their confederates met them, and there must have been some trouble because they hadn't arrived yet. Meanwhile, waiting and watching were wearing on all of them. He turned his attention back to Whitney, trying not to look too closely as she splashed contentedly in the shallow mountain stream.

Whitney smiled. The water was cold, relieving some of the oppressing heat, and it was clear and fresh, bubbling over smooth stones. Well-hidden by trees and bushes, the stream formed a rough bay that made a perfect bathing spot. Thick foliage sprouted on the sloping banks that were studded with rough boulders, providing a perfect screen from prying eyes. Whitney relaxed, elbows propping her up, body stretched out just below the water's surface, admiring the scenery. She could barely see Téjas's head as he stood guard on the banks, and knew he was prudent enough not to try to watch too closely.

It was invigorating in the water, and when she tired of finding new ways to flop about, she sat up and used as shampoo the pulp from a yucca plant that Téjas had given her. Swirling froth slid quickly downstream with the current, lacing the water with white bubbles.

For some reason, Whitney felt much more lighthearted than she had since being abducted. While she was splashing in the water she could forget for this short time that she was a captive with no rights and privileges, subject to the whims of her captors.

It didn't take long till she became bored with simply lying in the shallow stream and staring at cloud puffs scudding across the sky, and she sat up, her forearms over her breasts, casting longing glances toward a shaded spot within sight. A cascading waterfall splashed from a rocky crest twenty feet high, the crusty slopes leading downward surrounded by bushes heavy with leaves. Rocks carved by eons of wind and falling water had formed a deep pool at the bottom, and it was toward this appealing spot that she yearned.

Having learned to swim as a child, at her father's insistence, Whitney didn't feel the least hesitation about the obviously deep water. She worried more about upsetting Téjas. But it would be so nice to swim and dive from the flat rocks, and she soon convinced herself that she could do so without Téjas noticing she was gone.

She was right. Shivering at the chill air that made her flesh prickle with tiny bumps, Whitney pulled herself up on the bank, her bare toes digging into the smooth, slippery surface of a flat rock that jutted out. Water cascaded down with a musical tinkling that drowned out the rush of the stream, and her worries. A faint smile tilted her mouth as she paused for a moment, letting the sun-warmth of the rock seep into her feet and the sun bathe her skin. Then, rising to her toes, she curved her body into an arc and dove into the pool.

Breaking the surface of the water several yards beyond the banks, she came up gasping for air and shaking the hair from her eyes. Her arms moved through the water, and her legs treaded slowly, keeping her afloat. Tiny pinpricks of goose flesh dotted her skin, and she decided to take one more dive before moving back to the spot Téjas had chosen for her to bathe.

Apparently he hadn't missed her, so no harm was done. It was so quiet, with only an occasional bird call drifting through the roar of the water falling, Whitney was reluctant to leave it behind. But she knew that she'd better hurry, or Téjas would be impatient with her for taking so long, and he was the only ally she felt she had.

Pulling herself back up onto the wet rock where she'd balanced a few moments before, Whitney paused only briefly before she leapt in another dive, cleanly cutting through the surface and surging forward underwater before she came up for air. The water was silky, sensuous against her bare body, strangely erotic as she wriggled through the depths.

Her lungs were almost depleted of air when she came up, and she was gasping as she clawed at the wet ropes of hair in her eyes. Struggling to find her footing on the bottom of the rocky pool, she stood up in the waist-deep water and began to wring out her hair. Her head was bent down so that she had only a brief glimpse of movement before she was grabbed by an inflexible hand.

A startled scream burst from her throat, cut off sharply when she saw it was Cutter. He was looking at her quite intently, and there were lines around his mouth that she did not recognize as a struggle for iron restraint. Why should she? After all, he did nothing to stop her when she slipped lower in the water so that it slapped against her chin and shrouded her quaking body. His voice was light, almost casual, slightly teasing.

"Have I found a mermaid in the mountains?"

She decided to brazen it out, and looked over his shoulder for Téjas as she said, "You couldn't find me if I wasn't lost!"

"Then you *are* a mermaid, I take it."

This time his silky voice betrayed him with a slight tremor, and Whitney looked at him closely. There was still nothing in his face to indicate that she might be in danger, so her voice was cross. "Téjas said it was all right for me to bathe, and so I am."

Cutter followed her glance downstream and smiled. "Don't bother looking for your watchdog—I sent him back to camp."

Whitney swallowed the sudden bite of fear in her throat. Looking over his shoulder, she saw Cutter's horse was standing belly-deep in the stream, reins looped over its neck, and knew that Cutter must have been watching for several minutes. Why hadn't Téjas warned her? she wondered angrily, then answered her own question: Of course, he'd assumed that since it was Cutter, and she was his woman, it didn't matter. How distressing.

She couldn't know that wasn't quite true, that Téjas had tried to stand between her and disaster, but Cutter had flatly ordered him back to camp. And now Cutter was angry. It had nothing to do with the fact that she was bathing, but had more to do with the fact that he had not been sensible enough to deny himself the brief but dubious pleasure of voyeurism.

As she slowly became aware of the danger, saw in his taut expression that he was in no mood to pass pleasantries, Whitney sank even lower in the water, her hands moving beneath the clear surface to cover her wet, bare breasts.

"It's a little late for that, isn't it?" Cutter asked in a reflective voice. "You should have worried about spectators when you were posing up on that rock."

She flushed. He must have been watching her, and she had thought no one could see. He was right about it being too late for modesty, and she suddenly realized that she was in more danger from Cutter than she would have been from Lone Wolf. At least Lone Wolf would have stopped to think about Cutter; Cutter obviously had no one to answer to but himself.

As if he read her thoughts, Cutter smiled again, reminding her of the wolf in an old fairy tale, and—feeling remarkably similar emotions to what Red Riding Hood must have felt—Whitney suppressed the urge to say "What big teeth you have!" as she tried to recover lost ground.

"Cutter—if you'll let me get my clothes, I promise not to be so foolish again. I . . . I left them hanging on the bushes by Téjas, and . . ."

"Whitney, Whitney," Cutter chided her, "do you really think I intend to let you go back now?" His gaze dropped from her breasts lower, to that shadowy triangle the clear waters of the mountain stream couldn't fully hide.

Trembling, Whitney made a futile effort to cover herself and heard him laugh. Her chin lifted, and her gaze fixed on his broad chest. The pool level struck Cutter midthigh, but she realized that he must have been swimming also, because he was wet too, his dark hair slicked back and dripping, and his smooth skin gleaming and damp. She could feel Cutter's intent gaze lingering on her naked body, on her breasts and thighs, and the hollows and curves only one other man had ever seen. She tried to sink down to the stream's rocky bottom, but he curled his hands around her upper arms, his muscles knotting as he pulled her up.

Whitney saw with horror that the wet strip of buckskin he wore around his waist clung snugly, outlining his private parts, clearly exhibiting the fact that he was aroused. And when her gaze flew back up to his face, she saw with a sick feeling in the pit of her stomach that he had no intention of releasing her. . . .

Her pleas were futile, and the quick, jerky resistance of her arms and legs did nothing to slow him down as he lifted her against his wet chest and carried her from the stream to the grassy slope. Angry, half-sobbed, completely incoherent demands tore from her throat in a flood, and Whitney hardly realized what she was saying as she tried to catch his hands, tried to stop him from removing his own garment.

"You can't! Oh, I don't have any clothes on. . . ."

"That's the general idea, darlin'," Cutter broke in in a husky voice, and she shook her head.

"No one does this!"

His voice was amused as he caught her hand in one of his and said, "This is the way it's done, Whitney, I promise."

"No! Not . . . not like this! You don't understand what I mean . . . oh, you can't kiss me there!"

"Why not?" Cutter's thick voice drifted to her from the region of her rib cage, and Whitney squirmed miserably. His tongue explored the gentle indentation of her navel, and she jerked her hand free and tugged desperately at his hair.

"Stop it! That . . . that's indecent!"

"Not according to my definition," Cutter murmured, his mouth caressing the smooth velvet of her stomach in spite of her wildly tugging hands.

Whitney gasped with shock and dismay when he cupped her breasts, holding them, teasing the taut rosettes that fit neatly in his palms, making her writhe and renew her demand that he stop.

Ignoring her, and deftly catching her flapping hands with one of his and pinioning them over her head, Cutter shifted to lie atop her, one long leg thrown casually over hers, his eyes smoldering with desire. She could feel the hot length of him against her shrinking flesh, could feel the corded muscles in his legs as he shoved her thighs apart.

In desperation she summoned the welcoming shadows of oblivion that had saved her before, but to her despair they would not come. Only the sweeping fires of Cutter's touch pulsed through her, chasing away the black memories that could have kept her safe. *Oh, God—when will this stop?* she begged silently, but there was no escape.

Capturing her mouth with his, Cutter kissed her in spite of her efforts to evade him, using one hand to hold her head still, his fingers firmly gripping her chin. His lips dragged across hers in a lingering, arousing movement that made her breath catch, and he seemed to know it. Almost playfully, he ran the tip of his tongue over the outline of her lips in a moist, dewy caress, one hand shifting to cradle her wet head in his palms, the fingers doing strange, erotic things to the damp satin skin of her nape and below her ear. When Whitney trembled violently, his body maneuvered so that he was between her thighs, the heat of him nudging insistently against her, yet holding back, and Whitney felt as if she were drowning in a boiling sea.

Reality faded away, and the world narrowed to her and Cutter, the two of them afloat on some island of touch, taste, and scent. In spite of her resistance, the slow, coiling fire ignited, suffusing her body with a strange languor that slowed her movements as if she were moving underwater again. Cutter's mouth moved from her lips to her throat, pausing at the small hollow where she could feel her pulse racing.

Almost as if she were standing outside her own body, Whitney saw him move lower, his mouth trailing over her damp skin and leaving her shivering with reaction. When he cupped one breast in his palm and caressed the peak with his tongue, Whitney clasped him convulsively, not knowing or caring what she was doing.

It was all so strange, so confusing, and she suddenly wanted an end to the insistent yearning inside her, the fire that he had sparked. She'd never dreamed it could feel like this, could make her ache for him, and she writhed helplessly, arching her hips to meet him.

Then, without warning, she felt Cutter pause and put a hand over her mouth when she moaned a protest. It was only the sudden stiffening of Cutter's body and his muttered "Dammit!" that gave her any indication something was wrong. Whitney lay still and dazed, not quite certain what had happened. In the next instant Cutter was rising swiftly to his feet, reaching down and yanking her up beside him, his voice tight and frustrated.

"Get dressed, darlin'. Someone's coming."

"My clothes . . ." Whitney looked at him in confusion, still unable to grasp the sudden end to the emotions raging through her.

Cutter gave a short, low whistle, and his horse stepped obediently forward. Whitney recognized her clothes hanging over the animal's neck. Her embarrassment and confusion were only too evident as he tossed her the slightly damp trousers and shirt Téjas had given her, and Cutter laughed.

"God must have a sense of humor after all. Don't worry, darlin'— you've been rescued. For now." His soft, lazy drawl sounded more promising than reassuring.

Shaking so badly she could hardly pull the blouse over her head or step into her trousers, Whitney gave an incoherent gasp of sudden anguish, wondering why she had yielded for even an instant. How was the man capable of so easily dissecting her soul, removing it cleanly from her body without a trace? Tears stung her eyes, and she silently vowed to detest Cutter forever. Thank God she had been prevented from committing the most foolish act of her life!

Being a hostage must have deranged her, given her a strange form of brain fever that made her susceptible to half-Apache outlaws. There was no plausible explanation for what had just happened, for the fact that she had almost given herself to Cutter— had *burned* to give herself to him. Her cheeks flamed at the memory, and she prayed fervently to be rescued soon.

Cutter pulled her atop his horse, and they rode through the stream back to where she had left Téjas earlier. He was there now, his face creased with concern as he paced the narrow bank.

Téjas stopped short when he saw Whitney, his eyes on the way her clothes clung to still-damp skin, and how her eyes were like smudges of tarnished gold burning in her face. Cutter swung her down from his horse.

"They have arrived," Téjas said abruptly, and took Whitney's arm when Cutter pushed her toward him.

"Take her—before I do. How many of them?"

"Five," Téjas replied, feeling Whitney quiver beside him. He said something to Cutter in Apache, and Cutter gave him a sharp look and equally sharp reply.

Whitney felt Téjas shrug, but could not look at either him or Cutter. She felt as if the Mexican knew what had happened, knew how her own body had betrayed her. What had he said? Oh, what did it matter anyway? There was nothing Téjas could do, nothing she could do. Cutter would do whatever he wanted. And for some unknown reason, her traitorous flesh seemed to be on his side too.

"Whitney." Téjas shook her arm, and she glanced up at him, startled. His voice was gentle, and she realized that he must have spoken to her several times.

"Yes?"

"Are you all right?"

She smiled faintly. *Only if you can condone losing one's soul to the devil,* she replied silently, but said aloud, "I'm not hurt."

Téjas gazed at her white face, not believing her for an instant. He'd seen the determination on Cutter's face, and had known his *compadre's* mood when he'd ordered him back to camp. And looking at Whitney's flushed, defiant face, he knew she was lying. Perhaps Cutter had not physically harmed her, but she was wounded nonetheless.

"Come on," he said gently, and walked with her back up the grassy slopes.

Nine

Carefully keeping her expression blank as if she did not understand, Whitney listened to Cutter converse with the men who'd ridden into their mountain camp a short time before. These were the men the renegades had been waiting for, the Mexicans who had come to bargain, and she knew that whatever happened, it would affect her.

Her heartbeat quickened, and she tried to seem as if she wasn't listening. When she heard one of the men escorted by uniformed soldiers say in Spanish, "El Presidente will be most grateful for your contribution, señors." she felt a brief spasm of thanks that her father had insisted she learn Spanish.

The soldiers wore the garb of Mexico, bright red and blue uniforms with silver-hilted swords at their sides. It was Cutter who conducted the bargaining, and the Mexicans found him a shrewd negotiator. Several times one of them abruptly stood up, incensed, but each time his companions soothed his ruffled feelings.

Whitney gathered from the swift flow of words flying back and forth that the payroll Cutter had stolen was to be traded to the Mexican government for food, ammunition, and supplies, and before she could puzzle too long over who would need that great an amount, she learned that it was intended for the Apache families living at the San Carlos Reservation.

"You do realize, señor, that it is against our policies to undermine our own government," Capitán Lopez pointed out to Cutter. "Selling rifles to our enemies does not fall within those boundaries."

"Is it your policy to walk away from a great deal of gold for very little in trade?" Cutter countered, and the captain frowned.

"I suppose that President Gonzáles would approve the trade if we are not actually supplying renegade Apaches with the weapons," Lopez said with a smile. "It would only prolong a conflict that is certain to end in much unhappiness for all those involved."

Cutter's hard face did not change expression. His eyes were opaque, unreadable, and he did not move from the easy crouch he'd taken to parley. They would meet his demands because it was to their advantage. Just like the Mexicans, to try to wrest the last drop of blood from a man, but he guessed they were no different from most people. And Téjas had warned him they were excellent barterers. More like horse traders, he corrected his friend silently, and kept his gaze cool and noncommittal.

"We would not be so foolish as to ask for rifles for your enemies, Capitán," he lied smoothly. "We wish only to help the unfortunate people forced to live on a small bit of barren land at San Carlos. The rifles, of course, would be sold elsewhere."

"Ahh," Lopez murmured with a glance at one of his companions, merely to show he might be willing to accept Cutter's lie at face value. A slight shake of his companion's head forced another attempt at negotiation. "I suppose we can give you most of the things on the list you have shown us, except, perhaps, for the boxes of rifles and the cartridges. That might break the treaty we have signed with the United States, and . . ."

"Everything or nothing," Cutter said bluntly, suddenly tired of the pretense. He kept his gaze fixed on the captain. Lopez flushed, and glanced again at the man in the beaver hat.

They put their heads together briefly, muttering inaudibly, then Lopez sat up abruptly. "Since you are not actually using weapons against our country, we agree, Señor Cutter. You drive a hard bargain, but we agree."

"You have the supplies close by?"

Lopez nodded and stood up. "We will meet you in two days time, Señor Cutter, at the village of Rio Blanco, a day's ride from the border. Do you know the one?"

Rising to his feet in a smooth, effortless motion, Cutter nodded. "We will be there."

Whitney felt her heart lurch. A village—would she be taken along? And what if there were soldiers waiting? And if it would take them only two days to ride from where they were now well into Mexico, they must be almost at the border, she reasoned quickly. If Cutter took her into Mexico, she might never get back again, might never be heard from again. It wouldn't be the first time someone had disappeared without a trace, and she certainly didn't want to be the next missing person!

As Cutter's gaze shifted toward where she sat, Whitney looked quickly down at her hands twisting in her lap. She must not let him discover she knew anything. And she would have to seize the first opportunity to escape. . . .

But to Whitney's dismay, Cutter had no intention of taking her with him. He didn't bother to tell her, but if anything went wrong, he didn't want to risk Whitney ending up in some Mexican officer's bed. And he didn't quite trust the regime under President Gonzáles, who held his presidency by a thread. It was only a matter of time before Porfírio Díaz took control again, and he did not want to be caught between opposing factions. In the constant state of revolution, one never knew where to stand in Mexico.

So Cutter decided to leave Whitney in the care of Téjas, with complete disregard for her furious tantrum when she was informed. Jerking away from Téjas in spite of his effort to hold her, she sought and found Cutter.

"I refuse to be sent off to some little town and never heard from again!" she raged, not quite understanding why she was so angry. After all, with Cutter away, she might be able to convince Téjas to set her free. Why was she so angry at the outlaw leader?

Cutter wondered that himself. Tucking his thumbs into the narrow waist of his breech clout, he said with a slight smile, "I thought you'd be glad to get rid of me."

"Oh, you don't know how glad I am to be rid of you! I hope you never come back."

Allowing the shadow of a grin to flicker over his face, Cutter said softly, "You may get your wish if Lopez double-crosses us." Long-boned fingers grasped her chin, and his voice was unexpectedly soft when he asked, "Would you miss me, sweet?"

"Like a boil!"

Letting his hand fall away from her face, Cutter said, "And just when I thought you might have formed an affection for me, tiger-eyes."

At his light teasing, some of her anger faded, leaving a dull acceptance, and Whitney muttered, "Why didn't you tell me you wanted to help hungry people on some reservation? I would have understood that, and I might even have helped you. My father has a lot of money."

Mocking lights danced in his green eyes, and he allowed them to focus on her for a moment in an almost benevolent way. She was so earnest, Cutter almost could believe her. "Would you? I suppose you would have bought a city for them with your father's money. It's not quite that simple, Whitney. And to be honest, not all those supplies are for the San Carlos Reservation."

"But isn't that dangerous? You said—Téjas said"—she corrected herself quickly, not wanting him to know she understood Spanish—"that you were sending supplies to the reservation for the people who did not have enough to eat."

"I am." Cutter seemed amused now. "Can this mean that you are impressed with my noble cause, dear Whitney? That you are so bowled over by my philanthropy that you are worried about my safety?"

"Go to the devil!" she snapped, pushing at the hair in her eyes. "I don't know what I believe about you, Cutter! One moment you're pure Apache, fierce and mean and cruel, and the next you're speaking excellent English and talking about things only educated men could know. I don't understand you at all!"

"Then we're even." His voice was flat again, indifferent and cold. "You like me if I'm some kind of Apache Robin Hood, but if I admit to having some larceny in my soul, then I am immediately a villain. I think when this is over and we don't need you anymore, I'll be damned glad to be rid of you." He nodded to Téjas. "Keep her away from me—for her sake," he told the quiet man.

"You should not provoke him," Téjas said when Cutter walked away, and she wanted to scream.

"Not provoke *him*? What would you say if it was *you* who were abducted, dragged through all the cactus in Arizona, and continuously assaulted. . . ." She broke off, not trusting herself to continue.

Reasonably, calmly, as if to defuse the hysteria he heard lurking just beneath the tremor in her voice, Téjas said, "I concede your abduction, but I have not noticed any cactus spines in you. And as for the assaults—"

"Which *you* have done nothing to stop!" she flashed, making him lift his brow in surprise.

"You're baying at the moon if you think *I* can do anything about those," he said. "It probably won't do any good to mention this, but if you would try to speak softly to Cutter instead of fight him like a she-wolf, he might be more agreeable." He paused, politely waiting for the response he saw trembling on the tip of her tongue.

"Speak softly! When he . . . when he does the things he does to me? But I suppose, you being a man, you wouldn't understand that!"

"I might. An invasion of one's soul can be desolating." He waited for her to absorb the implications before he added, "And much worse than any physical violation."

Whitney—confused by the conflicting emotions tearing her apart and uncertain how much he knew—resorted to tears, and Téjas put an arm around her shoulders to comfort her.

"You're much stronger than you think you are," he tried to reassure her.

"But it's not over yet, is it?"

Slowly shaking his head, Téjas met her watery gaze. "No, it is not. But soon, I think. Soon."

Whitney held to that vague promise in the days to follow.

It was dark when they arrived at the hacienda where she was to be left with Téjas, and Cutter was in a hurry to move on. Exhausted by the long, hard day of riding down from the mountains and into the flat, arid valley, Whitney almost fell from Cutter's horse when he stopped in front of a shadowed building that gleamed dully in the moonlight. He pulled her down and guided her through a doorway and into a room.

She was so weary, she had only a vague impression of the house, of tall ceilings and tiled floors, iron grillwork and simple, functional furniture. They were in a kitchen, and she could smell the tantalizing odor of food cooking in pots slung over the fire. Several women chattered softly in Spanish, casting sidelong glances at her as she stood awkwardly in the doorway.

Cutter gave her a gentle nudge forward, and she took several steps and halted. No one spoke to her when she perched on the edge of a wooden stool, staring blindly ahead. And no one seemed surprised or frightened at the dangerous-looking men crowding into the house. Whitney briefly closed her eyes as Cutter and Téjas stepped to one side of the room.

"I'm leaving at first light," Cutter told Téjas, and nodded at Whitney. "Don't let her out of your sight, amigo. She'll try to talk you into freeing her."

Téjas slid his dark gaze toward Whitney's drooping figure. "Don't you think it's time?"

"Not yet." Cutter looked thoughtfully at Téjas. "Has she gotten to you?"

Shrugging, Téjas said, "She is guilty of indiscretion and willful stubbornness, but I do not think she deserves to be hurt."

Leaning back against the plastered wall, Cutter looked at his friend with dangerous eyes. "If you think I'm wrong, tell me, amigo. We've been friends too long to have a woman come between us."

Téjas dragged a weary hand across his eyes. "She has not come between us, but I admit I do not understand what is between the two of you."

There was a moment of silence with crackles of tension pulsating softly in the air; then, nodding, Cutter said, "I don't understand it either."

They exchanged long looks, and a faint smile curved Téjas's mouth. "I had that suspicion."

Both men looked at Whitney, now wolfing down food one of the women had given her. It was the first real food she had eaten since being abducted, and it was delicious, corn tortillas wrapped around bean paste. She ate three of them without pausing, then gulped long drafts of freshly squeezed orange juice directly from a pitcher.

As she finished, Cutter approached and lifted her up by one arm, taking her wordlessly with him. Now that she'd eaten, Whitney was too sleepy to protest his cavalier assumption that she would go willingly. What did it matter?

She hesitated only briefly when he showed her into a small room with a pallet on the floor. A single candle burned on a low table beside the pallet. Whitney quickly dismissed any objections she might make to the sleeping arrangements. It was late, she was tired, and after sleeping beside him for two weeks, she was hardly likely to object too strenuously this night. Besides, didn't he usually leave her alone except for a few cursory attempts to irritate her? Even though she had felt his obvious desire for her beneath their blankets, he had done nothing more than frighten her a few times.

Except for yesterday at the mountain pool, when he made me forget all my resolutions. . . .

"I'd like to wash," she said, giving a sullen glance around the small room that was little larger than the closet in her bedroom at home. "I'm dirty, and hate to sleep on even that crude bed without washing."

Cutter cocked a dark brow at her, his face impassive as always. "As you can see, there is no tub in here."

"Would it be too much to ask for a pitcher of water and a bowl?" she shot back, moving to the pallet and sinking down on it. With every passing moment she was growing more weary, and had even begun to entertain thoughts of sleeping in her unkempt state when Cutter gave a shrug and left.

He returned in a few moments with a pitcher of water and a large bowl, and even a few thick cloths and a towel.

"Will this do?" he asked, tossing her the cloths, and she nodded. "For now."

Cutter sprawled back on the pallet, watching as Whitney washed her face, her arms, and her feet. She shoved the rag up under her blouse with surreptitious wipes, though she would have much preferred removing her clothes. Hesitating, she wondered if he would leave so she could wash the rest of her, then decided against asking. He might decide to help her, and she certainly didn't feel like another battle of wills.

"There's enough water for you," she commented as she crossed to the pallet, and he grinned lazily.

"Is that a hint?"

Her gaze flicked over his lean, half-naked body. He still wore the breech clout and knee-high rawhide moccasins, and she'd almost forgotten what he looked like in regular clothes. Maybe these were his regular clothes, what he was most comfortable in, what he was. There seemed to be a wide discrepancy between Cutter the gunman and Cutter the Apache leader, but she was too tired to try to make the distinction now.

"Do what you want," she said wearily, and stretched out on the pallet beside him and closed her eyes.

In a few moments she felt Cutter move, and to her dismay, felt his hands on her.

"What are you doing?" she demanded, pulling away. She glared at him in the dim light, noting the reflection of the candle dancing in his wicked green eyes.

"You told me to do what I want," he mocked her, "and so I am."

"You know that's not what I meant!"

"Do I?"

Lurching sideways, Whitney half stumbled, and caught herself at the same time as Cutter reached her, drawing her back onto the straw-stuffed pallet in an easy motion.

"Ah, are you still trying to pretend you hate my touch?" he asked in a voice thick with intimacy, the subtle warmth of his fingers straying beneath her blouse to her just-washed skin, and lingering.

To their mutual surprise, she burst into exhausted tears. Leaning her head against his bare chest, she said, sobbing, "I don't feel like fighting you anymore . . . I just want you to go away and leave me alone, or ravish me, or whatever it is you're going to do to me, but no more of this! The suspense—"she hiccoughed noisily—"of waiting is driving . . . me . . . mad. . . ."

After a tense moment Cutter reached for one of the towels and gave it to her to wipe her nose. Then he used a dry corner to wipe his chest and said, "Go to sleep, *chica*. I won't bother you anymore tonight."

Whitney was too weary to wonder about it when he held her in his arms until she fell asleep. And when she woke in the morning, he was gone, and she felt strangely disappointed and deserted. He'd left without a farewell, and she might never see him again. . . .

The hacienda where she'd been left was composed of a large main house and scattered adobe huts. Sprawled across a low valley between two ridges of mountains, it looked to Whitney like the ends of the earth. Cultivated fields ran in neat rows along each side of a wide, tree-hung road that ended at the hacienda's front door. Behind the hacienda, where sunlight graced a bright-flowered garden and glittered from tiled roofs, vineyards looped dusty leaves from wood frames in thick ropes, nurturing the tiny gemstones of purple fruit that would be used in wine and jellies and fruit bowls. Beyond that stretched a searing blue sky brushed with cloud shreds, then infinity.

Whitney stood framed in the doorway of the kitchen for a long moment, gazing at the familiar yet unfamiliar reaches before her. She realized with a pang of resignation that she was just as far away from what she deemed civilization as she had been in the mountains, except that this was more agreeable. Fat geese waddled, honking demandingly, along garden paths, and a fountain splashed in the far corner, stone cherubs eternally spilling water from pitchers into a huge, ruffled basin. She could detect the sharp, tempting odor of fresh bread wafting on air currents, mingled with the rich, sweet fragrance of jasmine and gardenias. There was a feeling of comfortable domesticity that was vaguely reassuring.

Everything was changed, and she remembered Téjas telling her change was normal, but it was still hard to accept at times, especially when she thought of Cutter. It was just like him to dump her somewhere and leave, she thought resentfully, but what had she expected? There was nothing between them—nothing but dislike and a grudging tolerance of each other's company. That— and the bright, hard feelings he aroused in her. . . . Still, as she stared out the open doorway into the burgeoning garden that hummed with prosaic peace, she couldn't help but wonder if he'd be back for her.

"Are you hungry?" Téjas came up behind her and asked, and when she turned, he saw the questions in her eyes.

"Starved," she said simply, her sleep-swollen eyelids faintly blue with exhaustion, but her mouth curved in an attempt at humor. "I don't suppose you have something besides beef jerky and those wretched flat cakes?" she teased. Then her eyes opened as she took in Téjas's changed appearance. "Téjas! You look—civilized!"

"Please!" he said, laughing, his ebony eyes curving into crescents. "Don't let anyone hear you say that. Aren't I always civilized?"

"In manners, yes; in dress, no."

"This is better, then, than what I usually wear?"

Inspecting his slender build with a dutiful eye, Whitney told him that yes, it was much better. "Though, at least you always had enough self-respect to wear trousers and shirt, this—this is magnificent!"

Turning slightly, Téjas allowed her to inspect the short black jacket encrusted with swirling designs of silver and gold. Uncuffed trousers had matching designs on the side seams, and his boots were polished to so bright a sheen, Whitney swore she could see her reflection.

"I am pleased you like it," Téjas said with a smile, "and after you eat, we can find you more appealing clothes too. And then maybe you will feel a bit better, eh?" he added, turning her toward the wide polished table in the kitchen. "It is not so bad here after all."

And it wasn't so bad, except, perhaps, for Téjas's very young sister, who seemed to take an instant dislike to Whitney for some reason. The girl's name was Terésa, and if not for the sulky expression on her face, she would have been pretty.

"Pay no attention to her," Téjas told Whitney that first morning. Coming in to find her brother sitting at the table with Whitney, the girl had spit out a stream of abuse so swiftly, Whitney could catch very little of it. The only distinguishable words—repeated several times—had been *"puta"* and *"gringa,"* both derogatory adjectives directed toward her.

Frowning, Whitney asked bluntly, "Why is she so angry at me?"

"It's not you she's angry at," Téjas said, but his dark gaze would not meet hers.

Deciding not to press the issue since Téjas looked so uncomfortable, Whitney asked instead, "Did I hear her call you by another name?"

He grinned. "Here, I am known as Francisco Diego José Garcia y Vega."

"Oh. No wonder you chose to go by the name of Téjas. I suppose there's some obscure reason for you to be called that, probably having something to do with your descent into villainy, so don't bother explaining." Her smile flashed briefly as she reached for another ripe pear from the bowl of fruit in the middle of the table. "Is this your house, then?"

"The home of my ancestors, *sí*."

She flicked him a curious glance from beneath sleep-swollen lids. "Why do you ride with a band of renegades and outlaws if you have a decent home?"

"Ah, not every man known by the name of a bandit is one, and not every bandit has no home," Téjas said vaguely. He rose from the table and gave her a courtly bow, delighting her with his elaborate manners.

"Once out of the forest, the wild animal becomes tamed, I see," she quipped, and he laughed.

"And now we must find you some decent clothes," Téjas said, holding out his hand. "I think there are enough women in the hacienda to be able to find you a few things to wear until you can have your own garments made."

Whitney flushed slightly. She'd never worn cast-off clothing in her entire life! What would her father say if he saw her now? He wouldn't know her, and when Whitney saw her reflection in the mirror, she did not know herself.

Slowly putting up one hand to her cheek, she gaped at the changed appearance gazing back at her. Her face had been burned by the sun, and instead of being fashionably pale, had a sun-honeyed tint. Somehow, it made her eyes look brighter, larger, more exotic. And her hair—it had wide white streaks bleached in it, so that she looked as if she had bought a bottle from the apothecary to lighten it. Overall, in spite of the radical change, it was flattering.

She'd lost weight, so that her cheekbones stuck out at sharper angles, and there were interesting hollows in her face that had not been there before. Whitney smiled. Danger and stress obviously agreed with her.

Terésa de la Vega would not have agreed with Whitney. When her brother came to her and asked her for clothing for the woman, she had nothing to give, nothing that would suit the pale creature who seemed to have wormed her way into his affections.

"You will not insult my guest in our home," Téjas said shortly. "I will not allow it. I know why you are angry, and I sympathize, but you will not behave badly and be an embarrassment to the family name."

Whirling, Terésa's slender arms flung out as she demanded, "Me? An embarrassment? It is not embarrassing when you disappear, and everyone hears rumors of your activities as a hunted man?" She threw back her head with a proud shake. "And then you come back, bringing a woman with you, a *puta* you obviously share with . . . with Cutter."

"Ah, so that's it. You're jealous. Well, your jealousy is for nothing, because he is not for you, *niña*. He never was."

With that, he wheeled and left, leaving his dark-haired sister to stare after him with impotent anger. Even worse than the growing suspicion that her brother was right was the knowledge that she had behaved badly toward the wrong person. But the person who deserved her wrath had ridden out that morning, leaving his woman behind.

Unaware of the reason for Terésa's enmity, Whitney passed her days in lazy exploration. She rambled about the stucco and wood house, each new discovery better than the last. Téjas's home was fairly large and comfortable, with cool tile floors and high ceilings, and long doors flung open to allow in cooling breezes. Outside the room he gave her to use while she was there, a stone patio hid in leafy, jasmine-scented seclusion, providing her with shade and privacy, and a spot for waiting.

That was really what she was doing, Whitney thought, waiting for her life to begin again. Or was she waiting for it to be over? She wished she knew. She wished she could get away before Cutter returned—if he returned—so she could examine her feelings about him. *I hate this!* she would think, then decide that it was really Cutter she hated more than the limbo her life had become. But at night, when she closed her eyes, she would see his face, dark and sharp-featured, the features blurring slightly as his gaze grew greener, more intent with desire—but no other emotion.

Not that there could be anything else, not with a man like Cutter. She shuddered. What would her father say? What would anyone with any sense say?

In the long days that followed, Whitney wavered between despair and anticipation, planning what she would say to Cutter when she saw him—her demands to be freed now that he had no more use for her—and her despair that he might actually do so.

As dark fell on the eighth night, Whitney paced restlessly on the

101

small patio off her bedchamber. Night birds sang sweet hosannas to the dusk, and the air was heavy with the cloying fragrance of flowers that opened in a slow unfurling of white velvet petals. With the setting of the sun and the rising of the moon, she could not remain alone with her thoughts a moment longer. She sought out Téjas, and found him poring over the accounts in his comfortably appointed study lined with leather-bound books.

"Do you mind some company?" she asked softly, and he sat up from his account books and closed them.

"I would like your company very much," he said. He smiled as she walked toward him, admiring the gentle sway of her hips and the way the full, bright-flowered skirt she wore moved around her long legs, ending just above her neat, spare feet clad in open-weave leather sandals. The thin fabric of a soft-necked blouse fit smoothly over the curve of her breasts, and was tucked into the waistband of the skirt, flattering her small waist. Instead of wearing her hair loose, or in a braid, she had caught it up with Spanish combs one of the women had given her, and it frothed down in milky ringlets as crisp and tempting as spun sugar.

A brief smile flickered on her lips, and she said in a soft voice, "Thank you. I . . . I guess I'm restless tonight. I'm so tense, and I don't know why!"

Téjas knew, but he chose to divert her. "Has it occurred to you that you have been here over a week and haven't pestered me at all to let you go? Cutter will be quite disappointed."

It had definitely occurred to her, and puzzled, she said, "I don't know why. I meant to. As soon as Cutter left I meant to throw myself on your sense of chivalry and coax you into going against what he wants you to do."

"Do you think it would have worked?"

Her small, straight nose wrinkled impudently. "It might have if I had thought of something *especially* clever to say."

"But if it hadn't, you wouldn't have tried to go anyway, I don't think." Téjas's smile was gentle. "I think you are much smarter than to try to run away when you don't even know where you are."

"Don't credit me with sense I don't have," she murmured so wryly that he rose to put a hand on her shoulder in a comforting grip. "I'm not smart enough to get away while I can."

"A bit of advice, my dear—don't expect too much from Cutter. He's not fond of the polite little games a more cautious man might play with a woman, and though he has been very patient with you, I do not think he will remain as . . . restrained . . . as he has been."

Remembering Cutter's almost brutal touch at times, then the way he'd taken her to the brink of surrender, Whitney laughed skeptically. "Restrained? Are we talking about the same man?"

A rueful smile touched his lips. "Hard though it may be for you to believe, he has shown a much stronger restraint than I have ever known him to show."

"I don't think so!" Whitney's tone was definitely disbelieving now, and Téjas grinned.

"From your viewpoint, I am sure it is different. But try to remember that Cutter is a man unaccustomed to some of the . . . hypocrisies that float so freely in more *civilized* circles."

"I suppose, in your reserved way, you're trying to tell me that if he sees a woman he admires, he simply goes up, tosses her over his shoulder, and carries her off to a goosefeather mattress?"

His grin was mostly benevolent, with only a shade of reproach. "Perhaps with a bit more finesse—not to mention cooperation from the woman—but you could put it that way, yes."

"I thought that went out with prehistoric mammals," Whitney said gloomily. Shutting her eyes, she reflected that she had somehow entangled herself in a discussion that was revealing far too much of her inner feelings. "So," she said aloud, "because he hasn't brutalized me dreadfully, I am supposed to be grateful? Is that what you're telling me?"

"No." His voice came to her softly, seeping through the shell she was trying so hard to erect around herself, a kind, friendly voice. "I'm merely warning you to arm yourself for the inevitable."

Opening her eyes, Whitney said miserably, "It does no good whatsoever to tell me that. Don't you think I've tried? I don't know what happens, but when he does certain things, I melt like butter in the sun."

"Give yourself credit for being a woman," Téjas advised. "And think of your needs."

"My needs?" She looked at him with drowning appeal in her wide golden gaze. "What do I need? I don't know. I used to think I knew, but I've found out . . . Téjas, tell me about Cutter. I don't know anything about him, where he's from, what he's doing besides shooting people in gunfights and kidnapping women and robbing payroll wagons, and I can't imagine that's all there is to him. I don't even know if he has another name! Does he? Is Cutter the only name he has?"

A slight frown etched his brows, and Téjas shifted uncomfortably. "You will have to ask Cutter the things you want to know, my dear. It is not my place to say."

Frustrated, she snapped, "Then how will I ever find out anything? He's as tight-lipped as a South Sea clam!"

After a moment's thought, Téjas said kindly, "Does it matter so much to you to know about him? If he releases you, will it matter at all?"

Her head lifted, and her chin tilted proudly. "There's still my novel to write," she reminded him. "I haven't forgotten the reason I came to Arizona in the first place."

"Neither has Cutter," Téjas warned softly.

After thinking about that for a moment, Whitney said abruptly, "I think I can sleep now. Would you excuse me?"

Téjas rose and performed a small bow for her, smiling when she laughed. Tomorrow, he decided as she left the study, he would have to think of a way to convince her to listen. It might be the saving of her—and Cutter.

But the next day there was no opportunity to talk to Whitney. Late that night, while almost everyone slept, Cutter returned.

Ten

Stumbling in the dark, he cursed softly, wondering where Whitney was, and if she had somehow succeeded in convincing Téjas to release her. He wouldn't put it past her, nor would he be too surprised to find she had managed to have every Pinkerton detective at her father's disposal waiting for him.

Cutter grimaced. He'd already had a run-in with one of them, a burly man who had tried to convince him to surrender with the business end of a Winchester .44-.40. But that was what he got for stopping off in Nogales, a town swarming with men from both sides of the border. He hadn't realized that Morgan Bradford would work so quickly, or that he would put up so many wanted posters.

Grimly, Cutter reflected that the reward of twenty thousand dollars being offered was more than enough to bring out the worst kind of bounty hunter. And with the U.S. Army offering a reward for him dead or alive, it didn't make much difference that Bradford's posters specified alive. Some bounty hunters would take whatever they could get the best way they could, and only the best ones would try to bring him in alive.

The Pinkerton man had already discovered that taking him would not be easy, dead or alive. If it hadn't been for the laughing-eyed Luisa, who had smothered him with female companionship the night before, he might not have been forced to shoot, or forced to run. The Pinkerton agents were very thorough, he reflected. He hadn't remembered Luisa until he'd seen her peering out a window, but had stopped only on impulse, thinking she might get Whitney out of his system. Good thing the agent had not come a few minutes earlier, or he might have collected the reward. Such were the fortunes of war, and all things considered, matters had gone very well indeed.

Now he was back, and looking for Whitney, and she was not where he'd left her.

"*Caballero*" came a whispered voice, and Cutter turned to see Terésa beckoning to him from a shadowed doorway.

He went to her with a smile and gave her a brief hug and swift kiss on the cheek. "I brought you something," he said into the shadows where she stood.

"Not something like the last gift you brought me, I hope," she said in a voice that didn't sound quite right. Cutter peered at her in the dim light.

"What gift was that?"

"The blond *puta* down the hall."

Cutter's eyes filled with laughter. "Did I bring her for you?"

"No!" Terésa spat out. "You brought her for you, here, in my house!"

Sighing a little at this unexpected turn, Cutter said, "I can't always bring just the right gift, you know."

Terésa's eyes glittered with unshed tears, and Cutter realized that he had hurt her.

Slightly disgruntled—how was he supposed to know she had an affection for him?—he gave her another clumsy hug. This time Terésa felt the bulky bandage under the shirt he wore, and she gave a little gasp.

"You're hurt!"

"Not much. A scratch . . ."

"Come with me," she said, taking his hand and almost dragging him with her. "I will see to it. I still have my mother's bag of herbs."

Lighting a lamp in the small alcove off the kitchen, Terésa delved into a leather bag filled with old remedies and curatives. When she unwound Cutter's bandage, she frowned. It was stained with dried blood, and had obviously bled a great deal.

"I thought you said it was a scratch," she muttered as she dabbed ointment on the long gash running along his upper arm.

Cutter grinned. "It is."

Terésa muttered several colorful phrases about the stupidity of men, and wrapped a clean strip of linen around his arm, pulling it tight. After she put away her mother's bag of herbs and cleaned up the mess, she poured Cutter a cool glass of fresh orange juice and sat down at the table in the kitchen with him.

Pushing the hair out of her eyes, Terésa said in a matter-of-fact voice, "I think I misunderstood all those gifts and pretty words you've given me."

He didn't say anything for a moment, then looked at her steadily. "Yes, I think maybe you have," he agreed. "I meant them as a friend, but that is all."

Lifting her chin, Terésa said, "That is all I had to hear from you. Now I can accept Juan Castillo's invitation to go riding."

Cutter laughed, and leaned forward to kiss Terésa on the tip of her nose as he would have a younger sister. That was how he'd always thought of her, and had not known she might misunderstand. But then, she'd always been so much younger, and had only recently begun to blossom into a young lady.

Terésa grabbed him and gave him a quick, fierce kiss, whispering, "That is so you can see what you have missed!"

But to Whitney, standing in the shadowy doorway, it looked like much more than a simple kiss. Frozen, she saw Cutter—one arm bandaged, clad in denim trousers and guns again, his shirt off—with a smile on his face and Terésa's arms around his neck. Her quick gaze took in the fact that Terésa still wore her nightdress, and that her ample charms were well displayed. She didn't realize that she'd made a noise until she saw Cutter turn and look at her.

Instead of looking guilty, he laughed, his amused gaze flicking to Terésa, who did sit back with a guilty look on her face.

"Did you come to find me?" he asked lightly, and when Whitney turned and walked back down the hall, he got up to follow her.

"I think you're in trouble!" Terésa whispered after him, and he felt a wave of irritation.

Trouble? When Whitney was still his hostage? How could he possibly be in trouble?

To compound his irritation, he could not find the room she was in, and opened several doors—startling the cook and a maid—before he found the right one.

Anger showed hotly in his eyes as he slammed open the door. "What's the matter with you?" he began, but Whitney refused to answer. He reached out and whirled her around, wondering tightly if he should offer an explanation, when she reacted with an agility and speed he could never have foreseen.

After weeks of being shoved around, Whitney had finally recalled the moves Chin Yu had shown her a few years before. And she used one now on Cutter, swiftly grabbing his arm and with a quick twist of her body sent him over her back and crashing to the floor.

For a long moment he lay there, stunned with shock more than pain, listening to the sound of a lamp shatter and a table splinter where his feet had struck. Whitney did not move but glared down at him, not caring if he got up and killed her for her daring.

"Sweet Lord!" he said at last, and sat up as Téjas and Terésa arrived in the still-open doorway. They gawked, seeing Cutter sprawled on the floor, Whitney looming over him, and the ruined furniture lying in broken pieces.

While Terésa let out a small squeal of alarm, Téjas began to laugh, and when Cutter shot him a quelling stare, he laughed harder. Then, as Cutter vaulted to his feet, Téjas said quickly, "I'm right down the hall if you should need me, señorita!" and disappeared, dragging Terésa with him after closing the door.

Whitney faced Cutter boldly, her amber eyes spitting defiance, her entire body quivering with rage. How dare he! When she had thought of him the entire time he'd been gone, worried that he had been hurt, and he'd come back to the arms of another woman—a girl, really—right under her very nose!

"I guess I deserved that," Cutter surprised her by saying slowly, and his eyes were narrowed as he reassessed her.

Her chin lifted. "I'd say you did."

A faint smile slanted the harsh lines of his mouth. "Maybe I shouldn't have underestimated you, tiger-eyes."

"No," she agreed, "maybe you shouldn't."

"And maybe you shouldn't underestimate me."

She stared at him, the anger slowly fading away. "No, maybe we shouldn't underestimate each other anymore," she whispered softly.

Cutter stood there, poised between staying and leaving, his mind working slowly. He was tired, and had ridden a long way to get back, thinking of Whitney, wondering if she'd still be there when he arrived. For some reason he couldn't quite fathom, she'd been on his mind the entire time he was gone, even when he was supposed to be paying attention to the distribution of supplies.

Finally, he had left Lone Wolf in charge of the last small bit and ridden away, spurred by an emotion he didn't understand and didn't like. He wasn't a man who enjoyed entanglements, and he certainly didn't want to be involved with a woman like Whitney Bradford. She was trouble. He'd known that from the very first time he'd seen her, when she had stood frozen in his hotel room, too startled to move at the sight of a naked man but very capable of demanding that he kiss her again.

Whitney, staring at Cutter with wide eyes, found that she had missed him. It was a revelation, that and the sweep of jealousy that had pounded through her when she'd seen Terésa kiss him. Could it mean—? No, maybe not, but she knew suddenly that she wanted him to hold her in his arms, and she didn't care what came after that. To be near him, to have his arms around her and his breath stirring her hair, that would be enough for right now.

"Are you tired?" Whitney asked at last, and Cutter gave a short nod of his head, staring at her warily as she began to shove the broken furniture to one side. "I think there's enough room in this bed for both of us," she said, half turning, her voice nervous.

Cutter understood what it took for her to offer, and he unbuckled his gun belts and draped them on a chair.

Trembling, Whitney lay stiffly in Cutter's embrace, her entire body shaking as badly as if she were caught up in a storm. And that's what she felt like, battered and buffeted by a series of swiftly changing emotions, from dread to anticipation, to pleasure, and back to anxiety. She wanted him, wanted him beside her like this, his hard body pressed close to hers, his arms around her and his voice and touch gentle, yet—yet she was afraid, afraid of the inevitable end, when there would only be the indignity and insult of the final consummation.

She could feel him frown, his lips against the throbbing hollow of her throat, and stiffened even more.

"Relax," Cutter murmured. "I won't do anything until you're ready for me. I can wait, love. . . ."

His voice trailed away as he shifted to kiss her again, his mouth moving gently but insistently on her unyielding lips. Slowly, as he kissed her, his lips coaxing hers open like the slow unfolding of a summer flower, Whitney began to relax again, to kiss him back, shyly at first, putting her tongue to his so tentatively she was shocked at the sudden thrill that shot through her. Somehow the intimacy of his kisses was more shocking than the actual act itself. No man had ever kissed her like Cutter had, like he was now, his tongue probing deeply, exploring, making her heart thud erratically and her breath shorten.

"Don't be shy," he said when she pulled back, half afraid, half shocked by the violent tremors he caused in her lower regions. "It's all a matter of cause and effect."

"I know," she whispered. "That's the problem."

He laughed, his mouth pressing warmly against the small fluttering pulse in her throat, a husky sound ripe with sensuality and lazy determination. Dragging his lips from the sun-kissed hollow upward, he encountered the baby-soft spread of skin just beneath her ear, and focused his attention on that. It produced shudders that vibrated all the way down to her toes, and made her say soggily that she didn't know if she could bear too much of that.

"No? Then how about here . . . or here . . ."

Traveling in steaming, juicy kisses from her ear over the graceful line of her collarbone and down, Cutter's mouth traced the heavy swell of a breast with erotic moisture, a wet path that only heightened the brush of his lips against her rapidly hardening peak.

Gasping, Whitney arched into him. "That . . . that's not much better!"

"Not much better?" he murmured, barely pausing in his ministrations. "I'd guess that it was much better. . . ." But because he could feel the erratic tempo of her heart beneath the curve of his palm, and knew that she was quaking with apprehension, he moved upward again, returning to capture her lips with his.

It was a deep, exploring kiss, and somewhere in the midst of it Whitney felt herself straining toward him again in the bone-jarring need to be closer. There were things going on inside her body that she didn't understand, didn't want to understand. All she could focus on at that moment was the driving need to be part of Cutter. It was confusing and contradictory all at the same time.

When he pulled away, they were both breathing hard, and she could see in the dim light of the single candle left burning that his eyes were hazy and shimmering with vivid green lights. Shyly reaching up, she traced the winged arch of his thick brow with the tip of her forefinger, then skimmed over the straight line of his nose to his lips, outlining their sensual shape lightly. Cutter caught her hand after a moment and moved it lower, between their bodies, letting her feel the smooth bands of his chest muscles, then lower, where the muscle ridged his taut belly.

Quivering, Whitney stood it as long as she could before she took her hand away, and Cutter did not try to force her. Instead, he began explorations of his own, his hands skimming over her velvet curves in a touch as light as the brush of a butterfly's wings, teasing, touching, making her catch her bottom lip between her teeth and writhe with heated agony. It was so confusing; he was utterly different from anything in her experience, and she was afraid. There was only one ending to this, and she knew it, but could not stop herself from reaching out to Cutter, wanting him to make her feel the rush of sensation that would let her forget about what came later.

At least with Cutter there was the sweep of heat that left her weak and trembling with her heart pounding and a strange, unfamiliar ache throbbing deep inside. It was the ache that disturbed her most—it was so unsettling, leaving her with a swell of anticipation that she didn't know how to ease.

"Cutter . . . Cutter, I don't know how . . ."

"Hush, love. You're not supposed to know how," he said against her breast, then his lips moved to circle the tight peak and she felt the quickening deep inside, the growing fire that spread slowly, like heated honey, filling her with its sweet ache.

Whimpering softly, Whitney arched her hips when he moved gently between her thighs, pressing close, the heat of him insistent against her. Dimly, she wondered if he could give her the release she sought, but when Cutter edged forward that first tiny bit, hot and hard against her, the dark memories came flooding back, overpowering the yearning and smothering her with alarm.

"No!" she cried, wrenching away, shoving hard at him with the heels of her hands, terrified now, her eyes wide and glassy, her lips parted as she sat up, panting wildly.

Letting her go, it took Cutter a moment to digest the fact that she had—unpredictable as always—changed her mind. A rough sigh escaped, but his gaze rested on her gently. "It's all right, love," he said. "The first time is difficult for a woman, I know. . . ."

Whitney began to laugh hysterically, her voice choking as she changed to racking sobs. "You . . . you don't know!" she gasped out when he sat up and looked at her with a dark lift of one brow. "You don't know *any*thing!"

"Whitney, it's not as bad as you may have heard," he began with more patience than he was feeling as the moment, but she shook her head wildly, her pale hair flying, and put her hands over her face.

She couldn't look at him. She didn't want to see his expression change from tenderness to distrust, but she knew she had to tell him. He'd know soon enough, anyway. A woman couldn't hide something like that from a man, not a man like Cutter, who wasn't exactly inexperienced when it came to women. Shuddering with apprehension, Whitney kept her fingers over her face and her head bent so low the ivory fall of her hair brushed against her bare thighs.

"You're not the first," she said in a muffled voice, the words falling between her fingers like stones in the sudden silence. There was no response from Cutter, no reaction. A minute ticked past, then two, and still he hadn't spoken.

Whitney felt the mattress dip as he moved, and when she dared a glance up at him through her fingers, she saw that he was staring at her with opaque, unreadable eyes as hard and brittle as bits of green glass. Her heart dropped, and a cold lump grew in her throat so that she could hardly breathe.

"I can't say I'm too shocked," Cutter said after another moment passed, "but I am curious. Why the pretense all this time? Why act like an innocent virgin who's never known a man?"

His voice was flat, as if only mildly interested in her reply, and she felt her cheeks flame. She couldn't answer, but stared up at his dark face and remote eyes, and noticed for the first time that he'd gotten his hair cut. It was still long, not brushing his shoulders, just curling down the nape of his neck in thick black waves. Odd, how one's mind retreated from pain and rejection, she thought distractedly, barely aware that Cutter was leaning forward, one hand curling around her wrists to bring her hands down from her face.

"Well?" he prompted her. "If you're going to make a clean breast of it—no pun intended—why don't you tell all? I'm interested in knowing how many other men have felt as big a fool as I do right now."

"You don't understand," she said miserably, and saw his eyes begin to glitter with malice. "There haven't been—other *men*. Only one."

"Ah, still a novice, then. Well, I guess I could see how you might feel as if you were practically a virgin, but it doesn't explain why you felt it necessary to try to make me believe otherwise."

Her temper flared. "I never tried to make you believe anything! Can I help it if you assumed I was . . . that I had never been with anyone else?"

His voice was rough when he said, "Look, do you think I really care if you've been with one man or a hundred? It doesn't make a damn bit of difference to me, but I do object to being subjected to your melodramatic protestations of innocence and virtue these past weeks. I'm sure it was very entertaining to you to have me treat you as if you were so shy and innocent, but it doesn't impress me in the least."

Pulling away from his tight grasp, Whitney snatched up the sheet and held it up to her chin. Her voice did not betray her misery as she bit off her words. "I don't owe you any explanation, and I can't understand why you seem to think I do. My past is very private, and if you happen to have your male ego offended by the fact that I did not bare my soul, that is your problem."

"There's a name for women like you," Cutter said with such icy contempt that Whitney actually shivered, "but I'm sure you've heard it before from other men."

She watched numbly as he stepped into his pants and buttoned them, then lifted his boots and gun belts and left the room, slamming the door behind him. Reaction set in as she heard the distant slamming of another door, and Whitney put her face into her palms and wept bitter tears. Why hadn't she listened to Téjas's veiled warnings earlier?

Nathan would find it very amusing to know that he had left such a deep scar on her, she thought miserably. Nathan, with his cold hands and cruel mouth, casually hurting her and making her feel as if she were the one deficient, until she had armed herself with the only weapon she had—the waters of oblivion, Nathan had caustically called it. Her Lethe, her river of forgetfulness, like the river in Greek mythology. It had not escaped her notice that the Lethe of ancient myth was one of the five rivers surrounding Hades. But she had never felt such pain, such utter despair, until now, when Cutter had rejected the tenuous offer of her body and soul.

For the first time in a long time, though he would never have admitted it, Cutter felt the sharp prick of pain too, though not the same intensity as that Whitney felt. He wondered abstractedly who the man had been, then wondered why it mattered. He'd seen her with the young army officer, seen her in his arms and heard her call him Andrew, and seen the man gaze at her with adoring eyes. It had been Cutter who had ordered one of the men to club the lieutenant senseless, and had wondered at the time why it annoyed him to see them together. Of course, then he had thought her a coquettish virgin who didn't realize what she was doing when she teased a man. Now he knew differently, and it infuriated him that she had been able to play him so easily.

His mouth tightened. All those times, times he'd shown restraint when he'd really wanted to tumble her backward and take her, roughly slamming his body into hers until he could forget about her, walk away and not look back, just as he had always done. But somehow Miss J. Whitney Bradford had managed to sneak beneath his skin, worrying him like a sand flea, her memory and the soft feel of her in his arms returning again and again, even when he slept.

Swearing softly, Cutter dragged out the decanter of brandy Téjas kept in the lacquered cabinet and splashed the amber liquor into a large snifter.

Téjas paused in the open doorway and found Cutter finishing one snifter and pouring another. He observed mildly that he would have to purchase more *aguardiente* if Cutter did not show some restraint.

"I don't know what you're talking about," Cutter said shortly, and tilted back his head, pouring the fine brandy down his throat with complete disregard.

Téjas came into the room and shut the door behind him. A small lamp burned on his desk, and he crossed to it and turned it higher, then turned to Cutter and gazed at him in narrow appraisal. "I hope you did not hurt her," he said abruptly, and frowned at Cutter's sharp laugh.

"Hurt her? No, Téjas, I don't think that's possible. Our little hostage is quite resilient, believe me."

"Ah, so she did not dance to your fiddle? And are you sure that's what you want?"

Slamming the empty brandy snifter to the top of a table, Cutter jerked around. "Téjas, I'm in no mood to hear how mistreated she is. I've heard it before."

"*Sí*, and you will hear it again." Now Téjas was angry too, his black eyes glittering coldly as he faced Cutter. "We have been friends a long time . . ."

"That's right, so don't push this too far."

". . . so you will give me the courtesy of listening, for once." Téjas kept his gaze on Cutter's bland face, and said, "She is not the kind of woman you can take carelessly. Even though she is outwardly in control, her spirit is vulnerable. You would break it with rough handling. I think, amigo, that she has been hurt before. If you care about her, you won't do it too."

"You've made quite a study of this, haven't you?" came the polite observation, and Téjas shrugged.

"I've seen you both caught up in something you are not accustomed to. And I think you don't dare examine your real motives too closely."

Cutter was quiet when he finished, his gaze dangerously soft. Silence dragged heavily before he said in a voice like sheathed steel, "I'll keep that in mind."

Téjas felt a wave of irritation, and was surprised at its intensity. He had never before felt such anger at his friend, not in all their years of riding together. And now he did.

"I cannot approve of what is taking place under my roof," he said, then stiffened when Cutter said softly, "I'll leave first thing in the morning."

"And Whitney?"

"She's my hostage. She goes with me."

Téjas stared after him when Cutter pivoted and walked away, and wondered if he should have remained silent. A rift had been widened, and he didn't know if it would ever be bridged again.

Whitney didn't know why she was being dragged from her warm bed so early and told to dress, they were leaving.

"But where are we going?" she mumbled sleepily, not quite able to look at Cutter but feeling his anger.

He didn't answer, but propelled her outside with him, where two horses were saddled and waiting. Terésa was there, watching with a wide gaze, and Téjas stood with quiet misery in his eyes. Feeling the tension between them, Whitney suddenly understood that she was not being set free, and that Téjas did not like it.

Freeing herself from Cutter, Whitney took several running steps toward Téjas, her eyes wide, her unbound hair flying, before Cutter caught her, pulling her with him and flinging her atop the horse. She screamed once, and his hand closed around her wrist in a biting grip.

"Don't start that again, or I'll make you scream for real," he said so menacingly that she subsided into silence at once.

"*Ay di mi!*" Téjas said softly, but when he would have stepped forward, Cutter—unbelievably—pointed his rifle at him.

"Don't make me, *compadre*. I don't know what she's done to you, but I'm not sticking around to find out. Just stand back, and I'll see to it that she gets back to her father one day soon."

"Why not now?"

"Let's say I need a little extra insurance, and she can give it to me," Cutter said, then swung atop his horse and wheeled it around, leading Whitney behind him.

There were no words of farewell, nor did Cutter glance back, but Téjas was to remember Whitney's face for a long time, her tawny eyes wide with fright as she looked back in bewildered silence.

Eleven

The sun, hot and searing, sucked the life once again from her body and left her listless. Whitney tried not to yield to the sharp questions that she wanted to ask, but clung, instead, to the back of her horse with grim fortitude. Cutter rode swiftly, as if he knew where he was going; the landscape looked the same to her, with no marks to indicate direction, except the sun.

When they rode through a vast prickly forest of cactus that stretched toward the sky like huge pitchforks, Whitney asked where they were, and Cutter bent a sardonic glance on her.

"Plotting to escape?"

"Would it do me any good?"

"None whatsoever."

"Then I hardly feel disposed to explain that I only wondered what country we're in, whether I'm still in the United States, or being dragged across Mexico or Peru!"

Grudgingly, it seemed, he replied, "You're still in Arizona. These are saguaro cactus."

"As opposed to?"

A faint smile tucked the corners of his eyes as he looked at her. "Barrel, pipe organ, Spanish needles—there are a lot of variations."

"Fascinating."

"Isn't it?" Cutter's smile was bristling with animosity now. But later, when he showed Whitney how to get water from one of the round tubular plants by cutting off the top—no job for the fainthearted—and finding the hollow reservoir with its tidy storage of life-giving liquid, she felt a prick of interest. So this is what had interested Lieutenant West, the way the Apaches could find survival in so many different forms, and the way the seemingly barren desert could give it to them. Yucca plants yielded fruit in the form of a small blossom, that when cut and baked, tasted sugary. Mesquite trees showered beans on them, edible but not her favorite. Even rattlesnakes, she discovered, were a source of food, though she obstinately refused to try it, resorting, instead, to the tough beef jerky and dried cakes she hated.

They rode up into the mountains, higher and higher until the air was thin and cool and Whitney shivered with the chill. Tossing her a filthy serape, Cutter spared her a brief glance and the comment that she did nothing but complain.

Her stony gaze matched his. "It was hot in the desert, but up here it's cold. If you had any feelings yourself, you'd understand."

"Spare me your whining." Cutter tugged at the lead rope of her horse, and they continued on the narrow rock ledge that clung to the side of a peak so precipitous Whitney was afraid to look down.

She tangled one hand in the horse's mane, grateful for the saddle horn and the fact that Cutter had been too self-absorbed to pay much attention to her. They'd been riding for three days now, three long days of constant movement that left her too weary at night to do anything but fall onto the hard blanket roll and sleep instantly. Cutter still slept beside her, as he'd done before, but rolled up in his own blanket, not touching her. And he'd taken the precaution of stringing a rope from his wrist to hers, as if afraid she might try to escape.

Where would I go? she thought bitterly, but said nothing. Let him think she was planning a revolt. It would keep him on edge.

If they spoke at all, it was only to exchange the most necessary of comments, and on occasion a few tart remarks meant to prick. Whitney still ached from Cutter's abrupt rejection of her, his refusal to understand. Why hadn't he stayed to listen to her explanation? Couldn't he understand it had been difficult for her to confide in him? And when she began feeling too weepy, she would recall that he had been only too willing to believe the worst, and would steel herself again. She'd had years of practice at hiding her feelings, stuffing them way down inside where no one could see and where she could forget them for a while. And it had worked pretty well until she'd met Cutter and he'd reopened old wounds. Now she had to start all over again, learning to cope with the pain she had felt, running from those old feelings that still haunted her.

Sometimes, when she woke up early, she'd hear Cutter's deep, even breaths beside her, and she'd wonder why he had no more desire to touch her. Was it because she'd been married? Maybe she wasn't a virgin anymore, but she'd never before felt those sweeping rushes of emotion and sensation that she'd felt with Cutter, and how could she tell him that? He would only think she was pretending again, and besides that, her pride wouldn't allow her to say anything he might mistake for begging. Not her, not J. Whitney Bradford! A Bradford never backed down, isn't that what her father had always said?

It was the same stubborn pride that made her rebel when he pushed her too far, when he ordered her to help with the horses, or cook the evening meal.

"This is your show!" she snapped, glaring at him like a wild creature, her tangled hair tumbling over her shoulders and her mouth taut. "If you want anything done, do it yourself!"

"No work, no food," Cutter replied in his cool, polite voice, the one that made her want to shake him to get an honest reaction. He eyed her mutinous expression with an uplifted brow. "It's too damn much trouble for me to have to wait on you like I'm one of your servants." His voice took on a caustic edge. "It'd be interesting to see how long you could survive without me."

"As long as I needed to!" Tossing her hair out of her eyes with a flick of her hand, Whitney had no intention of letting him see her sudden concern. Damn him for being such a hateful, incomprehensible creature! And for assuming—correctly—that she needed him.

But when he refused to share his food with her, saying that she was a burden and would have to work to eat, she found that stubbornness had a very bleak future. Sullenly, she made a clumsy attempt to cook her own food, but succeeded only in burning the salt meat so badly it was inedible. Cutter watched her with an amused expression on his face, his eyes mocking as he ate with obvious relish and enjoyment.

"Damn you!" she cursed, and finally settled for the hard dried strips of beef jerky that he knew she hated. "I hope you choke!"

"And leave you out here alone?" He waved a hand at the empty expanse of sky and plain, and Whitney shivered. "Ah, I see you don't really like that idea. Don't worry," he added, his long legs straightening as he stood in a smooth, swift motion, "I have no intention of being so obliging. You will have to put up with me a little bit longer."

Kneeling by the fire, Whitney turned her head to look into the licking flames, and said coldly, "I assure you that I will be only too happy to be rid of you!"

"Really? We'll see if that's true," Cutter said in a thoughtful tone, and Whitney's eyes lit with hope.

"What do you mean? Are you releasing me? When? When are you taking me back?"

"Don't worry about it, darlin'. Now, see if you can curb that sharp tongue of yours long enough to get some sleep. I'm tired, and I certainly don't feel like listening to your vituperations."

Pressing her lips tightly together, Whitney sat in sullen silence as he tied the rope from her wrist to his, then rolled up in his blankets and fell asleep. How could he do that so easily? And why, oh, why, had she ever thought she might want to give herself to a man like Cutter? He was nothing but a renegade, a dangerous outlaw, and she should have listened when her father and Mary tried to warn her about him. She'd thought she could handle anything, but that was before she had met Cutter. . . .

When they finally rode down from the peaks into a small valley hidden from casual eyes by thick stands of fir and pine, Whitney was pleased to see signs of settlement. Crude fences made of split logs ran in an erratic pattern over ground that looked too hard to plow, and a few head of fat cattle grazed on lush grass and drank from a clear mountain pool. She slid a glance at Cutter, but he was indifferent to her curiosity, and Whitney would not ask.

Then, as they rode over a crest thick with tall grasses and down the other side, she saw his destination. Brush huts lined both sides of a meandering stream, and small children ran and played, shouting to one another. Camp dogs barked a noisy welcome as they rode in. It was an Apache village.

"Cutter," Whitney began, but his fierce glance in her direction stopped her in mid-sentence. Slumping back beneath the folds of the serape, Whitney tried not to look as frightened as she felt. People were staring at her curiously, and one old woman with wispy gray hair even reached out to touch the toe of her shoe as she passed. Did she look that different from them? she wondered, then knew that she did. These people were burned dark by the constant sun and worn by the elements. Whitney felt almost obscenely healthy, looking at them, trying not to see the sunken eyes in some faces and the disdain in others.

When Cutter stopped his horse in front of a brush hut, a man came out, his old, wrinkled face splitting into a welcoming smile. He said something to Cutter in Apache, and Cutter dismounted and they talked briefly. Whitney sat in numb silence, feeling the sharp bite of apprehension when Cutter waved an arm toward her and the old man laughed. What was he saying? What did he intend to do with her? Surely he wouldn't leave her here, alone and unable to speak their language?

Cutter gave her no explanation when he pulled her from her horse and put her on the ground close to the old man. Whitney stood quietly, but refused to play the part of a good squaw as she had for Lone Wolf's hearing. Her chin rose in angry defiance as she met the old man's disdainful gaze with one of her own. They took each other's measure in that glance, and even though Whitney had no idea what he said to Cutter, she felt as if she had passed inspection.

Whatever he'd said, it made Cutter laugh, then glance at Whitney with the mocking lights in his eyes that she'd grown to hate.

"Are you worth two mules?" he asked her, and she met his laughing eyes with stony silence. "Red Shirt seems to think you are. I told him you were as stubborn as two mules, but I would not waste a good mule on such a worthless squaw."

"You're quite amusing," Whitney replied. "Am I being traded, then?" She couldn't still the quiver of fear in her voice, and cursed silently when it was apparent that Cutter heard it.

"Maybe. If I can trade you before anyone finds out how useless you are."

Their eyes clashed, and Whitney refused to look away. Damn him! If he thought he could make her beg, he was wrong, and she'd see him dead before she would ever humble herself again! She made a silent vow to refuse to let him goad her into a visible reaction to anything he did.

But when Cutter pushed her inside a small hut he called a wickiup and told her to clean it, Whitney had to bite her tongue to keep from screaming at him. She looked down at the dirt floor and half-rotted grass mats, then at the scattered wooden eating utensils that still had dried, congealed food on them, then back up at Cutter.

"I have never done domestic work in my entire life, and I don't intend to start now," she said distinctly, her gaze daring him to force her.

"Ah, I forgot. You're the daughter of Morgan Bradford, the wealthy newspaper magnate! You don't even have to dress yourself if you don't want to." His voice was silky now, soft and somehow more dangerous than if he had been voicing threats. "So, Miss Bradford, I suppose you are expecting the same luxurious pampering now?"

"I don't expect anything from you." Her gaze flicked to the opening of the wickiup, where a rawhide flap had been swung up to form a door. "Except some privacy," she added.

"Oh, you'll get that, all right." His voice held a note of laughter in it, and Whitney began to wonder what he had in mind. Hooking his thumbs in his belt, Cutter said flatly, "You are going to get all the privacy you can stand, Miss Bradford. If you want to sit here in the filth, you can. If you want to sit here without a fire and food, that's up to you too. No one is going to wait on you hand and foot, or even acknowledge your existence." He smiled at her frown. "You may think that doesn't sound too bad, but try and feed yourself and gather your own wood for a fire. It ought to be very interesting to see how well you do."

Pivoting on his heel, he ducked beneath the open flap and out the opening. After a slight hesitation, Whitney ran after him, hating herself for it, but unable to still a surge of fear.

"Cutter! Cutter, you can't mean that you're going to leave me here!" she blurted out, catching his sleeve and holding him. "What will I do? What will happen to me? I can't hunt my own food, or . . . or clean! I'll starve!"

Feeling the hot spurt of tears fill her eyes and her nose, Whitney tightened her grip on his arm, but he gently uncurled her fingers and pushed her away. "Don't worry, Miss Bradford. I'm sure you'll think of something."

To Whitney's horror, he crossed the grassy clearing in the center of the collection of wickiups and caught up the reins to the horses they'd ridden. She could feel the eyes of interested observers, but didn't care. Nothing mattered at the moment but that he not leave her behind.

She ran along beside him, her skirts lifted so she didn't trip, her words tumbling out in a rush. "Cutter! I'm sorry for every nasty thing I ever said! I'll do anything you say if you'll only . . ." She swallowed hard, realizing her voice was pleading, and continued. "Only take me with you." When he ignored her, she began to sob, harsh racking sobs of fear and despair, sobs that tore at her throat. It did not have the least effect on Cutter. He continued walking as if she weren't running beside him, weren't grabbing at his sleeve again.

"Please!" she sobbed, the hot tears streaking her face and making her hate herself almost as much as she hated him at that moment. "I'm begging you!"

"Don't."

"Cutter!"

He stopped and turned to face her, and his eyes were as cold as she'd ever seen them. "I'm not taking you with me, and that's final. But, since you seem so eager to please, I will let you keep the bay horse and supplies. Do what you can with them. Maybe a little imaginative bargaining will keep you fed and warm." He raked her with a speculative gaze. "Of course, you can always barter that soft little body of yours, but you seem to have an aversion to that."

She grabbed his arm, her voice tight with humiliation. "Is that what this is all about? If that's what you want, I'll—"

He cut her short. "Stop. Don't debase yourself. That's not what I want. If it were, I'd have already taken it." He added harshly, "Just because you caught me off guard once, don't think you can ever do it again."

Thrusting the lead rope to the bay in her cold hands, he vaulted atop his mount and wheeled it around, pausing to say over his shoulder, "By the way, Red Shirt agreed to keep an eye on you for me. Don't make any plans to leave this valley."

With that he was gone, leaving Whitney standing in the middle of the Apache village staring after him. When he had disappeared over the grassy crest beyond the village, she turned slowly around, heedless of the hot tears streaking her cheeks. A few of the women were watching her with more curiosity than anything, and she could see Red Shirt standing outside his wickiup with his arms folded across his chest.

Hesitating, Whitney had to still her first impulse to mount the bay and ride after Cutter as fast as she could. It would do her no good. He'd made that plain enough. And there was always later; later, when the sun went down and it was dark and shadowed, she would slip away.

But now she had to pretend acceptance of the situation, and she knew the Apache women were watching her to see what she would do. Pride would not allow her to let them know how frightened she was. Whitney stalked past them with her head held high, going back to the filthy hut where she supposed she was intended to stay.

No one stopped her, or tried to speak to her, or even made any indication they noticed her as she stopped in front of the hut. The bay horse nickered softly and nudged her, and Whitney realized that it needed to be fed and watered, and the packs removed. Her head began to ache, and she stared at the animal crossly.

Cutter had always taken care of the horses, and she had no idea what she was supposed to do, or how to take off the saddle. After several minutes of trying, she did manage to remove the few packs, but it took much longer to unfasten the long leather straps that held the saddle on. And when she tried to pull it down, as she'd seen Cutter do so effortlessly countless times, she staggered beneath its weight and fell to one knee. The horse stomped impatiently, obviously smelling the water from the nearby stream, and Whitney glared up at it.

"I don't need any comments from you!" she muttered. Sweat streamed down her face in spite of the cool mountain air, and her blouse and skirt were smeared with dirt.

Shoving the saddle aside, Whitney brushed off her skirts and led the horse through the camp to the stream. It looked cool and inviting, and she noticed that several children were playing in the shallow depths. They were naked and giggling, splashing one another playfully, their dusky skin gleaming in the late afternoon sun.

The leather reins were too short to allow the horse to wade out far, and it jerked, shaking its head, straining to reach water deep enough to drink. Gritting her teeth, Whitney lifted her skirts and waded out into the stream, sucking in her breath at the icy wash of the water over her shoes and stockings.

"There, you big bully," she grated out, "I hope you're satisfied now!"

Unfortunately, the bay did not like the spot she'd chosen. It took several more steps, virtually dragging Whitney along even though she dug her heels into the mud and tried to stop it. Straining against the steady tug of the horse, Whitney felt her feet begin to slip on the slick bottom of the stream. Panting with effort, she struggled for balance, trying to hold back the determined horse, and slid abruptly down into the water.

At her startled scream, the spooked animal snorted and jerked free as water came down, breaking the leather rein. She gasped with dismay and the shock of the icy water, choking on the spray sent up by flying hooves.

At her scream, the children came running, staring at her with big, wide eyes. Whitney stared back, not knowing what to say or do, realizing how ridiculous she must look with her wet hair in her eyes and sitting in the shallow stream. One of them laughed, and she flushed but managed a tight smile.

"I suppose I do look rather amusing," she muttered, and grimaced as she rose clumsily to her feet, half fell, then waded from the water to the muddy bank. To her surprise, one of the older children had run and caught the bay for her, and shyly handed her the remaining rein. The broken rein dangled uselessly.

Murmuring a thank-you she knew he didn't understand, Whitney took the rein and led the horse back to the empty wickiup. She stared inside at the dirty eating utensils and scattered grass mats, then turned and looked at the bay. It rolled its eyes and snorted, not seeming at all sorry for running away. What was she supposed to do with it? She couldn't take it inside, and yet if she turned it loose, she'd probably never catch it again.

Use it for barter, Cutter had said, yet if it was gone, she wouldn't have anything with which to bargain. *Or escape,* her brain echoed. A frown creased her brow, and Whitney tied the animal to a sapling nearby and rummaged through the packs. She gave a soft crow of delight when she found a knife, and tucked it into the waistband of her skirt, feeling much safer. When she found a length of rope, she worked for several minutes on a clumsy knot like the ones she'd seen Cutter and Téjas use.

Testing it several times, she finally thought it strong enough to hold, and slipped it around the bay's neck and tied him to the sapling at the edge of the wickiup. With the animal grazing on grass behind the hut, Whitney set to work on starting a fire.

As the sun began to sink behind the high mountain peaks ringing the valley, it grew quite cool, and her damp clothes did not make her any warmer. She was far too aware of the other campfires, and of the odors of cooking food in pots slung over them. The wickiup was dark, and it took her a moment to find the packs. Her stomach growled angrily, and she chewed on a piece of jerky as she struck the flint against stone again and again. A few feeble sparks flew, but even though she blew on them quickly, no fire ignited in the dry leaves she'd heaped in the center of a ring of stones.

After several minutes, in which her fingers grew numb and scraped from gripping the flint so hard, she managed to ignite a tiny flame. Quickly, she blew on it with soft puffs of breath, until it grew into a small but respectable blaze. Satisfied, Whitney sat back on her heels and fed it small twigs and sticks she'd found scattered across the floor.

As the fire began to die down, she realized to her dismay that she had run out of wood to feed it. Glancing outside, she saw that the light was almost gone and she'd have to hurry.

The first few sticks of green wood she cut with her knife only smoked and hissed, refusing to ignite, and Whitney coughed against the smoke burning her eyes. She would have to find dry, seasoned wood if she expected to get a decent fire going.

But when she began to search for wood, she found that any near the camp had already been taken, and she had to range far out. Her wet shoes squished with each step she took, and the tall grass slapped at her unprotected face. Finally, using her skirt to carry it, she managed to gather enough wood to last the night, and hurried back to the wickiup.

The untended fire had died in her absence, and Whitney collapsed on the dirt floor of the wickiup with a soft cry. Then she began to sob, tears rolling down her cheeks in warm, wet paths. She was cold and she was hungry and she was frightened, and she wished she had never set eyes on Cutter. He had brought her to this with his stupid plan to steal the payroll and abduct her. Damn him! And damn him for stealing much more than money. . . .

Whimpering, Whitney crawled into a pallet made of the filthy serape and blankets Cutter had left for her, and rolled up snugly. Lying in the dark silence, she heard the sounds outside the wickiup as if they were magnified. She could hear the muffled blur of distant conversation and muted laughter. Babies cried and dogs barked, and there was a loud humming of insects. Whitney clutched the knife closely, lying in tense expectation, but no one came near the wickiup. She had never felt so alone in her entire life.

Twelve

Exhausted, Whitney fell asleep in spite of her discomfort, and when she woke it was morning, and she had not made her escape. And worse, she discovered that her knot in the rope had come undone, and the bay horse was gone. Dispirited, she slumped in the open flap of the wickiup and stared dully across the clearing bare of grass. Cooking fires blazed, and the Apache families were eating their morning meal. Whitney's stomach growled, and she sighed and reached for the packs and beef jerky.

As she chewed, she surveyed the mountains around the valley. They were high and rugged, and she tried to recall which way Cutter had brought her. He'd ridden through the saddle of the peak beyond the village—but after that—which way did she go? She frowned as she stuffed the last of the jerky in her mouth and tried to recall her former direction.

As it turned out, she was too closely watched to have an opportunity to do anything but remain on the fringe of the women gathering wood and plants. Red Shirt—true to his promise to Cutter—posted guards on her, as Whitney found out that first day.

As she tried slipping away from the camp through the tall grasses, a man appeared from seemingly nowhere. His face hard, he blocked her way. Whitney stifled the scream that sprang to her lips and turned around abruptly. She was frustrated, but sensed that she wouldn't have gotten far anyway. Without a horse and sense of direction, she would have soon been dead.

She tried to make the best of it in the long days that followed. Cleaning the brush wickiup was no small task. Whitney painstakingly washed the wooden eating utensils and bowls in the stream, scrubbing at them with rocks and grass, then rinsing them until they were reasonably clean. She beat the grass mats outside, choking on the dust she stirred up, but glad for the relative comfort they'd give her at night. Surveying her hands as the day faded, Whitney had the rueful thought they would never be the same.

Wood-gathering, she discovered, did not get any easier. As wood in the valley was becoming scarce, the women seemed to have arranged a rotation system, and jealously guarded their places in it. When Whitney reached for a tree limb or branch, she frequently found herself shoved away while one of the women would grab it, shouting something at her in Apache. Though she fumed, there was very little she could do about it.

And when she tried to watch what type of vegetation they gathered to cook, she discovered that some plants were for entirely different purposes, like dying hides, or using for salves and ointments. None of the Apache women would help her in any way, or allow her close.

"I feel as if I'm a leper," she muttered resentfully, and wondered if Cutter had arranged that too. Only at night, when she lay in her dark shelter, did she have the time and energy to curse him, and then she recalled every epithet she'd ever heard, repeating them until she fell asleep.

Days were better than nights. She still did not have a decent fire going, and began to feel much like the Greeks before Prometheus gave them the gift of fire. She'd watched the women carefully nurse their embers, never letting the fire go completely out, but somehow she could not manage it. If it blazed at all, it went out quickly.

And she discovered that she was lonesome for the sound of a language she could understand, or even for a friendly word in any language. The women largely avoided her, and whether it was by choice or design did not matter to Whitney.

Only one girl lingered near, her belly swollen with child, and when Whitney tried to speak to her, she ran away as if afraid. If not for the fire, she might never have had the chance to speak to the girl.

Weary of the tiny blazes she'd been able to spark with a great deal of work and little success, Whitney rummaged in the packs Cutter had left and found a small bottle of alcohol. It was for medicinal purposes, but she recalled the way rum blazed on flaming desserts, and decided it would do to get a nice fire going.

"Too bad this isn't the drinking kind of alcohol," Whitney muttered to herself with a wry face, and sprinkled the liniment liberally over the barely glowing fire in the center of the wickiup.

Unfortunately, she poured too much alcohol on the wood, and when the flames leapt, they roared into a towering conflagration that caught the roof of the wickiup on fire. Squealing with alarm, she kicked at the carefully stacked sticks of wood she had arranged so neatly in the stone circle, but succeeded only in setting her shoe ablaze. She quickly stomped it out and snatched up a pouch of water.

It was useless. The fire blazed out of control, and when she saw that the small amount of water she had in the leather pouches would do nothing to put it out, she began beating at it futilely with her blankets.

Smoke billowed up, alerting the other residents of the camp, and they came running. Fire in the camp could be devastating, especially in dry weather, sweeping through an entire village and destroying everything in its path.

A jumble of excited voices and shouts assaulted Whitney's ears, and she turned a soot-streaked face to see people running toward her with water pouches and blankets. When the fire had been put out and she was left alone again, she saw the girl she'd spoken to earlier still lingering.

"Thank you," Whitney said with a weary smile, hoping she'd understand the sentiment if not the words. On impulse she added, "*Gracias,*" and the girl immediately erupted into a torrent of Spanish.

Reeling, Whitney quickly saw that the language barrier had been partially broken, and she smiled delightedly. "Can you stay," she asked her in rusty Spanish, "and talk to me?"

The girl, who said her name was Elisa, was Mexican, and had been taken by the Apaches when she was a child. "I will stay a few minutes, but not too long, for Red Shirt will grow angry," she said shyly. "I am so happy to hear my tongue spoken again! They will not allow me to speak it anymore." She gave a slight shrug. "It is easier not to argue, and they have been kind to me since I became the wife of one of their best warriors."

Flicking a glance toward Red Shirt's wickiup, Whitney asked her quickly, "Can you help me gather food? I have very little left to eat, and do not know how."

Elisa stared at her with huge dark eyes. She would have been pretty under normal circumstances, but the harshness of her life and her advanced pregnancy had left her looking haggard. "Perhaps," she whispered, and poised as if to flee, added "tomorrow! Walk close to me when the women go out to gather *it ai*, and I will show you."

"Gather what?"

"*It ai*. It is a wild spinach, and very good." She flicked another glance toward Red Shirt's hut, then said softly, "I must go, before he notices."

"No one is allowed to talk to me?"

Shaking her head, Elisa whispered over her shoulder, "You are the woman of Corte de Navaja, and he has said you must be left alone."

A shudder rippled down her spine, and Whitney wondered whom she had been given to, and where he was. She would have asked Elisa more, but the girl slipped quietly away in the dusk, leaving her quite alone with her still-smoking ruin of a hut.

Later, curled up against the far side of the wickiup where the fire had not reached, Whitney reflected on the little she had learned. Corte de Navaja roughly translated to cutting edge of the knife. She frowned, then her brow cleared. Of course—Cutter! And he had said she must be left alone. Her mouth tightened. Left alone to die was what he meant, and he wanted her to suffer first! Oh, what she wouldn't give to have him there, and at her mercy!

But things were getting better, and since meeting Elisa, she felt a spark of hope for the first time. She'd show Cutter that she could survive without him. And when the first opportunity arose, she would escape this remote village and do her best to have him caught and hung for his crimes. . . .

Elisa proved to be her salvation in the days that followed. With her sly assistance, Whitney found enough to eat, and she was able to start a fire with shared embers from Elisa's. The Mexican girl even showed her how to repair her ruined hut, where to get the sticks and soak them in the stream to make them pliant enough to bend into position. All in all, Whitney was quite proud of herself. She bartered for a new set of clothes for herself as her skirt and *camisa* had become too tattered to wear, trading away the now-useless saddle for them. She traded the length of rawhide rope for a pair of moccasins to replace her burned shoe, and found them very comfortable.

And she learned to fish.

Fish was the luxury of her diet, as she found some of the Apache staples too strange to eat.

One night, when she sat in her lonely hut and placed one more smooth pebble into the empty gourd she was using to keep track of her days, Whitney decided to keep a journal of her experiences. There was a small supply of paper in the packs Cutter had left, and she wrote with tiny, painstaking script to save space. Who knew who might read this one day? she wondered bitterly, and hoped her precious supply would last as long as she did.

Now at night, instead of using the time to curse Cutter, she wrote her impressions of life in an Apache camp and her imprisonment there.

Self-reliance, she wrote, *is a major satisfaction, and I cannot think why I never knew this before. I feel as if I have triumphed over the one who brought me here in some small way, as if I have taken adversity and turned it to my advantage.*

And along with her thoughts she included small details of everyday life in the camp, the scraping and tanning of hides from the animals the men brought into camp, and how the family structure was developed. There were strict rules to be obeyed, she discovered, and the Apache prized marital fidelity very highly, as well as honesty. It was faintly surprising to her to find such necessary social skills in a people she had considered extremely primitive. The children were loved and cared for, the family honored.

Not too surprisingly, Whitney began to adapt because she had to for survival. She kept her eyes down and her mouth shut around the men, not wanting to endure the quick, harsh words she didn't understand but knew were rebukes. It was a form of slavery, in a way, she thought with hot resentment, but the women didn't seem to mind. On the contrary, they laughed and sang cheerfully as they went about their tasks, and if not for the occasional squabble that would sometimes end in an actual physical violence, the village could have been any small settlement. Cutter, she found, had not been tormenting her when he said Apache husbands beat their wives for disobedience; and worse, if infidelity was proven, the offending wife would have her nose slit or sliced from her face.

Thank God for civilization, she told herself, and prayed fervently that rescue would come soon. Elisa, however she had lived before, was content with her life, and could not understand why Whitney longed for freedom.

Laughing at her one day, Elisa said that if not for her pale face and hair, Whitney would look like the rest of the Apache. "You will fit in well when your man returns!"

They were gathering wood, and had drifted away from the others, a frequent ploy to be able to talk together, and at her words, Whitney slowly straightened. She glanced down at her full cotton skirt and deerskin ankle boots, and the long braids dangling over each shoulder. She'd tied them with strips of rawhide, leaving long ends, Apache style. At that moment she hated Cutter more than ever, but she could not let Elisa know.

Somehow, she made a noncommittal reply, remembering how Elisa had said Corte de Navaja was a valued member of the village, and how he frequently came back to visit Red Shirt.

"Why?" Whitney had asked, and Elisa had shrugged.

"Red Shirt is his uncle."

"Uncle?" Whitney repeated, then recalled that Cutter was, after all, half Apache. The fact that he had brought her to a relative made her angrier than before. How dare he! And Red Shirt had never said a word to her, just come and stood in the doorway of her wickiup on occasion, his dark eyes flicking over her as if taking inventory. It had made her angry, knowing he was only making sure she was still alive, and didn't care how she fared.

Slowly, Whitney managed to pull tidbits of information from Elisa about Cutter.

"So, his father was Apache?" she asked casually as they gathered wild spinach together.

"*Sí,*" Elisa said with a nod. She put one hand to the small of her back as if it ached, a common complaint now in the final month of her pregnancy, and smiled. "They say Long Knife was *muy mal hombre,* just like his son, and rode with the *chishende*—Cochise, of the Chiricahuas."

"Not Apaches?" Whitney asked in surprise, and Elisa laughed at her ignorance.

"The Chiricahuas are Apache, but a different tribe, like people from the United States come from different places, *comprende*?"

"I see. And this Long Knife, Cutter's father, is he still alive?"

Shaking her head, Elisa said no, that he had been killed in a raid many years before. "That is when Corte de Navaja's mother took him with her back to her people, but he never forgot his father's people, though he was only a boy then."

"He comes back often?"

Elisa grew vague, shrugging her shoulders and saying, "When he wishes. You are the first woman he has ever brought with him," she added as if that was important.

"How fortunate for his other women!" Whitney snapped, startling the girl.

"Do you not like your man, señorita?"

"No. He is rough and cruel, and . . . and I hate him!"

That statement brought a nervous glance from Elisa, and an end to information about him. She talked instead of her own husband, Six Feathers, and how brave and strong he was, and how she wished he would return from the reservation.

Curious, Whitney asked her why he was there and she was not, and Elisa replied that conditions were very bad at San Carlos, and her husband had sent her with Red Shirt while he stayed with Geronimo on the reservation. She frowned as she added slowly, "The medicine man Noch-ay-del-klinne has been preaching that the dead chiefs will rise again, come back in life to give the Apache back their former greatness in battle. Times are tense there, and my husband feared for me and our child." She smiled softly, and touched the great mound of her belly as if the unborn infant could feel her hand.

Recalling Lieutenant West's sneering contempt for the Apaches and Geronimo at San Carlos, Whitney remained quiet. She hoped that matters would be settled peacefully, because she liked Elisa. But she also hoped that she could escape soon and return to civilization. How much longer could she survive?

But Whitney found, to her vague surprise, that she was capable of doing a lot of things she'd never considered she could. The pampered, sheltered daughter of Morgan Bradford had evolved into this hard, determined survivor in less than three months.

Whitney's newfound strength gave her confidence enough to face her tormentors one hot afternoon when dust lay in a fine haze over the camp and the sun beat down. The wind had died away, and most of the village's inhabitants were drowsing. Unable to sleep or even write in her journal, Whitney wandered down to the stream to wash out her eating utensils. She carried them in a cloth sling, and squatted on the banks to scrub them with rocks and the cloth.

A soft laugh reached her ears, and she half turned, glancing over her shoulder. Her heart skipped a beat when she recognized the bay horse Cutter had left her, and it was being led to water by Prairie Woman, one of her worst tormentors.

Whitney stood immediately, without thinking, her voice ringing out over the water, "That is my horse!"

Though the Apache woman did not understand the words, she certainly understood the meaning, for she laughed again, her mouth curling in a sneer. Prairie Woman said something back, her voice mocking, and Whitney reacted.

Leaping over the narrow space between them, Whitney snatched the rope from Prairie Woman's hands and repeated, "That is *my* horse!"

Prairie Woman reacted with a hard shove, reaching for the rope. Whitney kept her balance and held the rope out of her reach. Tawny eyes blazed with fury, and Whitney felt the hot rage of righteousness as she shoved back.

With a shriek of rage, the Apache leapt for Whitney in a crouching rush. Whitney managed to avoid her grasp, and reacting instinctively, she half turned, grabbed her attacker's arm, put her weight into it, twisted, and flung Prairie Woman over her shoulder and into the stream.

By this time a crowd had gathered, and the men were laughing and shouting encouragement to the drenched woman spluttering in the water. Whitney flicked a wary gaze toward the spectators, but Elisa motioned behind her. She turned, and saw Prairie Woman coming for her again.

Remembering Chin Yu's admonition to stay calm, Whitney took two steps back to regain firm footing and waited. Prairie Woman charged—bellowing, Elisa was to say later, like a wounded buffalo. Waiting until the last possible moment, Whitney let her almost reach her before she sidestepped and brought her hand down in a chopping blow on the Apache's neck as her momentum carried her past.

When Prairie Woman shook her head and made to get up again, Whitney gestured with the knife she always carried in the waist of her skirt. Her heart was pounding furiously, and she had no idea if she could actually use the knife on another human being, but she fully intended to bluff as long as she could. The wicked length of the blade glittering in the sunlight gave Prairie Woman pause, and while the crowd hooted and laughed, she slunk away, leaving Whitney the undisputed victor.

It took her a moment to catch her breath, and then she stepped over to the bay and picked up the rope around its neck to lead it from the stream. She wondered, suddenly wary, if Red Shirt would be angry that the white captive had bested an Apache. She need not have worried.

A faint smile crooked the old man's mouth as he stood on the banks of the stream. "It is not always the dog with the biggest teeth that wins the fight," he said in Spanish, and Whitney knew then that he had been aware of her sly conversations with Elisa the entire time. She met his gaze with her head held high, and gave a slight nod of acceptance at his offhand tribute.

Red Shirt briefly inclined his head, then turned and walked away.

"You are very good," Elisa enthused, her eyes laughing. "Prairie Woman has never been outdone!"

"She has now," Whitney said grimly. The crowd parted as she led the bay through. She walked slowly, wondering if she had reverted to a primitive state. Had she actually drawn a knife on the woman? Shuddering, Whitney had the thought that almost anyone could be pushed too far.

And when she reached her wickiup with the bay and found Cutter standing there, she knew she had reached her limits. Whitney halted only a few feet from him. Her brain registered all of him with detachment, and she felt as if she had been physically struck. There he was, his brilliant green eyes as mocking as ever, his face darker, his body leaner, somehow, than she remembered it.

There was the distracting thought that she had missed him before the reality hit that he was dressed as an Apache again, his firm body clad in only a breech clout and moccasins, his black hair held by a red cloth headband. He smiled faintly, and Whitney felt a sweep of white-hot rage.

"You've survived, I see," he said when she remained silent, and she gave a terse nod.

"No thanks to you."

He shrugged. "I knew you'd make it."

Moving at last, Whitney strode past him to tie the bay to the sapling at the back of the wickiup, making certain the knot was secure. When she turned around, Cutter was right behind her, his gaze unreadable.

"Why did you come back?" she snapped, fighting the urge to use her knife on him as she had so often dreamed of doing.

Cutter grinned, and his voice held buckets full of sarcasm. "I missed you."

His casual reply, coupled with the delayed reaction from her struggle with Prairie Woman, made Whitney careless.

"You bastard!" she said slowly, distinctly, and saw with a mixture of satisfaction and apprehension that his iron self-control wasn't invincible. There was a quick, hostile flare in his eyes, and an almost imperceptible tightening of the skin over his high, sculpted cheekbones before he regained control.

Taking her by the wrists, Cutter pulled her unhurriedly toward him, and his voice was as cold as his eyes. "You didn't learn much while I was gone, did you? I had hoped for a little more humility."

His hand moved, fine-boned and lethal, to the arch of her throat, where it lingered in a caress that was more threatening than a knife. Brushing his finger pads downward, he felt the erratic pulse in the slender cords of her neck, and smiled with all the friendliness of a panther. "Let's not degenerate to random insults again, Whitney darlin'. I just got back. Maybe if I had a nicer homecoming, I'd be easier to manage."

If nothing else, the last weeks spent in Red Shirt's camp had taught her a little more restraint. She gazed up at him with a hostile stare to match his own, but refused to bite at his last comment. He smiled.

"Excellent! I'm proud of you. You have learned something while I've been gone, after all." The fingers at her throat fell away, and as he turned, he said over his shoulder, almost casually, "We leave in the morning, by the way. See if you can be ready."

Whitney didn't know whether to be glad or gloomy. After all, he hadn't mentioned where he was taking her.

Thirteen

Whitney was silent, whether from sheer exhaustion, relief, or anger, he couldn't tell. But at least, Cutter thought grimly, she was quiet for a change. They were almost there, and he wondered how she would react when they arrived.

Rubbing a hand across the stubble of beard on his jaw, Cutter had the thought that he'd be glad of a respite from the constant riding and running for a while. After he had left Whitney with Red Shirt, he'd gone back to retrieve the last of the supplies. Some of them would, as he'd admitted to Whitney, go to the San Carlos Reservation. But the rest had been taken to a small cave hidden deep in the mountains, a cave only the Apache could find. They would be there for a last effort.

A faint frown tucked his brows, and he flicked a glance toward Whitney. She slumped wearily atop the bay, and the setting sun behind her cast a rosy glow that made her fair hair gleam. Pale circles of lavender graced the apricot-tinged cheeks in faint circles, and her delicate brows were drawn together over half-closed eyelids that had a definite bluish tinge to them.

His frown deepened, and he felt a surge of impatience at the pang of guilt that shot through him. Was it his fault she'd provoked him into leaving her behind? If he'd taken her with him, she'd have been in danger. Soldiers were everywhere, and the men Morgan Bradford had hired seemed to sprout from every bush. No, he'd had to leave her behind. She was too much of a liability, and leaving her with Téjas had been an open invitation to trouble. Of course, she wouldn't have agreed with him and neither would Téjas, but he couldn't worry about that. Now he had to free her before he changed his mind. And before he gave in to the spurring urges of his body and drew her down on the next tuft of grass . . .

It was just as well, Cutter reflected with another glance toward Whitney, that they were almost there. Even though her endurance was much greater than it had been two months before, the steady riding had taken its toll. Each time he'd spoken to her, she had stared at him like someone awakened from deep sleep, her lids half opening, her gilded eyes faintly bewildered and shadowed with exhaustion.

Dark shadows shrouded the land with lingering wisps when Cutter quickened his pace, ignoring Whitney's moan of protest.

"Within an hour you'll be in a bed" was all he said, the words flung over his shoulder. He rode slightly ahead of her, pulling the bay by a lead line, so that Whitney had no more control over the horse than she did the wind.

Holding on to saddle horn and whipping mane, she ground her teeth together in determination. She would not show him how tired she was, would not give him the satisfaction of uttering a single protest. She'd heard his words, but she'd been promised beds before, and none of them—except for the one at Téjas's hacienda— had been more than a brief respite.

They crossed a river that Cutter told her was the San Pedro, and she saw a collection of adobe and wood houses on one side, and clapboard structures stringing along the other. The Galiuro Mountains humped along the eastern horizon, with the Santa Catalina Mountains ridging the near west side of the river, and a broad, fertile valley lay between them. While Whitney cast longing eyes toward the lights in the small town, Cutter pushed on, saying they were almost at their destination. But to Whitney, time passed in a blur of endless riding as night fell.

Through bleary eyes she saw a shadowy herd of fat cattle, grazing in grass that was so high it tickled the bay's belly. Cattle. Then that meant they were close to some form of settlement, though not necessarily to civilization. Cattle had grazed near the Apache camp, too, had dotted fields of dust and scrub at some of the other places Cutter had taken her. She couldn't remember most of them; they'd been waystops easing the worst of hours of bone-racking rides through mountains and across burning plains. She had merely the vaguest memories of faces, most staring at her curiously, only a few showing any concern at her pitiful condition. And why should they? She certainly wouldn't have been too quick to show any concern over the bedraggled woman whose man was draped in gun belts and danger. At least the Whitney of a few months ago wouldn't have, she amended with a gathering of newly discovered fortitude. Perhaps her physical strength was only slightly improved, but her mental condition had shown vast reforms.

The old Whitney would have wept huge crocodile tears and pleaded with Cutter to stop. Now, she might be falling out of the saddle, but she'd rather have been dragged naked through acres of cactus than show him how tired she was by the first word.

Not for nothing had she spent a terrifying month in an Apache camp where her mettle had been tried and tried again. Cutter had made a mistake; it would have been much better for him if he had left her in an ivory tower with scores of servants at her disposal, because this new Whitney Bradford had no doubts about her ability to survive. And that meant surviving anything that the capricious Cutter might decide to do with her.

Lifting her chin, she stared ahead, her lustrous eyes dimmed with weariness. Wherever they were, Whitney thought hazily, Cutter was glad to be there. She could see the slight straightening of his shoulders at the glimpse of lamplights in the twilight, twinkling orbs that dotted the horizon with a welcoming glow. Even his horse seemed to be eager, pricking its ears forward and snorting, its step quickening.

A wave of relief washed over Whitney when she saw the grove of trees ahead, gnarled branches lacing the lights with flickers of movement, and dogs ran barking wildly as the horses trotted down a wide lane leading to a house. In the deep dusk, with the purple shadows lying like wisps of fog over everything, Whitney could not distinguish how large the house was, but it looked comfortable, and that was all that mattered. Low stone walls bedecked with pots of flowers enclosed a small yard, and when they finally stopped at a gate lit with lanterns, she felt the first faint waves of embarrassment.

Cutter had obviously brought her to the home of people who would look askance at a female with soiled clothing and tangled hair. Self-conscious, she tucked the long strands beneath a battered hat, pulling it down to hide her face. Her throat tightened, and she felt a wave of irritation that gave her enough strength to protest.

"Cutter! You can't take me here like this!"

He was already swinging down from his horse even before it had come to a halt, his movements as easy, as if he hadn't just ridden for over fourteen hours. The gate swung open noiselessly, and he led the horses through before he replied.

"Like what? Don't tell me you've stayed quiet this long only to start up now?" His voice was impatient, and in the dim light his eyes reflected the lamps with a harsh glitter. "A word of warning—don't."

She would have protested more, but the door to the house was swinging open, and voices could be heard. Light from the house silhouetted a tall figure that paused, then seemed to explode with energy.

"Cutter!" came the greeting, and the shadow burst down the shallow front steps, coming to a halt beside Cutter. Light eyes glowed with pleasure, and a fall of straight brown hair covered a boyish forehead.

Swinging around, Cutter's mouth curled in a smile, and there was a note of genuine warmth in his voice when he said, "Davy! How is everything around here since I've been gone?"

A white grin flashed in the dusky light, and the boy said cheerfully, "Dead as bricks! God, I'm glad you're back! Now maybe things will start getting lively again. They usually do when you're here. Hullo! Who'd you bring with you? That's not Téjas back there, is it?"

Cutter's voice held a note of amusement when he said, "No, it sure isn't." Reaching up, he swung Whitney down in spite of her brief, futile struggle, and brought her closer into the light. "Miss Bradford, please meet my impetuous young brother, David Coleman."

A rush of air left her mouth, for whatever Whitney had expected, she certainly hadn't expected to be taken to Cutter's family home—especially as a bedraggled hostage!

For once she spoke her mind. "How dare you!" she snapped. "You drag me around half the country like a mongrel on a leash, and then you have the utter audacity to take me to your home as if I were a stray you'd found? I won't tolerate it, do you hear me?"

"You'll tolerate a lot more than this if I say so," Cutter said with jade fire in his eyes.

In a voice rich with laughter, David said, "I knew things would pick up when you came home, Cutter! Ma, here's Cutter back, and he's brought a guest with him."

Cutter turned, and with lighting eyes called to his mother, "It's been a while."

"Not by my choice. You seem to have forgotten how to get here." A rustle of petticoats and perfume scented the air, and then the cool, soft voice asked mildly, "Who is your guest, son?"

If it had been humanly possible, Whitney would have sunk into the ground, melted into the pebbled lane without a single trace. But as it wasn't, she had to face the gaze that was turned to her.

The woman facing her in the shadows was slender, with soft brown hair parted in the middle and huge eyes that Whitney was certain would be as green as her son's. There was no condemnation or judgment in the gaze, only a polite curiosity that was somehow even more damning. How would this obviously well-bred woman react to the information that her son was guilty of kidnapping? And that he had brought his hostage to her home?

She heard Cutter say in a voice tinged with slight irony, "This is Miss J. Whitney Bradford. Whitney—my mother, Mrs. Deborah Coleman." There was a short, sizzling silence in which Whitney wondered with a certain degree of malice how he would explain her, but he didn't.

Then she knew why, because his mother lifted a brow and said, "The Whitney Bradford who's in all the newspapers?"

"The same," Cutter said without a trace of remorse or guilt, and Whitney had the disbelieving feeling that she was the only one there who didn't understand the punch line of a cruel joke. Newspapers? she thought dully, then understood immediately—of course. Her father would have done his dead-level best to paste stories of her abduction all over every newspaper in Arizona in the hope that someone would recognize her and free her. Which also meant that the entire world now knew she had been alone in the keeping of a notorious renegade for just a shade over two months. And of course, human nature being what it was, there would be plenty of salacious comments and crude conjecture over what she must have suffered.

I might as well have been thoroughly raped for all the good of it, she thought with dismaying accuracy. *People will expect it.*

A hot flush crept up to stain her neck and pink her cheeks becomingly. Beneath the floppy brim of her hat, Whitney's eyes began to glitter like newly minted gold, and her lips thinned into a straight line.

After the barest of pauses, Cutter reached to sweep the hat from

Whitney's head, and her gilded hair swung down into the lantern glow in a bright spill. Anger and embarrassment made her voice tart.

"Excuse me for not appearing at my best, but one of the disadvantages of being a hostage is that you get none of the small amenities of life!"

There was the faintest tremor of laughter in her voice as Deborah Coleman said, "I know, dear. It's been very unpleasant for you, hasn't it?" She stepped forward, her smile reassuring. "I'm sure you're hungry. Come into the house with me. I'll have you a bath poured while you eat, and then later we can talk."

Gently disengaging Cutter's hard grasp from Whitney's arm, Deborah drew her with her, still chatting conversationally. "Did you know that I've read several of your books, Miss Bradford? They're very good. You seem to impart a great deal of humanity to your characters. . . ."

Whitney, who was more exhausted than she could remember being in her entire life, was given into the care of a Mexican woman who worked with soft efficiency to make her comfortable. Whitney wondered what Cutter was thinking or if he was thinking of her at all. He certainly hadn't seemed to care for the fact that his mother had quietly but firmly told him they would discuss matters later; nor had he seemed too pleased by his young brother's barrage of questions and comments, most of which were reproved by Deborah when it was obvious they were embarrassing to Whitney, and Davy was sent off to bed in a high dudgeon.

At the moment Whitney was too grateful for creature comforts to ponder the strange situation, though it did occur to her that Deborah Coleman certainly did take things in stride. How many women would react so calmly when their son brought home a widely publicized hostage—especially a hostage *he'd* abducted? Something was definitely very odd, Whitney thought drowsily.

It wasn't until after she'd soaked for a half hour in a brass hip bath, had her wet hair brushed dry in front of a fire by the maid, Juana, and eaten a delicious meal of thinly sliced roast beef, small green peas, and sliced potatoes smothered in sour cream and onions, that the answer came to her.

Of course. Cutter was a half-breed, so his mother must have had some experience with this sort of thing herself. It stood to reason. Not many women who were so obviously refined actually strolled through Apache camps and chose a suitable husband, so Deborah Coleman must have been a hostage herself at one time. It was, Whitney thought sleepily, a sort of roundabout requital.

She would have been quite gratified to know that as she was being tucked cozily into bed by Juana and the lamps blown out, Cutter was facing an inquisition of sorts. Not that Deborah shouted or ranted; she was not that kind of woman. And Cutter would not have borne it, even from his mother. No, Deborah's instrument was one Cutter employed himself with a fair amount of skill—sarcasm.

"It's so nice to have you back in the family fold, son," she said softly, and her smile conveyed only maternal pleasure. "Of course, I've been able to read all about your latest exploits in the papers, but that's not at all like an actual letter or visit."

Straddling a chair close to the settee where his mother sat with a book in her lap, Cutter didn't flinch. He knew she was after blood, and he'd be damned if she'd get it.

"No, it isn't, is it? But now I'm here, and as soon as we get this part of the visit over with, we can enjoy our time together."

It was a challenge, a gauntlet thrown down, and Deborah did not hesitate. "It was very enlightening to discover that my eldest son was clever enough to engineer a robbery and a kidnapping at the same time. Not many men would think to do that. A masterstroke, I'd say."

"Thank you. I was rather proud of it myself." Irony tinged his voice as he waited, and Deborah didn't disappoint him.

"And to take a woman so well known! Why, if you'd been craven enough to abduct some lesser-known female, you might not have been the object of so many searches, or rewards offered." A smile touched her lips. "How long has it been now? Two months? And you've managed to avoid capture. How proud you must be!"

"Bursting my buttons with it." Cutter flicked a glance around the room filled with solid wood furniture and stuffed pillows. It all looked the same, with very little changed since he'd been a boy. The same braided rugs, the same heavy tables and overstuffed chairs, and the same air of homey comfort. Brass gleamed, the tables were polished to a high luster, and the tile floors beneath the rugs were as smooth and cool as his mother's voice.

"Of course, I'm certain you have just as brilliant a plan to release your hostage and remain alive at the same time?" came his mother's soft, pleasant voice, and his dark head turned.

Green eyes met green, wills clashing for a moment, as they always had done. Deborah Coleman was no weak-willed female, but a proud, determined woman who met life head-on.

"As a matter of fact," said Cutter equally pleasantly, "I do."

"How wonderful. I'll be able to sleep well tonight now that I have your assurance." There was a brief pause before she said, "Since you have deigned to honor us with your presence and that of Miss Bradford, I am assuming that you want us to send her back to her father."

"It would certainly expedite matters."

"Odd," said Deborah with a deliberate curl of her lip, "but I'd never considered you cowardly before."

Her remark was rewarded with a tautening of the skin across Cutter's high cheekbones, and a slight narrowing of his eyes.

"I suppose you think it wiser and *braver* for me to stroll into Tombstone with Whitney trussed and gagged and tossed over my shoulder?" he returned tightly.

"Isn't that how you took her?"

"No!" he burst out. Then, with the faintest trace of a smile, he added, "I forgot the gag, much to my sorrow."

"You must plan better next time." Deborah gave him a long look, then asked, "Cutter, whatever possessed you to invite this kind of trouble? To take a young woman of good background as if she were of no consequence?"

"Insanity" was the prompt reply, embellished with, "And an odd notion of intimidation. I can't imagine why I ever thought she'd be intimidated. Nothing I've done so far has succeeded."

"Would it be prying if I were to inquire where she has been the past two months?"

"Over most of Arizona Territory, I'd say."

"Really?" Deborah said with a smile. "Somehow, it's what you *don't* say that I find the most intriguing."

Suddenly opaque and unreadable, Cutter's eyes drifted from his mother to a spot on the far wall, focused, and remained for a full thirty seconds before he said slowly, "I think you probably know some of it, and can guess the rest. But whatever you're thinking, I didn't hurt her."

"How chivalrous. I shall recommend you for a medal at the next Ladies League meeting."

Cutter's mouth tightened. "I don't intend to defend my actions . . ."

"That's probably best. . . ."

". . . but I did what I had to do."

"Spoken like a true man."

"So, you've now decided that I should be hung out to dry too? How maternal," he continued acidly.

Deborah settled back against the settee, staring at the dangerously tight expression on Cutter's face. "What you're doing won't help, you know," she said suddenly. "They've lost, and nothing you do can change that."

The thread of the conversation had altered, looping to a frequent subject. "I know," Cutter said. "But I felt that I had to do what I could." There was a brief pause before he asked, "Where's Daniel?"

"In Prescott." Deborah's smile was wry. "When he read about your . . . activities . . . he decided to do what he could to delay your execution."

Grinning, Cutter said lightly, "He must be pretty worried to go all the way to Prescott."

"That's where Morgan Bradford is. It seems he's acquainted with Governor Fremont too."

"Why is it I'm not surprised?" Cutter murmured. "So, Daniel thinks he can coax Bradford into retracting his bounty? Or has he gone to collect it?"

Sternly, she replied, "Your stepfather is quite concerned, Cutter. You should be too. I understand Morgan Bradford is tearing up and down the territory, enlisting the aid of everyone he thinks might be able to find his daughter."

"Maybe I should take her to him myself, after all," Cutter said with a faintly mocking lift of his brow. "The reward would be only a small payment for the trouble she's caused me."

"Daniel managed to trace you to Téjas, you know." Silence greeted this statement, but Deborah pressed on. "He seemed to think you might bring her here."

"Did he?"

"That was a month ago."

Cutter's eyes met his mother's. "I took her to Red Shirt."

Deborah nodded. "And how was he?"

"As usual. Just glad to be off the reservation. At least he has enough to eat now, with the cattle you've sent to the camp."

"And how did Miss Bradford adjust to life there?" Deborah inquired.

"I didn't stay to find out firsthand, but Red Shirt assured me that she adapted well." He grinned.

"I can recall Red Shirt's methods quite well, thank you." Deborah's eyes were soft with laughter. "I used to complain about him to your father, but, of course, it did no good whatsoever."

"No, it wouldn't."

A comfortable silence fell between them, as it always did after one of their discussions.

"Tell me about her, Cutter," his mother said gently, and drew his gaze.

Shrugging, he said, "She's beautiful, smart, and rich. And arrogant and dictatorial and hardheaded."

And . . . ?"

Cutter's brows lifted, and a smile smoothed his lips. "Are you waiting for betraying sentiment? I'm afraid you're wasting your time. The only sentiment I could reveal would be one I would not want my mother to hear."

"How shocking."

The smile squared into a grin. "Which is why I didn't mention it."

"I suppose you know that Téjas thinks the two of you have much deeper affections for each other than you'll admit."

Cutter's grin became mocking. "There are times Téjas bears a remarkable resemblance to a piñata stuffed with romantic conceits."

Clasping her hands together, Deborah matched his mocking smile with one of her own. "After all these years as friends, you're suddenly enemies? Why?"

"An unaccountable difference of opinion, I'm afraid."

"This is not the first time one of your feminine companions has gone to Téjas for comfort, yet, for some reason, this time you resent it."

Shaking his head, Cutter said, "No, that wasn't it," in such a closed voice, Deborah did not pursue it.

Instead, she said, "Well, I find her refreshing. Much more entertaining than mundane young women who can only darn socks and bake bread."

"Whitney has a variety of talents," Cutter said dryly. "It would quite surprise you to see her in action."

"It's been a while since I've been surprised," his mother said sarcastically. "I'll have to explore her acquaintance more thoroughly."

Cutter rose from the chair he was straddling, put it back in its place, and said pleasantly, "Just watch your shoes too. She's very good."

When he had gone, Deborah sat mulling over their conversation for some time.

Fourteen

Daniel, David, and Deborah, Whitney reflected. *Alliterative and biblical . . .* And entirely different from Cutter. But it wasn't just Cutter's name and heritage that set him apart from his family. Except for the green eyes and iron will, there was very little to connect him to the peaceful people with whom he'd spent his childhood and a rather turbulent adolescence.

"Turbulent," Deborah had said, "by his choice, not ours. He never quite adjusted to the more stable life here, and always ran away to the village where he'd been born. It was a great worry for a long time, until I came to realize that he was capable of living with one foot in each world." A faint smile had touched her mouth at the memory. "Daniel, who has tried to guide and discipline Cutter since he was a wild young boy, has been much more understanding than I have."

It occurred to Whitney to wonder what kind of man would take on the responsibility of an Apache warrior's widow and son. With the world the way it was, marrying a woman who had been captured and married to a fierce Apache invited ridicule and conjecture, but the absent Daniel Coleman had not seemed to care a whit. Not that she could blame him, in a way, because Deborah Coleman had made him an excellent wife. She was beautiful, polished, confident. And she had certainly learned how to deal with adversity.

At first Whitney had been somewhat skeptical when Deborah began to talk to her, thinking, perhaps, that she was going to try to excuse and exonerate Cutter. But instead, Deborah had related how she'd felt upon being captured as a young girl, taken from her home and forced into servitude by a man who had been frightening and harsh.

"But I survived. And in time I saw the good things about him, the tenderness of which he was capable. When Long Knife died, I was quite grief-stricken. But when I returned home, I found Daniel. He was the young attorney who had been responsible for the sale of the ranch after my parents' death, and felt dreadful that he had not been able to find any trace of me. I was their only child, and as there were no other heirs, the ranch was auctioned. He worked very hard to see that I got a portion of the money, and in time we found that we loved each other."

"So, all ends happily ever after," Whitney had said in a tone that revealed more than she would have liked. Deborah had said nothing, and she was glad, but the sudden emotion she'd felt still disturbed her.

She was even more disturbed by her reaction to Cutter in the settled atmosphere of his home. To please his mother, she supposed, he wore no weapons, not even the knife she was accustomed to seeing stuck in his belt. He'd trimmed his hair and was clean-shaven again, and he dressed in dark, slim-legged pants and a white shirt open at the neck, looking the picture of a rancher's son. That was something else—Cutter used his stepfather's surname of Coleman, taking it to his advantage. Who would look for an outlaw beneath the civilized exterior he now presented to the world? It made her furious to think that he would get away with everything—the robbery and her kidnapping, and even the men he'd killed.

Beneath that civilized exterior, however, she knew he was still the same. Just below the surface of those jade eyes glittered the same predatory inclinations. She found it out very quickly when they were left alone on the stone patio at the back of the house.

Looking fresh and more handsome than she could recall, Cutter sauntered onto the patio where Whitney and Deborah were having pleasant conversation. His beautiful eyes flicked over both of them as he greeted his mother, then rested on Whitney.

"Enjoying yourself, Miss Bradford?" came the pleasant inquiry in a tone that displayed only a polite courtesy.

"I was until *you* joined us," she returned tartly, and was annoyed by his soft laugh. She looked down at the skirt of the rose-colored gown she wore, pleating the muslin between her fingers with irritation at Cutter's response.

"Shall I leave, then? I thought my mother wanted us to chat cozily out here, pretending we like each other."

"Cutter," said Deborah as she got up from the chair where she'd been sitting, "why don't you pretend that you're a gentleman while I go into the house and ask Maria to prepare us a light lunch. It may not be easy, but I have confidence in your abilities."

With that smooth comment she was gone, leaving Whitney feeling suddenly vulnerable.

Cutter's eyes sought and held hers with all the polite pretense she hated, and, suddenly moved to strip away his masquerade, she said, "How distressing for you to have to behave like a human being instead of a savage."

The quick, fierce flare in his eyes told her she'd managed to pierce his guard, but she still wasn't prepared for his swift reaction. In a fluid movement, he grabbed both her wrists in his cool, hard fingers, pulling her up from her chair in a manner that was outwardly playful but for the painful pressure of his hands on her delicate wrist bones.

"I haven't forgotten how to be savage, if that's what's bothering you," he said in a lazy tone that did nothing to hide the menace in his words.

"I hadn't assumed you had," she returned coolly. "And from the bruises you're putting on my arms now, I'm certain no one else here will be mistaken about it either."

"Quite the little diplomat now, aren't you?" he asked calmly, and released her arms. Whitney sank back into the cane chair, glancing up at him sullenly as he leaned back against the low stone wall enclosing the patio. Casually crossing his arms over his chest, Cutter kept the polite smile on his lips as he studied her flushed, angry face. What was it about her that intrigued him? he wondered with a familiar twist of irritation. It certainly wasn't her sweet temper, and as he hadn't allowed himself to ease his urges in her soft, honeyed body, it couldn't be that either. Or maybe it *was* that, he thought then. If he did what he'd wanted to do since the first evening she'd come into his hotel room, he'd be able to stop thinking about her. That was usually the way it went; the pursuit and challenge engineered his interest, and after attaining his goal, he lost interest rather quickly. And it wasn't as if she were an innocent girl. She'd admitted. . . .

Squinting against the bright prick of sunlight in his eyes, Cutter asked abruptly, "Would you care to take a ride with me?"

Warily, Whitney countered, "Ride where? I seem to have been riding a great deal with you, and I can't imagine why you think I might want to do so much as cross a room to spend a moment in your company! Especially when all you want to do is fight with me."

"For God's sake, Whitney!" His tone was exasperated. "Don't you think I get tired of the fighting too? I had the revolutionary notion you might want to discuss your release, but if—"

She stood abruptly. "Discuss . . . my release?" Her breath caught. "Do you mean—is that why you brought me here?"

"It certainly wasn't so I could endure my mother's lecture, or the lecture still to come from my stepfather." His voice was grim when he added, "If I'd had any other option, I assure you I would have taken it."

Fiercely glad that he had been inconvenienced by his family, Whitney didn't bother to hide it. "Seeing as how you thought very little of *my* feelings, I think it's only fair you should suffer now!"

"Ah, so you'd like to see me horsewhipped and hung on the barn wall?" Cutter mocked lightly, and in spite of his irritation, he felt a surge of amusement. "You're a bloodthirsty wench."

"You'd feel the same if you'd been through what I've been through!"

"Don't give up, tiger-eyes. You may yet get your wish. In my younger days Daniel wielded a riding crop with great agility. I imagine, if pushed, he may resort to such crude tactics again."

Whitney sniffed her disbelief. "It's much more likely that my father will take whip in hand if he sees you. Or a pistol."

Laughing, Cutter took her hands again, gently this time in spite of her resistance. "A duel at twenty paces? Just my idea of a good time! I only hope no one is cruel enough to leave me at *your* mercy. . . ."

Disturbed by his light teasing, and wondering why he was making the effort to be so friendly, Whitney gazed up at him. He was looking down at her with his sensual lips still curved in a smile, and when she saw the slight widening of his pupils and the hot flare of desire that he quickly veiled, she was startled.

"Your fears are well-founded!" she returned tartly, still unable to quiet the lurch of her heart at the light in his eyes and the soft smile on his mouth. Why did she react like this to him, especially after all he'd done? Why was she noticing the way his eyes tucked at the corners when he smiled, and the erotic outline of his mouth?

With her head tilted back and the light behind her, Cutter could see the conflicting emotions written on her face. The luminescent eyes gathered and held a fleeting response, but then she gave a toss of the pale hair flowing loosely around her shoulders and said abruptly, "I think I'll see if I can help in the kitchen."

Thoroughly amused now, Cutter said, "I thought you didn't do domestic chores. Isn't that what you once told me?"

"That was before I was thrown to the wolves and forced to fend for myself!"

"Then maybe I've had a good influence on you after all, tiger-eyes."

She paused, and slid him a reflective glance. "Yes, Cutter, I think you have. If nothing else, I've learned not to depend upon anyone but myself."

"It's about time," was all he said, but after she'd gone and he was alone on the patio, Cutter felt a rush of annoyance. So what had he expected? One couldn't take a sheltered and autocratic young woman like Whitney and subject her to such enormous change without either breaking her or making her stronger. And isn't that what he wanted? Wasn't that one of the reasons he'd taken her to Red Shirt's camp and left her there? It didn't matter that he knew she would come to no harm; she hadn't known. But now her self-assurance was irritating, and even more irritating was not knowing why it should bother him. Cutter quickly masked his chagrin as his young half brother came out onto the patio to join him.

"Hullo, Cutter!" David grinned, his youthful face alight with affection and delight. "You sure did stir things up a bit last night! Ma gave you a good raking over the coals, I'll bet!" Sliding a glance toward the kitchen, David said in an admiring tone, "She sure is a looker, Cutter. I've never seen hair that color before, or eyes like a cat on a woman."

"Tiger eyes." Cutter corrected his brother with an amused twist of his mouth. "And she is a tiger. Don't let her fool you."

David's grin was infectious. "Yeah, so I saw last night. Gave you a good pop, didn't she?" At Cutter's shrug, he continued. "Pa's due back in the next few days. What do you think he's going to say about this? He sure was mad when he read in the paper that you'd kidnapped her and made off with the army payroll. Hey, did you hear about Billy the Kid?"

"What about him?"

"He's dead. Shot dead up in New Mex, by a fellow named Pat Garrett."

For a moment Cutter didn't say anything. He remembered the day in late April when he'd compared Billy's notoriety with his own reputation, and not soon after learned of the Kid's escape from jail. Justice, it seemed, came to every man sooner or later.

"You don't say," Cutter replied when it seemed as if David expected some sort of comment. "I figured he'd get careless one day. Not many outlaws die in bed."

That gave young David pause, and he gazed anxiously at his brother. "But you're going to give it all up, ain't you, Cutter? I'd hate to think of you . . . getting it like the Kid did."

Cutter teased, "I don't have but one warrant out on me, Davy lad. All the other charges couldn't stick to flypaper."

"Yeah, but this one is a pip! Word is, Bradford wants your hide nailed to the wall."

"So does his daughter."

"But Cutter—he may be able to do it."

Cutter's smile was reassuring. "What makes you think I can't avoid it a while longer?"

Giving a miserable shrug, David said, "I don't know. I guess, like Billy the Kid, everybody gets caught sooner or later."

It was almost an exact echo of his own thoughts, and Cutter laughed. "Look, if it will make you feel any better, I intend to give her back to her father and disappear for a while."

"Where will you go? You're always going off, and one of these days you're going to never show up again. Pa says I shouldn't worry so much about it, that you're like that wolf bitch I had once. Do you remember?"

Cutter nodded, and his voice was tight. "Yes. I remember."

Wiping a hand across light eyes suddenly grown wet, David said, "I thought Silvertail liked me as much as I liked her, but then she went off and never came back. Now you're going to do the same thing."

"What else did Daniel tell you?"

David bit his lip. "That you can't change a wolf from being a wolf, no matter how much you treat it like a pet."

"Well then, maybe you should apply that to people," Cutter said gently, and wondered wryly why he didn't follow his own advice. A wolf would be a wolf and a tiger would be a tiger, and even dressed up in a silk suit and top hat, he'd still be restless. "It's the laws of nature, Davy boy," he said, ruffling his brother's fine brown hair with an affectionate hand.

Slyly, David said, "Speaking of nature—you ain't really going to give her back, are you? I sorta hoped that maybe you'd gotten attached to her."

"Attached? I've seen gut-shot grizzly bears I liked better." Now Cutter was grinning, and David laughed.

"Just the same, it's going to be interesting to see what Pa has to say when he gets home. I bet he likes her."

It would, Cutter reflected grimly, be *very* interesting to observe Daniel Coleman's reaction to Whitney Bradford. He just hoped he'd manage to be gone before then.

"I'm going visiting," Cutter said abruptly, and when David asked to go along, he laughed and said it would not be a good idea.

"Oh. I guess that means you're going down by the river."

"And what do you know about that?" Cutter couldn't help but ask with an amused expression. "You're only fourteen. I hardly think you've started wandering those paths yet."

Belligerently, David said, "And how old were you when you first visited?"

After a moment's consideration, Cutter shrugged. "Well, you still can't go. I may not be back for a while. Tell Ma I won't be home for supper."

It suited David to remain silent as to where Cutter had gone, and dinner was a quiet affair that evening. In the light of the tall candelabrum placed in the middle of the table, Whitney looked as if she were about to fall asleep. Her pale hair gleamed like polished ivory, and her cheeks were devoid of color. Only the bright glitter of gold eyes reflecting the candlelight gave her any animation, and Cutter's absence was felt as vividly as if he'd been the main topic of conversation.

Later, when everyone had gone to bed and the house was quiet, Whitney lay wakeful. Annoyed with herself because she couldn't get Cutter out of her mind and couldn't concentrate on anything else, she at last gave up the idea of sleep and shrugged into a thin white wrapper that matched the sleeveless muslin gown Deborah had given her. She would go and sit on the patio in the moonlight and listen to the night sounds. Perhaps that would make her sleepy.

Night brushed the air with soft shadows, and a single lantern glinted light from the profusion of blossoms that twined along the garden walls. The jasmine and gardenias mingled with the rich, heady scent of moonflowers, the plant Deborah had told her opened only at night, unfolding large white petals and releasing its fragrance into the shadows.

Perching on the seat of a cane chair, Whitney stroked the flower with a light finger, watching it tremble beneath her touch, the silky bloom as light as a butterfly wing and just as fragile. A profusion of blossoms rambled delicately over the wall, and she yielded to impulse and pulled one from the vine. She would take it back to her room with her so she could smell its sweet fragrance during the night.

"Did you know that flowers are the sex organs of a plant?" came a light, inquiring voice, startling Whitney into jerking around and dropping the blossom. It drifted like a giant snowflake to her feet, and she stared at Cutter with wide eyes. He was leaning lazily in the doorway leading to the patio, his left arm above his head and his right arm at his side. A rifle dangled from his hand, and as he levered his body away from the doorway and crossed the patio in fluid steps, Whitney had the thought that he was drunk. Very drunk. She stiffened. Cutter didn't usually drink to excess.

As he passed a small table, Cutter dropped the rifle onto its surface without pausing, crossing to Whitney and bending down in the same fluent motion as he swept up the dropped blossom. Twirling it between his long fingers, he said in the same pleasantly blurred voice, "Your flower, milady," presenting it to her with a flourish.

Whitney took the flower because she didn't know what else to do with it. Then she wished she hadn't, because Cutter cupped his fingers around her hand, and began to stroke the velvet furring of the blossom with his fingertip as he explained the function of the flower in the plant world.

"This, m'dear, is a petal, as you probably know. But cupped inside this showy blossom—or corolla—are the inner sex organs . . . have I said something to upset you? No? You gave a start. My mistake. Now . . ."

"Cutter . . ."

"Shhh. This is a botany lesson, and if you will lissen caref'ly, you'll learn something." His breath, spiced with fruity fragrance, warmed her cheek.

Just being this near him made Whitney's throat tighten, and she was much too aware of his lean body pressing lightly against hers, and how thin her wrapper and gown were. She shivered slightly, a tremor that rippled from neck to ankle, but Cutter seemed not to notice.

"See these tiny little stalks?" he was asking. "These are the stamens, I think. Or maybe they're pistils . . . well, whatever, it's hard to tell, they're tucked so far inside the petals." His finger smoothed across the petal in a light touch to tickle the tiny filament. "Reproduction is performed—you do understand about reproduction, don't you? I thought you did. Anyway, tiger-eyes, for the plant to be fertilized, it requires help." His other hand, until this moment propped against the low wall behind them, shifted to work under her hair, lifting it from her shoulders and smoothing it away so that his fingers could slowly massage her neck.

The tense, corded muscles—taut and screaming—began to slowly liquefy under the satiny pressure of his fingers, and Whitney lost the thread of his conversation, drifting in and out like grass in the wind.

". . . plants whose reproduction is aided by night-flying insects are often pale in color and heavily scented—am I going too fast for you?"

A shake of her head, and she gathered the presence of mind to take a step away from him. He let her hair spill over her shoulders again, but now his hand dropped to her hip, pulling her against him.

"Cutter . . ."

Turning her slightly, he took the flower and tucked it behind her ear, the back of his fingers grazing her cheek in a slow caress, his thumb sliding beneath her chin to tilt her face to his.

"Even the plant world does it, sweetheart. It's simple. I know you know how. . . ."

"Cutter!"

Drowsy eyes widened slightly, and his sensual lips quirked in a smile. "It's no good, tiger-eyes. I went down by the river—hell, I went *in* the river, and it still didn't work."

"I don't know what you're talking about."

"I know. It's probably better that way."

Her eyes narrowed fractionally, and she gazed up at his face, at the lazy smile and eyes and the dark hair falling over his brow. "You're drunk."

"That I am, sweetheart. Drunk on wine, drunk on desire and . . . just drunk."

Dropping her gaze, she saw that his white shirt—so immaculate this morning—was rumpled and stained, and gaped open to reveal his smooth chest. The neat cord trousers that had been tucked into knee-high leather boots earlier were just as wrinkled.

"What . . . what will your mother say?" she asked lamely, and then flushed at his gathering laughter.

"Somehow, I think she has more on her mind than th' state of my clothes right now." His hand caught her again, curling around her wrist in a light clasp that wasn't threatening, just firm. It was the damnedest thing. He'd spent most of the day and a good part of the evening with a very obliging young lady, yet coming home and finding Whitney on the patio dressed in a thin white gown that did not do a great deal to hide the shadowy curves beneath had taken him right back to where he'd begun earlier. Even the dip in the river hadn't dampened the fires he now felt.

Whitney, staring up at his wind-ruffled raven hair and seeing the slight widening of his eyes with the yearning she knew so well, felt her chest begin to constrict. She'd promised herself in the past weeks that she would never again be so easy as to let Cutter seduce her with sweet words or a caress, but it was much easier to defend oneself against the intangible than the tangible. And right now, with his hands stroking up her arms in soft nuzzles of lean fingers against skin, it was very hard to remember any vows she might have made.

Cutter brought her hand to his lips, and keeping his eyes on hers, began to kiss the small pink palm that still held tiny calluses. He kissed each one, then touched his tongue lightly to the center of her palm, listened to her quickly drawn breath, and moved up the rounded hill to her wrist. The fabric of skin stretching over her wrist held faint bruises from the day before, and he kissed them each, light brushes of his lips that made her entire arm tingle.

Sliding his hands up her arms to her elbows, Cutter cupped them in his palms and pulled her gently forward, angling so that her hands slid inside his open shirt. The soft touch of her hands on his skin had a paralyzing effect on Whitney. She could feel the smooth bands of muscle on his flat stomach, the light hair that covered him, and the rapid thunder of his heart beneath her fingertips.

As Cutter's hands progressed in silken caresses up her arms to her shoulders, pulling her forward so that her breasts were pressed against his bare chest, Whitney heard the bells of warning that signaled she needed to get away as fast as she could. But it was hard when his mouth was discovering that soft, vulnerable stretch of skin beneath her ear, nuzzling it so that licking fires ran molten through her veins.

Knowing she should stop him—stop herself—Whitney drew up the heel of her hand and pressed against his chest. His muscles contracted, and he pulled her even closer so that her arm was trapped between them. Cradling the back of her head with one palm, Cutter slowly massaged her scalp as his mouth left her ear and moved to her throat. His other hand cupped her buttocks and lifted her into him, holding her.

"Cutter . . . Cutter, don't!" she managed to gasp out, but it was hard to be coherent when he was making shudders race through muscles she hadn't know she had, making flames leap in the pit of her stomach as if she had a volcano inside.

"Don't? Don't what? Don't stop?" Capturing her lips, he coaxed a kiss from her, a tidy, neat kiss, hardly one that would satisfy. "Open your mouth, tiger-eyes," he murmured against her lips. "Just think of yourself as a flower, and these"—his thumb dragged across her bottom lip in a caress, then soothed the curve of her upper lip—"are the petals. Give me some of your nectar, love . . . that's right . . . open for me." His tongue slicked over her lips and slipped inside, the moist contact lubricating senses already out of control.

"I thought it was pistols or something," she said shakily when the kiss had ended, "not nectar."

A light laugh broke into the air, and Cutter eased her down atop the flat ledge of the low wall, facing him, one arm holding her up as he pulled her slightly forward so that her hips were level with his. Whitney was wreathed in a shimmy of green leaves, snowy blossoms, and crushed perfume, cascading over the wall, filling the night with incense. Spreading her thighs with a gentle hand, he put one of her legs on each side of his, and her white muslin gown flowed around him like falls of cream.

"Pistil, stamen, corolla—I don't think it matters right now." Easing between her legs, he could feel them tremble as his palms traced their slender contours, gently kneaded the tender flesh, then moved slowly up beneath the froth of muslin to her hips, pulling her against him.

Startled at his touch against her bare skin, at the press of his hard body between her thighs, Whitney tried to protest through the heated haze enveloping her.

"Cutter, no!"

"No?" he murmured against the pulse pounding erratically in her throat. "Are you sure?"

Her head fell back as his mouth came down to press against her throat, and the flower fell from her ivory curls to lie between their bodies. Its heady fragrance scented her breasts, was inhaled with every breath they took. Bringing one hand up in a slow motion, as if it were an effort, Cutter gently pushed aside the gathered neck of her gown, freeing her breasts. She whimpered at the sudden attack of night air, and her hands clutched desperately at his shoulders.

"Cutter! Yes!"

"Yes?" His palm cupped the hardening peak of one breast in a soft caress, moving in slow circles that made her burn with multicolored flames.

"No! I mean—yes, I'm sure. . . ."

"Sure of what, tiger-eyes? If you mean do I want you, yes, I'm sure I do."

Faint racking shudders rippled through her body, and Whitney tried to drag her overheated senses back from the fire into which he'd plunged them. It was hard to concentrate when he was manipulating the rhythm of her breathing so expertly just with his touch, and for a moment she couldn't think how the flow of conversation had begun. Then she remembered.

"Yes, I'm sure I want you to stop," she said, but even to her own ears her voice sounded weak and unconvincing. It felt so good to be in his arms, to have him kissing her, but Whitney would rather have him sweep her off into the plains and lie under the stars with her than to take her like this.

A choking sob wove itself into her voice as she said without much hope that he'd listen, "Not like this, Cutter. Not like this!"

Hearing the desperate note in her tone, Cutter paused in his dedicated attention to the lush weight of her breast and looked up at her. Tumbling hair fell like silk around her face and shoulders, and her eyes were enormous in the shadowy light of the single lantern behind them. And in her urgent gaze, there was a silent appeal. It took a moment for it to sink through the heated fog of wine and desire, but he finally recognized the finality in her panicked voice.

Urgency galloped through his body with each beat of his heart, and Cutter struggled against the inclination to bend her back against the wall and toss her gown over her head. *Not like this*—like what, then?

Taking a step back, Cutter released her, watching as she rearranged the neck of her nightgown and worked the hem back down over her hips and thighs. The crushed flower still lay between her breasts, nestled in bruised fragrance on the soft skin, and he resisted the impulse to reach for it.

"You'd never make a gardener," he observed in a voice that was remarkably calm for a man who was fighting violent urges to toss her over his shoulder and take her to his bed.

Whitney looked up, her eyes wide. "What?"

"A gardener. None of your plants would reproduce, and what would you do then?"

She stared at him, unable to form a reply. How could she tell him that she wanted him, but not on his mother's patio? The words wouldn't come, and she had no experience with saying them, so she just sat and gazed up at him.

Reaching out, his hand cupped her chin in his palm, and if it weren't for the hostile tone, she might have thought he was trying to be kind. "It's all right, sweetheart. I'm beginnin' to grow used to your particular brand of teasing. At least you're not retreatin' into melodramatic vows about your damned virtue—or lack of it—again."

Flushing, she said, "It's not what you think!"

His hand fell away. "It never is."

The overindulgence in alcohol and drugging passion made Cutter's reflexes slower, so that when they both heard the noise behind them, it was Whitney who turned first. Her eyes grew larger, the dark pupils absorbing light from the lantern, and he turned in a smooth motion, taking a step in front of her as if to shield her. He needn't have bothered. It wasn't Whitney who was in danger.

"Should I have knocked?" came the coolly polite voice, and Cutter had the fleeting thought that he shouldn't have returned. It would have been much better if he'd kept on riding today, leaving Whitney with his mother.

But none of that showed on his face as he said in a light tone, "Daniel. You're back early."

"From the looks of things, I'm back a bit late."

A brief shrug lifted Cutter's shoulders, and he spared a moment's inclination to tell the truth before he decided to at least try to shield Whitney. "She had something in her . . ."

"Don't say it," Daniel Coleman stopped him, and took another step forward so that the light from the lantern illuminated him. His gaze took in Whitney's disheveled condition, flushed face, the hem of her gown up around her knees, and Cutter's slightly unsteady stance, and he added pleasantly, "I think we need to talk."

Oh, Lord, Cutter thought, *not now! Maybe when I'm sober, but not now!*

Aloud he said, "Tomorrow would be a better time for me, and besides, you must be tired from your trip."

"You mean the trip I took to try and save your neck?" Daniel took another step forward, and Whitney saw that he was as tall as Cutter, maybe a shade taller, and his light eyes were narrowed with anger. "After—Miss Bradford, isn't it?—goes to bed, I'd appreciate your lingering here so we can talk. Please oblige me."

The soft voice reminded her of Cutter's, the words sheathed in icy steel, and she shivered, sliding from the wall to stand on bare feet, her gown swaying against her legs. Looking from one determined face to the other, she murmured a good night and fled, not looking back.

Fifteen

Glancing from Cutter's rifle on the table to his face, Daniel saw the guarded expression in his eyes, and thought grimly that it was a trifle late to be cautious.

"You do recall, I hope, that there are certain things I expect of those in my home," he began, pleasantly polite. At Cutter's nod, he continued in the same voice. "Seducing young women on my patio is not one of them. Nor," he added when it seemed as if Cutter might speak, "do I condone abducting young women and forcibly dragging them around the territory, no matter what spurious reasons one might have."

Cutter's eyes glittered with angry lights, but he'd endured just this sort of unpleasant interview with his stepfather before, and he knew the futility of trying to do verbal battle with the eloquent lawyer. It was no small wonder Coleman was considered the finest—and most ruthless—attorney in the Arizona legislature. The respect he'd always felt for his stepfather had not lessened through the years, for in spite of Cutter's wild adolescent years and rebellious spirit, there was a genuine affection between them. If there hadn't been, Daniel's lashing contempt would not have mattered to him.

Raking Cutter with his cold light eyes, Daniel said smoothly, "I've spent a most interesting few days with Miss Bradford's father, and am now inclined to agree with him that you should be tarred, feathered, and hung from the nearest oak. I find it rather galling that I argued so persuasively for a deferment of justice until the girl could be found and delivered safely into her father's hands. Governor Fremont was most reluctant to sign a blank warrant giving permission to shoot you on sight, but Bradford is a very persuasive gentleman."

When Daniel paused and looked at him, Cutter said into the heavy silence, "So Fremont gave in, I presume? Damned inconvenient of him."

"It would be," Daniel said coolly, "if I hadn't managed to convince them both that to shoot on sight would endanger Miss Bradford's life too."

"Ah, so it's the tar and feathers now." Cutter's mood was not improving, and, he noticed, neither was Daniel's. This sort of confrontation always left them as wary as two strange dogs, circling each other and trying to sniff out any sign of weakness.

Taking a step forward, Daniel let his hand rest on the table beside Cutter's rifle, and from the pale glitter in his eyes, Cutter had the thought he was tempted to use it. But he merely lifted a brow and gazed contemptuously at his stepson.

"You know, of course, that her father expects her to be returned to him as soon as possible."

"That's why I brought her here," Cutter said, and wished he hadn't consumed quite so much wine. He should be able to think more clearly, to defuse a potentially explosive situation without alienating his stepfather.

In a pleasant voice that did not deceive Cutter for a moment, Daniel said, "Has it occurred to you that by taking her back, you are signing your own death warrant?"

"Are you suggesting I keep her as a hostage?"

"Not by any means." Daniel ran a hand over the smooth wooden stock of Cutter's Winchester, then to the bluish metal of the barrel, his fingers lingering for a moment. "There are not many options open to you. However," he added, "I believe that you and Miss Bradford have just provided both of you with a means to escape almost unscathed from the biggest scandal in years."

"Really?" Cutter's tone was lightly mocking. But his sense of honor demanded that he hear his stepfather out. "And what means is that?"

Daniel's smile did not lessen the shock of his words. "Marriage."

There was a long moment of silence. Cutter's iron-hard control slipped sharply, and he heard his voice, faintly disbelieving, repeat, "Marriage?"

"But of course. How else could you so neatly escape a rope?"

"Given the choice, I'd prefer to take my chances with the rope," Cutter said. "And besides, there's always the little matter of the army payroll. Marrying Whitney would hardly erase *that* offense."

"As you are surely well aware," came Daniel's cool voice, "I am capable of resolving the misunderstanding with the army. The thorn in this problem has been Bradford's obdurate refusal to back down a single inch. He's out for blood, Cutter, and he can get it."

"Let him try."

"Do you care so little for your mother, or for my reputation?" Daniel shot back, harshly now, his polite facade dropping away. "If Bradford so chooses, he can drag us all through the muck. When will you understand that your actions affect the others in this family? I expect," Daniel continued grimly, "for you to be honorable enough to do the right thing."

"What makes you think she'd marry me anyway?" Cutter asked, his voice cool but his temper showing hotly in his eyes. "She hates me."

"That didn't look like an exchange of hatred when I came in," Daniel said, "but if she does, I must say she shows remarkable good sense. And good sense will certainly dictate that she marry you in order to still some of the worst of the gossip that's spread from East Coast to West. A woman of her standing can hardly be abducted without comment, but a romantic elopement will only enhance her reputation in time."

Forcing a coolness into his voice that he didn't feel, Cutter said, "I've never entertained thoughts of marriage, and if I had, I would not choose a mate as arrogant and hardheaded as Whitney Bradford."

A tight smile played at the corners of Daniel's lips as he brought up Cutter's Winchester with a smooth motion, and slid back the bolt. "Your capitulation is preferable to an unfortunate *accident*. Although even *that* would be more desirable than a public hanging."

In spite of the bonds of affection between them, Cutter knew full well that Daniel Coleman did not make idle threats. Nor, in a way, did he blame him. There was a lot at stake, not the least of which was his mother's well-being. Coleman had worked hard to build up his reputation, and no politician was inviolate when it came to gossip.

In spite of his wine-drugged responses, Cutter had the thought that agreeing to marry Whitney would calm everyone down for the time being. *Doing* it could be delayed indefinitely—maybe forever.

So, in spite of the licking flames of fury searing through him, he said in a tight, mocking voice, "How can I resist when you put it so nicely?"

"I do have your sworn word on a quick wedding, I presume?" The muzzle of the rifle lifted when Cutter remained silent. "Your word, please."

For one unreasoning moment of blind fury, Cutter considered leaping for the rifle, and just as quickly knew he wouldn't. Where he didn't have much doubt that Daniel would not hesitate to shoot, he wasn't certain *he* could do so. Though his fists were clenched at his sides, his voice was light and pleasant.

"Shoot and be damned."

Coleman actually curled his finger around the trigger, then he said softly, "If you cared at all about that girl, you'd save her from some damned unpleasant gossip."

There was a short, tense silence, and Cutter struggled with himself. His first impulse was still to refuse, but the memory of Whitney in his arms, and her soft body curled trustingly against him while she slept, returned to haunt him. Worse was the memory of that night at Téjas's home, when he had behaved so badly. Christ! Was she the first woman who'd ever made such a confession? And he'd behaved like an ass, condemning her for not being more trusting. A self-mocking smile curled his lips. She'd been right not to trust him.

"Very well. You have my word. I'll marry her. But I would love to be there when you inform Whitney. That should make for a very interesting conversation indeed."

"I have no intentions of informing Miss Bradford. That is up to you. You are the one who abducted her. You will be the one to marry her, so you will inform her yourself." The rifle dropped back to the table as Daniel looked at Cutter. "And don't look so morose. Talk to her about gardening again."

After Daniel disappeared into the house, Cutter fought the inclination to laugh. What a ludicrous situation! Never in his entire life had he dreamed he would find himself caught so neatly in a trap of his own making. And never had he dreamed that he would submit to a forced marriage, almost literally a shotgun wedding. He supposed that when the effects of the wine he'd drunk earlier wore off, he would not feel so inclined to laugh, but now there certainly seemed to be a fair amount of ironic humor in the situation.

* * *

Whitney saw no humor in the situation, ironic or otherwise. Marriage to Cutter?

"I'd rather marry a fence post right now!" she'd stated calmly, but no one seemed to pay the least bit of attention.

After Cutter's polite, cool proposal of marriage—which she had refused with a favorite expletive of her father's—he had lost patience and told her that he didn't like it either, but unless she wanted to be the target of malicious gossip the rest of her life, she'd best agree and get it over with.

"Don't you understand anything?" he asked harshly. "You won't be allowed in any decent home after being abducted by Apaches and kept as a plaything! Do you really think you'd enjoy the lascivious sneers of 'polite' society? Think again, princess!"

"And you believe marrying you would save me from all that?" she'd shouted, not caring who heard her. Hot tears stung her eyes, and she faced him like a furious feline, her lips curled into a snarl. "I can see us now, living out our years with you running all over the country while I sit in an apartment over Central Park, watching out the window for you!"

"No need to worry about that, darlin'." One eyebrow quirked when she looked at him. "I have no intention of going to New York. As my lovely bride, you may either stay in Arizona, or go home with your father. Whichever, I don't intend to stick around to watch."

Whitney felt her heart plummet. *Oh, Cutter—couldn't you love me?* The silent plea made her backbone stiffen with self-loathing and anger. It was obvious how he felt, and just as obvious that he was proposing marriage only out of a sense of duty. She'd been in one loveless marriage, and had no intention of being in another. No, not even to the man who haunted her every waking moment. She didn't quite understand it, but somehow she'd fallen in love with him. It defied logic, defied credibility, defied everything she'd ever considered sane and reasonable in her entire life. But she'd know, after almost surrendering body and soul to him on his mother's patio, that Cutter was the man she wanted to be with the rest of her life. But not unless he wanted it too.

"Oh, do what you want to," she said, suddenly weary. "You will anyway."

"Is that an acceptance of my impassioned marriage proposal?"

"No. Just go away. I'm beginning to get a headache—and don't tell your mother. She's poured so much herbal tea in me, I slosh like a sponge every time I move."

"Poor little tiger-eyes. No one can please you, it seems."

Eyes flashing, Whitney rounded on him. "Look, you have done the honorable thing by proposing! I've refused—for which you should be grateful—so go away and leave me alone!"

"Gladly. Talking to you is like trying to carry on a conversation with a porcupine. I'm certain I can find less prickly company elsewhere."

"Going down to the river again, I take it?" she shot out in a scathing tone, taking him aback. Then he grinned. She must have heard about the clapboard houses and their female occupants by the river. The servants, of course. There was always gossip.

"I might." He stepped forward and lifted the strand of hair dangling over her shoulder, watching the play of light glimmer in the silky filaments. "But of course," he said softly, only half teasing, "with a lovely wife at home who fulfills my every desire, why would I need to go there?"

That had been too much. Whitney had screamed at him to get out of her bedroom before she began throwing things, and he'd left, saying cynically that she should be glad she was around people who understood the temperament of she-wolves. Not knowing what he was talking about, Whitney had thrown a silver-backed hairbrush at him, but it had bounced harmlessly off the swiftly shut door.

Deborah had come quickly and soothed her with soft words, none of them, unfortunately, permanent cures for the torment of her mind. The drapes had been drawn to shut out the bright sunlight, and she was supposed to be lying down, but she was too restless, too filled with nervous energy and a thousand questions.

Her mind was whirling too fast and her head was aching, and she'd hardly slept all night wondering what was being said out on the patio. Cutter's stepfather had looked so forbiddingly angry, and she'd feared that Cutter would provoke an argument that would end up causing a rift in the household. Whatever else might happen, she didn't want Deborah to be caused any pain. And oddly, in some way, she felt as if she might be to blame. Perhaps if she hadn't allowed him to kiss her hotly on the patio, if she'd refused to be drawn into his seductive game, Daniel would not have seen them. It was galling to think that just when she realized that she was beginning to love Cutter, she was being given her freedom. Marriage, of course, was out of the question. Not when Cutter didn't love her. And really, she could depend on herself to get by now—hadn't that month in Red Shirt's camp taught her self-reliance? Before, even though she knew her father would always take care of her, it had been *his* money, *his* name; the reputation she'd built as a novelist had been like a thin cloak hiding the real Whitney beneath. Now, she didn't need the critics' approval to make her feel as if she belonged. She didn't need to belong to any special group or place. Now all she needed was to find herself somewhere in the midst of this tangle of mixed emotions and half-formed ideals.

Cutter remained gone for the day, and Whitney stayed in her room with the drapes drawn over the windows. The house was quiet, too quiet; even Davy seemed subdued. And Deborah seemed especially considerate, as if Whitney had a violent disease. And then she learned from Deborah that Daniel had actually wired her father in Prescott, and Morgan Bradford had agreed with him! That had been the crowning blow for Whitney, and not even the news that her father was on his way to the ranch for the wedding could cheer her.

For the three days it took Morgan to reach the ranch, Whitney spoke hardly one word.

Her unexpected silence was as puzzling to her father as it was to Cutter. Whitney silent? The ranch was thrown into a frenzy of hasty preparations for the upcoming wedding of Daniel and Deborah Coleman's eldest son, yet the ashen-faced bride had very little to comment about the dress or flowers or hundred of other little details.

It wasn't until Morgan and Whitney were left alone on the patio that she switched from the pale, lifeless doll she'd resembled to an angry tigress. Wide-eyed, Morgan had the helpless thought that his daughter had changed a great deal. This was no tantrum or obstinate debate. Whitney quite coldly and somehow more ominously stated her objections to the marriage without mincing words or masking her feelings.

"You had no right to release the news of my wedding to the papers," she said, standing by a low stone wall and facing him. The cane chair creaked as he shifted uncomfortably and opened his mouth to explain. "Don't bother giving me your reasons," Whitney forestalled him. "They don't matter. And I believe I understand some of them, though you still should have talked with me first." After a short, tense silence, she said, "If I remember correctly, this is not the first wedding you've forced me into. I forgave you Nathan. I'm not certain I can forgive you Cutter."

Rising abruptly, Morgan said, "Whitney, you must understand that—though I deplore it myself—Coleman is right. If you were to go back to New York, or even stay here, you'd be a curiosity, like a two-headed dog." His voice became soft and pleading. "I've been almost frantic with worry about you, and when Coleman told me that you were well and safe, and that he believed you and his son had formed an attachment for each other, I—"

"Attachment!" Whitney's voice was cutting. "The man has dragged me from one end of this territory to another, abused me at every turn, and even abandoned me for a time in an Apache village, and you think he's formed an *attachment* for me? Next thing you know, he'll *attach* me to a stake with dry wood at my feet!" Cupping her forehead in her palm, she drew in a shaky breath before saying, "Marriage is not the answer."

"Perhaps not, but I don't see that either of you has much choice." When Whitney's head snapped up, Bradford continued. "He can marry you or hang, and you can marry him or spend the rest of your days locked away like a nun in some convent. There won't be many doors open to a woman who is widely known to have spent a great deal of time as an Apache prisoner, not the kind of doors you're used to."

"I don't think I care about those doors anymore!"

"And you don't care if Cutter hangs either?"

Morgan's abrupt question stopped her cold. She did care if he was hanged, and even her father could see that. What did it matter if he was more concerned with his daughter than with Cutter? The results would be the same. Cutter would hang, and then she might as well die too.

Shocked by the force of her feelings for Cutter, Whitney could not reply for a moment. This was still so new, still so fragile—how could she explain it even to herself? What was that saying—"Better to marry than burn?" Yet marrying Cutter would hardly put an end to the burning sensations he'd ignited in her. . . .

Whitney had only vague recollections of the marriage ceremony, the heavy scent of flowers and burning candles, her satin gown with heavy scallops of lace at throat and cuffs and hem, the good wishes of those attending—even David, who gazed at her with wide, perplexed eyes. Cutter, standing straight and tall in a white shirt, dark pants, and red vest, his black hair reflecting candlelight and his eyes filled with a glittering mockery that made her shiver with apprehension, was a stark, searing memory. That, and the brief interchange between them when a guest—she would never recall who—suggested that the new groom feed his lovely bride the first bite of wedding cake.

Whitney could not help the sudden intake of breath at the suggestion, or the quick glance toward Cutter, who seemed only indolently amused.

"How romantic you are," he said to the guest, and turned slowly, one eyebrow lifted. "Dare I, my love?" he murmured with a wicked slice of his eyes toward the cake Maria had painstakingly baked and decorated. "Or will it be like feeding raw meat to a tiger?"

Cutter was already lifting a slice of the richly spiced cake in his hand, grasping her chin with the other, his fingers digging into her soft flesh with a grip that would have held back six wild horses.

Reaction to his harsh grip was instinctive. Her lips opened to take in cake spiced with nutmeg, cinnamon, and cloves, and her small white teeth closed down on his finger as well, holding it firmly, but not biting. Her eyes met his with a fire she'd not felt since reluctantly agreeing to the marriage. Startled, Cutter met her angry gaze with a quick, wary, upward flick of his ridiculously long lashes, and saw in her tawny eyes his own reflection.

To her faint surprise, he smiled, a rather sardonic smile, but completely free of malice. "Truce, tiger-eyes," he said softly, relaxing his hurting grip on her jaw. The long-boned fingers of his hand became caressing instead of painful, and she quickly released his finger, much too aware of the sudden lurch of her heart at his gentle touch.

It was all too much for her, the frenzy of preparation, the ceremony beneath a flower-entwined trellis on the front veranda, and now the pretense while guests drank to their health and happiness.

She stood with cold hands and a fixed smile, Cutter at her side, wedding guests crowding around to bestow compliments on the bride and congratulations to the groom.

Why is that? she wondered idly, smiling at a dowdy matron who wished her, with rather malicious glee, a happy and contented life with her new husband. *Why does the bride receive compliments and the groom congratulations? Shouldn't it be mutual congratulations for having found happiness?*

Of course, that would not apply in this case. And one glance at Cutter's impassive face should tell anyone with a grain of sense that the groom was less than thrilled.

Lanterns that were strung in loops over the patio flickered like fairy lights in the night, and musicians played ceaselessly as the guests laughed and talked and danced. Whitney sat quietly beside Cutter at a linen-draped table, and waited for the inevitable.

Finally Cutter stood, and with mocking eyes proposed a toast to his new bride while everyone applauded. "And now," he added, his words falling like stones on her ears, "it's time we left. I understand there's a cozy cottage awaiting us in the mountains."

This last comment was greeted with laughter by some, cheers by others, but Whitney felt as if she had turned to salt. She looked up blindly, and saw her father staring at her with a frown. Did she look that terrified? She must have, because Deborah was coming to her, taking her by one arm and smiling. Then Morgan was there, too, taking Whitney by her cold hand, his mouth set in a taut line.

"There's no need for the newlyweds to rush off so soon, is there?" he said. "I've got a few words of advice for my daughter."

"Save them until later," Cutter said pleasantly, but there was no mistaking the finality in his tone. He and Morgan locked gazes, and the air bristled with tension.

Whitney couldn't speak. She was agonizingly aware of the avid stares in their direction, the curious looks they were receiving. Every person there knew that this was a rushed marriage, and some of them even understood why. It was not as if it were a well-kept secret that the Cutter who was the half-breed gunman was the same Cutter who was Daniel Coleman's stepson, but the politic opinion was that it should not be mentioned in most circles. The public had heard of the "romantic elopement" of the pair; it was a polite fiction that would be continued for mutual benefit. After all, there weren't many outside of Arizona Territory who'd ever heard of Cutter until he'd abducted Whitney—wasn't that why she had gone there in the first place?

And now Cutter was her husband, and he was giving her father a cold, dangerous stare that dared him to interfere.

"Don't worry, Bradford," he said blandly. "I promise to bring back her scalp"—he paused maliciously—"still on her head."

"If you harm one hair on her head, Cutter, so help me God, I'll . . ."

"I've heard it all before, and unless you want to further entertain these guests you and my parents were so kind to invite, I'd suggest we postpone our discussion. Whitney love, go and get ready," he turned to say, and she swallowed the sudden protest that rose.

With a hard look at her son, Deborah Coleman drew Whitney with her, taking her to the bedchamber she'd occupied since Cutter had first brought her there.

"Are you all right, dear?" Deborah asked with a worried frown. "Don't mind Cutter. He's always nasty when he feels he's been pushed into something—I beg your pardon?"

Pressing cold hands to cheeks that were white as ash except for two crimson streaks, Whitney replied, "I said—oh, God!"

Deborah looked at her closely. "I do believe he *has* hurt you! Hasn't he?"

"Not—" She gulped. "Not like you may think."

"Well, I know Cutter may seem a bit harsh at times, but he's not one to let his feelings show easily. Are you all right, Whitney?"

She'd begun to shake, and Deborah gripped her by the arms as she stammered out, "It's just that . . . that I don't know how I'm supposed to act now."

Searching delicately for the right words, not wanting to frighten this obviously skittish young woman with the pale face and glittering gold eyes, Deborah asked her quietly, "During all the time you spent with Cutter, dear, did he . . . did he . . . ?"

"Seduce me?" Whitney finished for her, and shook her head. "No."

Deborah's taut features relaxed with relief. "I'm glad. It shows that he still retains some sense of decency, at least." There was a stinging pause, then Deborah asked in the same delicate tone, "Are you afraid of what comes after the wedding, dear? The intimacy of a relationship with a man? The first time is the most difficult, but . . ."

Wrenching away from her, Whitney put her palms over her face and shook her head. "It's not that at all! Oh, you don't understand!"

"No, I'm afraid I don't. If you're not afraid of the first time, then what is it?"

Whitney whirled around to face her, and her eyes were like huge gold coins in a pale face. "It's the *next* time I'm afraid of! It's the pain and the degrading things that come along with it! And even though . . . even though Cutter has made me ache to be with him at times, I know that it will be no different than it was with my husband!"

"Your husband?" Deborah repeated in surprise. "I had no idea you'd been married."

Bitterly, Whitney replied, "Well, I have! And I can assure you that I know what intimacy with a man is like! I was glad when Nathan died, glad I would never have to endure that again!"

A heavy silence fell, and the noise from the patio drifted into the room, seeming to grow louder and louder. Finally, Deborah said, "Did you love your husband?" When Whitney gave a violent shake of her head, Deborah said more softly, "It will be different if you care about a man, child. Trust me. Do you care about my son?"

Whitney's eyes were pained. "I think so." How could she admit that she loved him so strongly it was like a constant ache in her heart? Especially when she knew how he hated being forced to marry her? It was too late for that now, too late for anything but more endurance.

"Then tonight will be different. Cutter cares for you, too, even if he's too proud to show it right now." Deborah touched her cheek lightly. "Be patient, Whitney. The love will grow."

Whitney didn't have the heart to tell her that love could not grow where it hadn't been planted. She allowed Deborah to help her change into a simple blue cotton blouse and skirt, then brush her hair. She stood listlessly while Deborah chattered about the little house in the mountains where she and Daniel had spent their wedding night. It would do no good to explain to Deborah that her son had no intention of remaining with his new bride, or that Whitney had decided to return to New York with her father. The proprieties had to be observed now, even if that meant riding off alone with Cutter.

Sixteen

Refusing the horse and buggy Daniel offered, Cutter had pulled Whitney up in front of him on his horse, saying that they were accustomed to riding that way. As the wedding guests stared uncertainly, he wheeled his mount around and rode into the night with her.

For a while neither of them said anything. There was only the pounding rhythm of the horse beneath them and the drifting shadows over the land. He rode up into the hills, keeping a steady pace, and Whitney wondered miserably what he was thinking. He was angry; she knew from the tense muscles of his arm around her waist, the clenched jaw and cold eyes, that he'd tolerate no lingering pleas for delay tonight.

This time there would be no timely interruption; there would be no persuasion she could think of to stop him. She was his wife, and he would be completely justified in being more than a little angry if she denied him. *But,* she told herself, *my being married to him doesn't give him the right to mistreat me!*

With that determined thought in mind, Whitney prepared herself for her first night as Cutter's wife.

Though he still wasn't very talkative, and still had that cold look in his eyes that used to mean trouble for her, he was pleasant enough when they arrived at the tiny cabin high in the mountains. Tall pines surrounded the log structure, swaying in the wind, making a ceaseless whispering rustle that sounded like singing to Whitney. It was dark, with only a sketchy moon glittering palely over the harsh ridges gnawing at the horizon.

As it was late, Whitney was almost numb from the steady jolt of the horse, so that when he swung her down to the ground, he had to keep one arm around her waist to steady her.

"I'll put the horse out back," he said in that hard, impatient tone that she'd once been so accustomed to hearing. "You can go into the cabin." His voice subtly altered to a mocking bite. "Don't change clothes yet—I may want to watch my wife undress."

For the first time, it occurred to her that she had not thought to bring any other clothes with her, and that she did not know how long they would be there. One night? she hoped. Surely, no more than two. She wasn't certain that prolonged proximity to Cutter would be good for either of them. And since they were only observing the proprieties anyway, one or two nights should be enough.

"Don't worry," she said more calmly than she'd thought possible, "I didn't bring any other clothes."

He laughed. "If you thought that would save you, tiger-eyes, you're wrong. I don't care if you wear anything or not. In fact, I think I prefer *not*."

Swallowing the hasty retort that clung to the tip of her tongue, Whitney whirled and pushed open the door to the cabin. After finding and lighting a small lamp and placing it on a table, she was pleasantly surprised. The light shed a warm, welcoming glow throughout the cabin. Though small and rather crude from the outside, the interior was furnished with highly polished furniture and gay rag rugs scattered across the floor. A massive stone fireplace dominated one wall, and pewter and brass dishes lined a wooden cupboard. Several chairs and a table stood in the center, and beneath a small alcove squatted a wide feather bed. She looked away from it, but then her gaze was drawn irresistibly back. It looked comfortable. A patchwork quilt was spread over the bed's foot, and fresh linens smoothed over the ticking of the mattress as if someone had just placed them there, and perhaps they had.

Yes, she supposed Deborah had seen to it. This was supposed to be a joyous occasion, wasn't it? Whitney gave a soft, bitter laugh. Two people forced into a marriage neither of them wanted!

Shivering, Whitney knelt before the fireplace and began to lay a fire with the tinder and wood from a small pine box. She had a nice blaze going by the time the cabin door opened and Cutter came in, and she stood slowly, turning to watch him.

Her mouth was dry, and her legs were shaking so badly she was certain he could tell by the violent quivering of her skirts how nervous she was. That thought alone gave her the courage to still her trembling muscles and lift her eyes to his. She saw by the sudden tautness in his face that she had somehow irritated him, and when he crossed the room to her, Whitney could not fight a sharp intake of breath.

"Dammit, Whitney! You look like a terrified rabbit in a trap!"

"Aren't I?" she countered shakily.

"You might recall that we're in the same trap," he shot back. He was more than irritated; he was furious that she obviously thought he would hurt her.

Cutter stared at her for another moment, not realizing how fierce and cold he looked, his eyes glittering with icy anger beneath the thick lashes. When he reached out to touch her, Whitney recoiled, and he felt a pang of guilt that he had caused such a reaction.

Dropping his arms to his sides, Cutter said quietly, "I think there's some food in the cupboard. Are you hungry?"

She shook her head, her eyes still on him, her lips quivering. Was this a new game he was playing with her? Why didn't he do what she expected? She prayed for strength to endure the hours ahead, to escape with her soul intact, to avoid the pain of humiliation.

She had the distracted thought that he hadn't changed clothes, and that he looked very handsome in the dark pants and starched white shirt, the red quilted waistcoat a vivid splash of color that made him look faintly reckless instead of more civilized. But he wasn't civilized, was he? She ought to know that by now. She recalled very well how he had ridden as carelessly as the other Apaches, looking as savage as they did with his face painted and body almost bare to the wind. It was remembering that well-muscled body that left her speechless now.

Cutter walked to a large chair near the fireplace and sat down, his intent gaze fixed steadily on her. Stretching his long legs out in front of him, he said in the same quiet voice, "Come here, Whitney."

Her gaze darted to the door, but she knew how quickly he could move, and wondered if she'd make it.

As if reading her thoughts, Cutter asked pleasantly, "Do you think you could outrun me?"

Whitney knew better. She'd seen how swiftly he reacted, his lithe, lean body as fluid and dangerously graceful as the uncoiling of a rattlesnake. And if she made him angry, she would be the one to suffer for it. Silently, like a sleepwalker, she crossed the room to stand in front of him.

Almost gently, he took her wrists in his and turned her around so that her back was to him, then exerted soft pressure until she sat on the rug between his outstretched legs. Whitney could hear the pounding of her heart in her ears, and the light pressure of his thighs on each side of her body made her quiver violently.

Yet Cutter did nothing. He sat without speaking until some of her trembling eased, then began to massage the back of her neck with his long fingers, gently easing with circular strokes the tension that corded her muscles. His hand worked up beneath her hair, loosing the coils and scattering lacquered pins on the floor as he freed the ivory mass. It spilled down over her shoulders in a fragrant flow of silky tendrils, crackling and seeming to have a life of its own.

"I've always loved your hair," he murmured, and she shuddered at the exquisite touch of his hands. The fire leapt on the hearth with a cheery crackle, and there was no sound in the room other than the stilted labor of her breathing.

She was beginning to relax when he asked softly, "Tell me about him, Whitney."

"Him?" she echoed faintly.

"The man you told me about." His touch was still soft in her hair, his fingers caressing, but she could hear the deliberate carelessness in his voice, and knew that her answer was important. "Your first lover," he added, and beneath the silky words lurked a layer of menace that made her stiffen. "I want to hear about him."

"He wasn't my lover!" she said more sharply than she intended. "He was my husband."

His hands stilled in her hair, and she could feel his quick recoil. Should she have said something else? The muscles in his thighs tightened as if he were about to get up, and she tensed. After another moment he said softly, "Tell me."

Then, while she sat stiff and still, the words poured out, her years of pain and fear, the feeling that there was something the matter with her, and Nathan's cruel taunts. When she'd finished, it was very quiet, and Cutter had not said anything else. She could hear him take a deep breath, but could not turn to look at him. Now he knew the reason behind her reluctance, knew that his wife was . . . defective.

Finally, he spoke. "Whitney, I assure you that there's nothing the matter with you." His voice was like a caress, his tone tender and protective. "You are a warm, loving woman, no matter what he may have said. All you need is a little time to . . . adjust." He drew in another deep breath. "I want to prove it to you, but if you think I'm going too fast, tell me. I don't want to frighten you or hurt you. Will you tell me?"

She trembled beneath the light touch of his fingers and murmured, "Yes."

Closing her eyes as he softly tilted her head back, Whitney felt his hand shift to the curving whorls of one ear, linger to explore the pink surface, then slide easily down to her shoulder. How could he make her react to his touch like this? she wondered hazily. It was so simple for him—all he had to do was caress her, and she melted. And, oh, God, what was he doing now? His hand had slipped inside the loose neck of her blouse and was caressing her collarbone in slow, smooth motions.

"Cutter, I—"

"Hush. I won't do anything you don't want me to do. Just feel."

Just feel? Dear God, what did he think she was doing? Everything below her eyebrows was aflame with feeling, and her heart was pumping so fast, she was certain it would stop from overexertion. She felt everything, the cadence of his breathing, the hard pressure of his thighs against her arms, and the caressing sweep of his hand. She even felt his heart beating, though she knew that had to be her imagination. Maybe it was her own pulses, pumping blood so fast through her labored veins that she could hear it.

Whatever she had expected, this patient side of Cutter was not it. He caressed her with smooth, soft motions, his hands warm on her, easing the worst of her fears that he would be harsh.

She was hot and cold at the same time, the heat from the fire staining one side of her body, but the chills of reaction making her shiver. What was it he had said one time about being hot and . . . *hot?* She couldn't remember now. It was hard to think of anything but his hands, the long fingers sliding beneath her blouse, toying with the lacy edge of her chemise, smoothing inside to gently stroke the curve of her breast. Her entire body tingled from his touch, and she wondered how reaction could travel so fast from her breast to her toes, lingering in the pit of her stomach and forming a tight knot that writhed and spread heated fluids like melting honey through her limbs.

"It's warm enough, isn't it?" he was murmuring. "Let's get rid of this blouse, shall we? That's right . . . you've still got your undergarments, and I won't do anything until you're ready. . . ."

His whisper was silky and seductive against her ear, his breath stirring wisps of hair and making her shiver again. It was hard to reconcile this Cutter with the Cutter who'd forced her down on the ground, his hard body slanting across hers as he'd taken insulting liberties. *But now,* her treacherous mind whispered, *now you want him to hold you like this, to caress you like this. . . .*

Cutter rose from the chair, slowly dragging Whitney up with him, his hands light and familiar on her, tucking her hips into the thrust of his, holding her close. Spreading his fingers, he cupped her buttocks in his palms, lowering his head to brush her half-parted, trembling lips with his. He kissed her lightly at first, as if it were her very first kiss, then slowly, subtly, increased the pressure, holding her all the while, his mouth teasing a response from her.

With her blouse gone and her bare arms lying atop the curve of his shoulders, Whitney began to kiss him back, almost shyly. She kept her eyes closed, half embarrassed at her surrender. It was inevitable, this slow yielding, yet somehow she felt as if she should be holding back, not giving all. Now he was her husband, and he had a right to be holding her like this, his hard body against her so intimately, but she was still apprehensive, even with the ache spreading through her.

Cutter's hips embraced hers with a hardness of detail that was paralyzing, and Whitney felt the breath pause in her lungs until she became light-headed with the need for oxygen. Pressing against the small round of her stomach, he let his hands burn across her bare back, fingers sliding beneath the pitifully small lace straps of her chemise to let them fall aside, dangling over her arms, freeing the curve of her breasts. Instead of moving to cup them in his hands, he let his palms rotate across her narrow shoulders, then stole up into the loose weight of her hair, fingers tangling in waves made curly by the bend of her braid. The silken fibers clung to his hands as he compressed them, slowly pulling her head back, his mouth moving from the honeyed warmth of her lips to the arch of her throat.

"Cutter," she moaned, the heels of her hands pressing against his shoulders, writhing toward him, yet straining away. There was still a small part of her that wanted to resist, but it was being rapidly smothered by the heated knot coiling up and outward from the center of her.

"Yes, love?" he murmured against the sweet scent of satin flesh beneath his seeking lips. "Are you ready for me? God, I'm ready for you . . . I've been ready since that first time. . . ."

His words were lost in the ivory tangles of her hair as he brushed his lips over her temple, then lower to capture her mouth again. He kissed her deeply, his tongue probing, flicking hot flames through her, and Whitney wondered how she could stand much more. She could sense that he was holding back in the taut quiver of his body vibrating against her.

Slowly, his finger pads moving like silken fire, he let his hands move up the curve of her ribs, curling into the lacy material of her chemise, drawing it slowly over her head and tossing it to the floor. Whitney shivered. The air across her bare breasts was cool, yet heated by contact with her skin. Oh, God, how could she stand the sensitive trailing of his hands over her breasts, his fingers pausing to coax the peaks to rigid buttons?

The motion ignited a curling fire inside her, a fire that seared through her belly and down into her toes, leaving her almost too weak to stand. If Cutter hadn't been quick to catch her, she might have fallen, but his arm went behind her back and bent her over to allow his mouth to follow the burning path of his hands.

"Cutter! Cutter, I can't . . . it just . . . please," she ended on a faint whimper, not knowing what she was asking, just knowing that somehow he could answer.

"I know, love, I know," he muttered huskily, his voice thick, seeming to drift to her ears through layers of heated gauze. "Here, let me hold you . . . where is the button on your skirt? Ah, I found it . . . no, love . . . I've got it. . . ."

It wasn't the first time he'd seen her naked, but Whitney could not help the slow flush of embarrassment that spread over her in a rush when the last of her undergarments slid down over her legs to a silken puddle on the floor. Instinctively, she tried to cover herself with her slender arms crossed in front of her body, and Cutter gently drew them away.

"No, don't cover yourself against me, tiger-eyes," he said in a thickly erotic voice, his words like a caress against her heated cheeks. "Don't pull away. I'm going to kiss you again, that's all. Tilt your head back, Whitney. That's right. Open your lips for me . . . let me taste you. You are all honey, sweet and soft and . . . it's all right. It's just my hand on you . . . touching you there, it's like satin and silk . . . don't you like it?"

Her head was spinning, and her senses were rioting at the touch of his hand on her, his palm between her thighs, the heel of his hand rotating slowly against her, making shudders race through her entire body. She was clinging to him shamelessly now, her fingers digging into his shirt, and she was vaguely aware that he was still fully dressed while she was not, but somehow it didn't matter. All that mattered was the hot urgency spreading through her, vibrating up through her body from his hand, making her cry out.

Panting, confused, not knowing why she felt this overpowering need to be even closer to him, Whitney felt him lift her in his arms, felt his long strides across the room, then felt the welcoming cushion of the feather bed beneath her shoulders and hips. Cutter's mouth fastened to hers when she might have protested, and his hand found her again, stroking her, making her writhe like a leaf in a wind eddy.

Then his hand was gone, and when she opened her eyes to look up at him, she saw that he was shrugging out of his clothes impatiently, ripping the buttons of his shirt and vest, stepping out of his pants. She quickly shut her eyes against the hard urgency of him, her throat tight. The mattress dipped with his weight, and he pulled her into his arms, his body lying next to her instead of atop her, one long lean leg thrown over her thighs.

"Cutter . . ."

Her voice was more like a sob, and he pulled her into the angle of his hip and flat stomach so that she could feel his heat. His breathing was uneven, his voice ragged.

"Look at me, Whitney," he said softly, but she averted her gaze, unwilling to stare at the lean, spare lines of his body. "Tiger-eyes— are you afraid to look at me?"

"Yes."

The blunt word, spoken so forcefully in the heated space between their bodies, amused him, and Cutter laughed.

"I didn't think you were afraid of anything," he teased gently, levering his body slightly away from her so that currents of air whispered between them. His fingers grasped her chin and tilted her head up so that she was forced to meet his eyes, hot green and liquid with desire. "There's nothing to be afraid of. I've never hurt you yet—not like I could have—" he answered the quick protest in her eyes, "and I'm not likely to hurt you now."

Taking her hand in one of his, he drew it slowly down the length of him, over the flowing muscles of his chest to the ridged band on his belly, then lower. Whitney heard the sharp intake of his breath when she brushed against him, felt the quick leap of response to her touch.

"There," he said tightly when a moment passed and he could speak again, "that's not so bad, is it?"

Her errant hair tickled his jaw when she shook her head, and he uncurled his fingers from around her hand and shifted slightly. Poor tiger-eyes, he mused in barely coherent thought, she was still frightened, and he felt suddenly as if it were his first time to experience passion too. It was a surprising feeling for him, this heated rush that left him shaking, left him wanting to please her. He hoped that somehow she could find it within herself to forgive him for his reaction that night she'd first tried to tell him of her fears. He hadn't listened then, but he was certainly listening now. . . .

Whitney's golden eyes were heavy-lidded with a sensuality that glimmered just beneath the surface, and her satiny lips were slightly parted and moist, swollen from his kisses, her delicate brows knit into a faint frown.

As she held him tentatively, not knowing quite what to do with him, Cutter let his hands slide back up her body in slow, erotic rhythms, massaging gently, gathering response from her body with his movements. When he heard the quickening of her breathing, felt her fingers tighten involuntarily around him, he eased his body between her thighs, nudging them apart, his mouth moving to capture her protesting lips with his.

Whitney twisted beneath him, wanting him, yet not quite sure how he wanted her. Oh, she knew he *wanted* her, as a man wants a woman, but did he really want her? Soul and all? And why did the doubt not lessen her desire for him, for the release he could give her? Her fears faded away in the face of this burning torment inside, so that all she could think of was Cutter . . . Cutter holding her . . . Cutter's hands, touching her, caressing her . . . his body easing the throbbing ache. . . .

Slowly, lacing his long fingers through hers, Cutter drew her arms up and over her head, easing his body forward. As he struggled against the raging urgency that had been pounding through his body for the past two months he had the brief, biting worry that he would rush her. What was it about this one stubborn woman that so possessed him? He could have taken ten—no, a hundred—other women, and yet not felt the same surge of desire and fever he felt now.

Whitney's warm body beneath his was a torment, and as he slid into her steaming velvet folds, he felt a heady rush that he'd never before felt. He remained still for a moment, half afraid to move, then began to rock slowly against her, her hips rising to meet him as he moved faster. He tried to stay the gathering tension until he heard her cry out, felt her warm breath brush over his cheek, her arms clasp convulsively around him. An instant later he joined her, his own arms tightening, his breath just as harsh and ragged as hers.

Still imbedded inside her, Cutter half rolled to one side, taking her damp body with him, his arms coiled around her slender, shaking curves.

"What's the matter, tiger-eyes?" he muttered against her ear.

"Cutter . . . I never knew . . . no one ever told me . . ."

Patiently, still trying to regulate the strangled gasps of his breath, he asked, "Told you what?"

"That it could be like this!"

Faintly disgruntled, his voice filtered through curls of her hair. "I tried to tell you."

There was a slight pause, then she murmured, "Yes, I think you did." Another pause drifted past before she moved, tilting back her head to look into his sleepy, passion-dazed eyes. "Too bad I didn't listen. Look at all the time we wasted." A laugh underlined the trembling words, and Cutter smiled.

It was a moment before he spoke, and then he said in between the surging movements of his body, "Let's see if we can make it up now. . . ."

Inside the small cabin the fire on the hearth flickered and died, yet the fires in the feather bed were leaping out of control. The room grew dark, shadows grew long as the sun pinkened the sky, and the lovers slept at last, weary and exhausted.

Seventeen

"Tell me again about the flowers, Cutter."

Lying with her head nestled into the curve of his chest and shoulder, Whitney let her fingers dance over the smooth skin of his flat belly in a light tickle, smiling when he drew in a quick breath.

His voice, drugged and lazy, drifted to her. "What flowers?"

"The *sensual* flowers on your mother's patio." She felt his chest rumble with laughter.

"Oh. Those flowers. What do you want to know?"

"I believe you were telling me about . . . reproduction. You remember—stamens, and pistils, and petals and such."

"Ah, yes, now I recall. I was rather inspired that night by the sight of you with that huge white blossom held up to your face, the kind of dreamy look in your eyes." He paused for a moment, then said in the voice of one reciting a school lesson, "The petals of the flower"— he drew a finger from Whitney's stomach down to the gossamer wisps at the juncture of her thighs—"hide the vulnerable stamens and pistils, without which fertilization could not take place." His fingers traced the delicate velvet folds with infinite care and felt her quiver. "While the fertilization process is not that complicated—it requires only that the seed be pollinated—it often requires assistance." His long body shifted to lie atop hers, while his hands remained softly stroking, sending shuddering vibrations through her body. "Sometimes," he said raggedly, his breath coming faster and his words spacing out, "this can be accomplished by insects or birds carrying pollen grains to another flower . . . *Lord!* Do you have to do that? I thought you wanted a botany lesson."

"I think," she said slowly, her tone languorous, "that I prefer biology, after all." Her clever hands held him in a firm grasp, listening with some satisfaction to the increase in the tempo of his breathing. "You're so easy, Cutter, " she murmured against his ear when he bent to place hot kisses on the arch of her throat, then sucked in a deep breath when his body surged forward. Her arms moved to wind around his neck, and her legs clasped him firmly as he buried himself inside her.

The patchwork quilt had been worked from the bed to the floor, and the clean linen sheets that smelled faintly of wind and sun remained only half on the feather mattress. In the urgent heat of the moment, only the fabric of skin over bone and muscle mattered, the acute mating of highly sensitive tactile senses until time and place spiraled into blind sensation.

To Whitney, still dazed from the discovery that the culmination could be exquisitely delicious instead of painful, this meeting of bodies was the most wondrous event in her experience. She could not get close enough to Cutter, could not draw him deep enough inside her, as if to allow him to remain too far away were to lose him entirely. Mind images that had once haunted her were banished now, removed to the nether regions of all bad dreams, and replaced with the sweet passion of Cutter's mouth and hands and body.

There had been no words of love, but somehow they would sound inadequate for the surge of emotion she felt. It wasn't as easy for Cutter to express himself, she knew, and in a way she was afraid. He'd been patient with her, and had not mentioned the past, but she wondered if he still thought about it.

Lying beside him with his taut frame stretched out like a great, lazy cat, Whitney thought that few moments could compare to the dulcet sweetness of this one. The nagging doubts faded away, and the sighing of the pines outside the cabin was a drugging serenade as she lay in the safe circle of his arms.

Shadows flickered in the cabin, and a breeze filtered in through the open window over the bed, carrying the scent of pine needles and summer flowers.

"Hungry?" Cutter asked in a soft murmur, and Whitney shook her head.

"No. Just . . . contented."

He grinned and rolled to his stomach, propping his head in the cup of his palm to gaze at her through half-closed eyes. Sable strands of hair fell across his forehead and veiled the green eyes, and his mobile lips twitched with amusement.

"You're greedy. I'm too exhausted to get up. Why didn't you tell me you were such an insatiable wench? I would have built up my strength for the past few days."

She drew his head down to her and lightly grazed his lips with hers. "Then you wouldn't have been surprised."

"True." His hand moved to stroke her skin, still flushed from passion, and his lazy eyes followed the path of his hand, skimming her face as his finger grazed her lip in a sweet caress. "Whitney—a while back, at Téjas's—I didn't really listen to you. I should have."

She caught her breath and her eyes grew wide. "Are you still angry?"

Shaking his head, his voice was rueful. "Only at myself for being so obdurate." There was a pause, then he added, "I'm afraid that's as close as I can get to an apology. Were you listening?"

Laughing softly, she pressed her face to his, brow to brow, nose to nose, and whispered, "Every wonderful word."

He kissed her, not with passion but with an aching sweetness that made her heart soar, and Whitney thought that she had never been so happy as at that very moment.

When Cutter finally rolled from the bed and began to pull on his pants, Whitney watched him with admiring appreciation. Why had she never before truly noticed how well made he was, with the smooth flex of muscles, slim hips, and long, lean legs? Perhaps, she answered herself, because it was too dangerous to think of him that way before. She supposed that she'd been intrigued and fascinated and drawn to him ever since that first day in Tombstone.

And then, later, when he had been so arrogant and objectionable, it would have been sheer folly to have recognized her true feelings. Odd, how matters had worked out. She'd never thought she would be married to the outlaw she'd come to Arizona to interview. And even two weeks earlier she would not have dreamed she would actually enjoy—invite!—his touch.

"I'm going to see to the horse, love," he told her, and smiled when she lifted her face for his kiss. He bent and briefly brushed her lips with his, then went outside. She lay back on the bed, staring up at the rough beams of the ceiling for a moment, stretching luxuriously.

Realizing that she was, in fact, hungry, Whitney rose and stepped into her chemise, lifting it from the floor. When Cutter returned, it was to find her smiling shyly as she set the table with the pewter dishes, garbed in the short chemise that reached only halfway down her thighs. His immediate response was not to the food he could smell cooking.

"Don't bother," he said when she turned toward the pot over the fire. "That's not what I'm hungry for."

Crossing the room in a fluid stride, his bare chest gleaming in the light from the fire, Cutter pulled Whitney into his arms in spite of her half-formed protests.

"Oh, but the food . . . here, Cutter?" A gasp, then, "Not on the table!"

"Why not?" His mouth found the hollow of her throat, his fingers curling into the edges of her chemise, and there was a slight rending sound as he pulled it away and tossed it carelessly to the floor. "A table is for lots of things, tiger-eyes," he murmured, laying her gently back, his fingers curling into her hands and pulling her arms up and over her head. "The first course should always be light," he murmured against the heavy underside of her breast. Hungrily, he found the aching peak and nourished it with his mouth, his hands loosing hers to slide slowly down her bare body, lifting her hips, his mouth traveling damply down over her breast to her rib cage, then over the gentle round of her stomach. "And the second course should be meaty and filling. . . ."

Whitney cried out with shock and tangled her hands in his hair. "Cutter, no!"

Cradling her hips in his arms, Cutter looked up at her with a love haze dimming his eyes, and his smile was crooked. "Remember the flower nectar? Nectar of Whitney. It's the same, love."

When she moaned and writhed beneath him, crying out, he finally slid his body up and over hers, the hard surface of the table providing an unrelenting mattress. His smile was soft and dreamy as he fumbled with the buttons of his pants. Leaning back over her, he said softly, "And the final course should be the best of all. . . ."

Whitney's thighs enclosed him in a firm grip, her hips pressing against the wood table as he entered her with a fierce urgency. Gasping, she arched to meet him, her hair spilling like cream over the table, draping over pewter dishes in an ivory fall. There was none of the previous sweet coaxing but only a driving need that swept her up with him, made her cling to him, her need as great as his. And when the release came, Whitney thought she would surely die from the aching pleasure of it.

*   *   *

They rode down together, detouring through the small town of Los Gatos on the San Pedro River. They'd spent a week in the mountain cabin, and neither of them was ready to return. "But," Whitney had said with a rueful laugh, "if we don't let my father know I'm still alive and in fairly good health, he may come up after you!"

Grinning, Cutter had informed her that he'd brought his guns, the .44s he usually wore. Whitney frowned.

"Why? Are you expecting trouble?"

"I always expect trouble, and that way I'm ready for it if it shows up," Cutter replied.

It bothered her that he so casually spoke of trouble and his guns, but she didn't say anything when he strapped them on before they rode down out of the mountains and into Los Gatos. The little town nodded sleepily in the noonday sun, its citizens drowsing in chairs beneath porch roofs or behind open doors to small shops. Cutter took her inside and bought her some ribbons for her hair, and, laughing, a book on flowers.

"It has illustrations!" Whitney said with an impudent wrinkle of her nose, and he'd pointed out the section on reproduction. The store clerk looked at them disapprovingly, but she didn't care. She was in love. There could be no disapproval in her life now. She had Cutter.

They walked outside, hands entwined, her purchases tucked beneath one arm as she leaned into him and looked up, laughing. He was explaining to her how he'd terrorized the Los Gatos furrier as a boy by bringing in a live bear for him to skin, when a noise drew their attention. Whitney turned more slowly, her reflexes not as attuned to trouble as were his.

Across the wide, dusty street, a single door swung open with a violent bang, scattering dust and the few pedestrians lingering on the sidewalk. There was time for only a brief start of surprise before Cutter was pushing her down behind a water barrel, telling her to stay there, his voice harsh and unrelenting. Whitney, however, had no intention of going anywhere. She waited tensely as Cutter crossed the street.

From her position behind the barrel, she could see Cutter approach three men, heard the voices lifted in anger and argument. One of the men was dressed in leggings, breech clout, and a rough shirt; the other two were garbed as cowhands, their manner aggressive toward the Indian they held. She couldn't hear what they said, but saw the two cowhands casting uneasy, faintly belligerent glances at Cutter and the guns he wore draped so casually around his hips. It was obvious they either knew him or knew of him, for she heard one of them say there was "no need for a man like Cutter to concern himself with this."

She didn't hear Cutter's reply, but she didn't need to. In just a moment the two cowhands wheeled and walked away, and Cutter talked briefly with the Indian. When he came back to her, his face was grim.

"Let's go," he said shortly, taking her by the arm and pulling her with him.

"Go where? Cutter, what's the matter? Why were those men angry at the Indian? Did you know any of them?"

His glance was faintly amused. "You sound like a wind-up toy, tiger-eyes. Yes, I knew one of them."

"The Indian?" she guessed, and he nodded.

"Yes."

His voice was tight, and she let a moment pass before she asked, "What's wrong?"

He didn't answer her until they reached his horse and he had lifted her up and mounted behind her. "Plenty's wrong," he said softly, reining the horse around and kicking it into a trot. "Geronimo and seventy-four of his warriors have left the San Carlos Reservation, and the army is hot after them. Noch-ay-del-klinne is dead, and so are several soldiers. It looks bad."

She felt a sinking feeling. "But that doesn't have anything to do with you, does it, Cutter? I mean, you won't do . . . do anything foolish?"

Whitney felt his body tighten, and knew even before he said anything what he would say. "That depends on what you call foolish. I knew it would come to this one day, and I made a vow to help if I could."

"But you'll be killed!" she stormed. "You just can't!"

"Whitney . . ."

"No!" She tried to throw herself from the horse, gripping his arm, her body twisting with the effort. Hot tears and rage rose up in her as thick as the dust choking the road, and for a moment it was almost like two months before—Cutter, his face tight with anger, trying to hold on to her without hurting her, the horse snorting and half rearing beneath them. "I won't let you go!" Whitney panted, his arm cutting off her breath like a vise beneath her breasts. "I . . . won't . . . be . . . a . . . widow!"

"Dammit, Whitney, listen to me!" he snapped in her ear. "It's not like I'm going to ride with them on raids. I intend to try to act as a negotiator with Geronimo. I can do it, I know I can. Someone has to try. There's been too much bloodshed, and there will be more before it's all over." As she calmed slightly, her rage subsiding into desperate tears, he added grimly, "The army butchered a whole village of people."

She knew he was telling her the truth. There was a bleak look she'd never seen in his eyes, and she felt a deep sadness.

"Everyone?"

"Everyone."

"But . . . but, Cutter, the army—they're soldiers. They wouldn't do that! Not . . . not . . ."

"Not white men? Is that what you're trying to say?" Cutter gave a harsh laugh. "Think again, tiger-eyes! I've seen villages after the soldiers have been through them, and sometimes there's not a recognizable man, woman, or child there. Bashed to pieces, mutilated . . . it's war, Whitney, and men of any color don't usually take time to beg your pardon before they shoot you. Atrocity knows no racial differences."

"And now you're going to try to make everything right by riding with Geronimo, is that what you're telling me?" Her voice was as angry and bitter as his, and her back was straight and stiff.

"I'm not that naive." He drew in a deep breath. "Look, Quanah Parker of the Comanche Nation has done it. Maybe—if Geronimo will listen—I can too."

Sullenly, she said, "I suppose you mean that chief who surrendered his tribe at Fort Sill a few years ago."

"Yes. His mother was white but his father was a Comanche warrior. Quanah is smart, and he's helping his people make the transition to reservation life." There was a brief silence, then he said softly, "I don't really hold out much hope that Geronimo will do the same, but it's worth a try."

"So you're going to risk your own life, not to mention capture and arrest by the army, to go on a mission you know you can't win."

Cutter didn't reply, and Whitney sat in miserable silence the rest of the way to the Coleman ranch.

Nothing Daniel or Deborah had to say mattered either. Cutter was unyielding in his decision.

"You know I have to," he said to his mother, and after a pause in which she gazed into his jade eyes so like her own, Deborah nodded sadly.

"Yes, Cutter. I know," she said in a whisper.

But Whitney didn't understand what drove him. She wished her father were still there. Surely Morgan Bradford could have talked some sense into Cutter!

Whitney followed Cutter into a bedroom and stood in wretched silence, calling upon the lessons she had learned in Red Shirt's camp to keep her from making a fool of herself again. She watched numbly as he changed from pants, shirt, and gun belts, pulling on leggings, breech clout, and moccasins again. His jet hair was shorter, but he still tied a headband around his forehead, a wide red strip of cloth that made his eyes look greener, his face darker.

He came to her, his touch gentle, and took her in his arms. "I'll be back for you soon, love." There was a brief awkward silence, then he added, "Will you wait for me?"

She looked up at him with drowning eyes, her heart aching so fiercely she thought she would die from it. "Can I . . . can I go with you?" she blurted out, but he was already shaking his head.

"No. It's too dangerous."

"Cutter!"

"*No*, Whitney." He pushed her slightly away, and his eyes became dark slits. "You'll wait?"

Fighting the urge to stamp her foot in frustration, Whitney gave a short nod of her head and said irritably, "I suppose I'll have to! I can't go with you, and I can't very well run off when you might be back soon, so I guess I'll just have to wait!"

He laughed. "It's nice to see you back to your sweet-tempered self again. I was beginning to worry that you'd changed."

Leaning into him, she said breathlessly, "Oh, Cutter, I have changed, I have! I think I'll die if you don't come back! Please don't go!"

Grimacing, he muttered, "Are we back to that again? Look, tiger-eyes, it's not like I'm going to stand up on a rock and make a target of myself, so—"

A knock at the door preceded Daniel's voice, saying, "Cutter! Trouble outside!"

Grabbing up his rifle and an ammunition belt, Cutter strode to the window and pushed aside the curtain. Cursing softly, he turned back to Whitney. "Soldiers. They must think I know something. Look, I'm going out the back way. See if you can stall them."

When she might have argued some more, Cutter grabbed her arm and yanked her against him, bringing his mouth down on hers so fiercely it cut off her protests. Then he was gone, leaving her standing in the middle of the empty room and staring after him.

In the weeks that followed, Whitney was to learn the hell of waiting. Staying in the bedroom at the Coleman home, she twitched with anticipation every time she heard a footstep in the hallway outside her door. And she lingered on the patio at night, breathing in the scent of the flowers and thinking longingly of Cutter.

Her only outlets for the long hours of frustration and waiting were talking with Deborah and her writing. Deborah helped with the worst of it, but there were times even she could not abate the pain Whitney felt. That was when she turned to her writing again, sitting down at the small secretary in one corner of her room and filling page after page with her impressions and thoughts of what she'd learned since coming to Arizona. It wasn't quite the exposé she'd intended it to be when she'd first come, but more of a commentary on the harsh way of life for all those brave enough to endure the rigors. And she didn't spare herself when she wrote of the unrealistic and biased opinions of people who'd never been farther west than the Mississippi River.

She wrote about Cutter, and the conflicts of a man caught between two worlds. The words flowed from her pen as she tried to convey the difficulty any man would have in dealing with prejudices from both sides of his heritage. It was not the book she'd first intended, but it was more true than she had ever thought it could be. What would her father think? she mused. Before returning to New York, Morgan had said testily that he thought Whitney had lost her common sense, and should go back with him.

"Why are you staying?" he'd demanded the morning he'd left. "Let him come after you when he's through chasing and being chased all over Arizona Territory!"

Whitney's smiling refusal had been firm, and Morgan had left, thoroughly exasperated.

Finally, late one night when everyone had gone to bed and Whitney had exhausted herself writing, she went out onto the patio and stared up at the moonlit sky. Stars were everywhere, twinkling so brightly they almost hurt her eyes; the familiar ache in her throat when she remembered the nights spent lying beneath them with Cutter was almost overwhelming.

It was September, and the flowers were fading as the night air took on a faint chill. She shivered slightly, pulling a lacy shawl more tightly around her shoulders, and reached out to touch the blossom of a moonflower.

"Hey, tiger-eyes," came an achingly familiar voice from the shadows beyond the patio, "still interested in gardening?"

"Cutter!"

When he vaulted over the low stone wall and onto the patio, she was in his arms immediately, crying and kissing him wherever she could reach—his chest, his neck, the underside of his jaw—and he laughed.

"God, I never thought I'd get this kind of homecoming from you!"

"Where have you been? No one has heard from you in weeks, and I've been so worried. Your mother—Cutter, are you back for good?"

She looked up into his dancing green eyes with a worried frown, and he pulled her more tightly into his embrace. "So many questions! No," he answered the most pressing one, "I'm here for only a few hours. I just had to see you." He folded her against his naked chest, and she could smell the sharp scent of wood smoke and leather on him.

Whitney thought he had never looked so good to her, even in the breech clout, leggings, and rawhide vest open over his smooth, bare chest. His long knife was stuck in the waist of his breech clout, and his hair seemed to have grown out again, brushing against his shoulders in raven strands. Whitney raked her hands through it, bringing his head down to her face. She brushed her lips over his, lightly at first, then more firmly, and with a muffled growl he swung her up into his arms and strode across the patio with her.

They passed Deborah, standing in her night shift in the hallway, a lamp in one hand, and Cutter said over his shoulder, "I'll talk to you before I leave!" then pushed open Whitney's bedroom door and slammed it shut behind him with the graceful nudge of his foot.

In moments they were naked, a sense of urgency making their fevered movements almost frantic. There were no preliminaries beyond hot, searching kisses, and Whitney was opening her body to receive him, arching her head back, her cries muffled by his mouth as he took her, slamming into her with a pressing need that she shared completely.

The fiery release, when it came, was so shattering that Whitney sobbed into his shoulder, holding him close, his body pressed so tightly to her not a whisper could have come between them. Lifting his head, Cutter gazed down into her teary eyes with a faint smile. He traced the tear-track with a curious finger, smoothing its dewy moisture over her cheek, then to her trembling lips.

"Tears, tiger-eyes?" he murmured, and she nodded numbly. "For me or for you?"

"Both. Cutter, oh, Cutter, time is so short, and I need you so much! Please—don't go back. Stay awhile with me." She hated to beg, but she couldn't help the tumble of words that spilled from her lips, even when she saw the regretful shake of his head.

"I can't, Whitney. You know I can't."

She clutched at him. "But Daniel said that Geronimo is wreaking havoc everywhere, staying in Mexico and crossing the border in sporadic raids—are you a part of that?"

He evaded her piercing gaze, and she felt him shrug. "I do what I can to stop him. Geronimo is wild with anger right now. I'm trying to negotiate for peace." He sounded tired, and Whitney saw the sudden bleak expression in his eyes when he added, "I don't think he's going to listen. Not now. He's too filled with hate and the memories of his life on San Carlos."

"And you can't convince him to turn himself in to the army?"

Cutter's ironic gaze drifted from Whitney's hope-filled eyes to her lips, and he pressed a light kiss on her mouth before he shook his head. "He listens politely, then proceeds to destroy anyone unfortunate enough to be in his path."

"Oh, Cutter, I'm afraid for you!"

Amused, he rubbed his finger across the tip of her small, straight nose. "Why? I'm safe enough with Geronimo. Unless we run into cavalry. But that isn't often. The army can't seem to run him down. Geronimo's too crafty for them. He knows every small niche in the mountains, and all he has to do is go to ground when he sees a patrol."

After a short pause Whitney said softly, "Daniel says that you're back in the same trouble you were in before. He seems to think that Governor Fremont won't be lenient if he finds out you're riding with Geronimo."

"I'm sure he won't be, and it wouldn't do any good to tell him that I'm trying to convince Geronimo to give up. I find that hard to believe myself, especially knowing some of the things I know."

"What do you mean?"

A hard note crept into his voice as Cutter said, "The army is not exactly blameless, you know. They're slowly going back on every agreement they've made with the Apache. The land belongs to the Apache just until a white man wants it. As long as it's worthless, it's good enough for the Apache, but if gold is discovered, or silver, or copper, or even coal—well, you get my meaning. Do you blame Geronimo? The Apache has run free on this land for hundreds of years, and now the United States government wants them to stay in one small area no one else wants, and shut up and be happy about it. Instead of hunting food, the proud warriors are supposed to stand in a line and hold out their hands for an allotment of spoiled beef and weevil-infested grain! It's an insult to the dignity of any human being."

"And you, Cutter? Whose side are you on?" Whitney asked after a moment.

He sighed heavily. "My sympathies are with the Apache. But common sense dictates that I argue for peace. There can be no other way to save the entire tribe from being exterminated."

Another long silence stretched between them, and then Cutter was kissing her again, his lips and hands removing any coherent thoughts she had as he took her, his body sweet and hard against her. When he left several hours later, and she heard the fading hoofbeats of his horse, the brave facade she'd put on for his sake dissolved, and Whitney succumbed to the hot press of tears.

Eighteen

Daniel Coleman glared at the army captain angrily. "Now, see here, Captain West—"

"Sorry, Mr. Coleman, but I have my orders." Andrew West looked from Daniel to Whitney, and nothing in the hard set of his expression indicated he felt any sympathy for her. "Your daughter-in-law is married to an outlaw and a renegade, and I'm taking her in for questioning. As a smart attorney, you surely appreciate that I can do this."

"I'll have a writ on you so fast, Captain, you'll be back in private's stripes before you can turn around!" Daniel snapped.

West's eyes were grim. "Sorry, Mr. Coleman," he repeated. "She goes with me. Feel free to come to Fort Grant after her. Of course, if we are not through questioning her, or have decided to press charges, you may do what needs to be done then."

Whitney, white-faced and quivering, felt a wave of anger wash through her. "How dare you!" she spat out. "Do you think I am a renegade? That I am in . . . in league with Geronimo?" Her voice dripped with scorn when she added, "It should be very interesting, indeed, to see you prove any charges against me, Captain West!"

Bravado was fine when she was standing in the Coleman home,

but once alone with the troops of soldiers and riding across the Galiuro Mountains, visions danced in front of her eyes of Cutter's capture and hanging, and Whitney found herself shuddering with apprehension. She wasn't afraid for herself really; she was afraid for him. But hadn't Daniel said he had been pardoned by the governor? Of course he had, and no new charges had been filed. It would all be over soon, and she would be sent back to the Colemans. All she had to do was tell the truth, within reason, and wait until someone came to get her.

Captain Andrew West had other ideas. Upon arriving at Fort Grant, he took Whitney immediately to a small room with no furniture but a table and two chairs. Weary from the long ride, hungry, thirsty, and irritable, she glared up at him.

"Is this the best you can do, Captain? I would hardly call this the best accommodations!"

Stiffly, West said, "It's the best that I can do right now, Miss—Mrs. Coleman."

Whitney gave a start. Mrs. Coleman? Oh, yes, Cutter used his stepfather's last name. She'd thought of him only as Cutter. Cutter. She conjured up a vision of him as she'd last seen him, his green eyes glittering with that reckless light, his body so bronzed and hard and—and dear to her. Her throat ached suddenly, and she found it difficult to force words past the lump in it.

"Your best is sadly lacking, Captain," she said, weaving all the coldness she felt inside into her voice. "You do realize that I will complain to your superior officers?"

Leaning over the table, his palms spreading on the surface, West said harshly, "By the time I've accomplished what I set out to do, my superior officers will be giving me a recommendation, not a lecture! I have a plan that will bring them all to heel this time! Yes, I will have a recommendation from President Hayes himself before this is over!"

Whitney felt the bite of dread gnawing at her. There was such a malicious, triumphant light in West's eyes, she knew it had to involve Cutter. He would not forgive Cutter for making a fool of him about the payroll, and she knew instinctively that he would not forgive her for marrying Cutter, no matter the reason.

She heard, as if from a distance, West saying, "How do you feel, having a husband who leaves you to face such a time alone? While you are here, being questioned and interrogated as to your activities, your renegade husband is free."

Recognizing the hatred and contempt for Cutter in his voice, Whitney suddenly realized this would be much more uncomfortable than she'd first supposed, and she hoped that Daniel or her father would come quickly. Lifting her chin, she looked into West's eyes calmly.

"Then, so far my husband is ahead of you, isn't he, Captain West?"

Recoiling, West glared at her. "Only for now, I promise you that!"

Whitney turned her head away, and stared coldly at the opposite wall. "Unless part of your inquisition is to browbeat weary women, I suggest you find me a place to lie down, Captain."

Switching to polite coolness, West inclined his head. "I will see to it that you have a bed for the night. And in the morning perhaps we will have a little more to discuss," he added obliquely.

Whitney was to think of that remark later.

She woke with a headache. The sun was shining into the small room where she slept on a cot, streaming through a curtainless window to spill onto the floor, dust motes swimming in the beams. She lay still for a moment, listening to the sounds outside the room. Male voices drifted in and out of earshot, and she could hear harness jingling and saddle leather creaking. Dogs barked, and somewhere she heard the shout of a child. A child at the fort? Must be one of the officer's.

Swinging her legs over the side of the cot, Whitney gazed down at her rumpled skirt and blouse. She wondered what West had done with the clothes he'd allowed her to bring, then wondered where Cutter could be. It had been only a few days since he'd come to her on the patio, and she worried that he might still be in the area. West would be merciless if he found him.

It must be late, she decided, because the angle of the sun through the window was high and sharp. Her stomach growled, reminding her she hadn't eaten, and she wondered if they'd somehow forgotten she was there.

But then she knew they hadn't, because she heard shuffling footsteps outside the door and the turn of a key in the lock. A woman entered, bringing a tray of food, her smile wide and shy. She spoke to Whitney in Spanish, a dialect that was hard to understand, and it took Whitney a moment to figure out that the woman wanted to press her skirt and blouse for her. Reluctantly, and mostly because the woman was so persistent, gabbling at her and pulling at her clothes, Whitney agreed.

She ate, some kind of bean paste wrapped in a tortilla, and drank hot, bitter coffee. Sitting on the edge of the cot with her arms around her body, the chemise much too brief for her comfort, Whitney was relieved when the woman returned with her pressed garments. She shrugged into them gratefully, and then Captain West was at the door, telling her she was to be questioned now.

Haughtily, Whitney swept before him down the narrow hallway. He showed her into a large room, where four men sat waiting. One man stood beside her chair, his arms folded across his chest, but his expression forbidding. He was obviously meant to be her guard, and Whitney's eyes narrowed contemptuously. Were they that afraid of her?

And then began the questions:

"Who is your husband?" "Where is he?" "Who has he gone to meet?" "Do you know where their camp is located?" "What did he do with the payroll he stole?" "Did he use it to buy weapons for the Apaches?" "Did he hide it?" "Where?" "Who rides with him?"

They came at her from all sides, one after the other, and Whitney kept shaking her head with stubborn defiance, saying "I don't know" until she thought she would scream. Then a knock came at the closed door, and Captain West crossed to the door and spoke to the man on guard.

When he returned, he had an enigmatic smile on his face, more like a wolfish curving of his lips than genuine amusement. "Perhaps, Mrs. Coleman, you will feel more talkative in a moment," he said smoothly, and she glared at him.

"I hardly think so, Captain," she said icily. She heard a metallic rattle and half turned, staring with horror as Cutter was brought in, his arms and legs shackled with heavy chains. His shirt was gone, and the leggings he wore were torn, as if he'd been in a fierce struggle. Beneath the fall of dark hair, his eyes were hard and glittering, colder than she'd ever seen them. Whitney hadn't realized she'd risen from her chair until West put a restraining hand on her arm.

"Cutter! Oh, God, what—how did they find you?"

"It was easy enough," West answered for him. Cutter was looking at him through narrowed eyes, his face battered and bloody and untreated cuts still oozing on his body. "I simply let it be known that I had arrested his wife, and before you knew it, he was banging at the gates of the fort demanding to be my prisoner!"

"Oh, Cutter!" she whispered hoarsely, and tried to go to him. West held her fast, his fingers digging cruelly into her wrists.

"Not so quickly, Mrs. Coleman. I believe there are a few questions we'd like to ask before we allow you to speak with your . . . husband."

Whitney's gaze was fastened on Cutter, and she recognized the cold, mocking light in his eyes, the one that always preceded danger. She also saw the almost imperceptible shake of his head, then his gaze slid away from her.

Cutter was furious—at West, at himself, and at Geronimo. He knew better than to allow himself to become vulnerable, yet he had been taken because of a woman—his woman. When the Apache scout had found him, he hadn't wanted to believe that Whitney was in danger. West was smart, he gave him that. He'd sent an Apache to trail an Apache. When the scout had lured him from hiding by simply waving a few articles of Whitney's clothing, that had convinced Cutter it was no bluff. Even then he thought they wouldn't harm her, just frighten her. But in the end it hadn't mattered, because he couldn't stand the thought of her being subjected to even the slightest danger. Damn Geronimo for being so stubborn! If the wily old fox had only listened, perhaps some sort of equitable solution could have been worked out, but he was still too hate-filled to consider it.

So Cutter had ridden to Fort Grant, knowing that he would be arrested, maybe even executed. And it had come to him on the fast, furious ride that he would never have done this for any other woman. The idea of Whitney being at the mercy of hard men had compelled him to rescue her at the risk of his own life. Was this love? he wondered somewhat sardonically. He, who had always prided himself on being able to remain emotionally detached, in love? Yes, he must be, because even now, seeing her with her pale hair tumbling around her shoulders and the glitter of tears in her eyes, he wanted to comfort her.

But there wasn't time for that, not when West was still gloating, his pale eyes filled with a malice that indicated no good for Cutter.

"After you've answered a few of my questions," the captain was saying when Cutter dragged his attention away from Whitney to him, "I will decide what to do with you. But of course that all depends on the answers I receive."

"You want answers?" Cutter mocked. "You don't even know the right questions, West!"

Stiffening, West fixed him with a baleful eye. He had his position to protect; the other soldiers in the room, all officers under his command, were watching to see how he would handle this stubborn half-breed. And of course there was the still-lovely Whitney—oh, yes, he would definitely bring this renegade to heel before the day was gone!

"Perhaps I don't know the right questions," West said with a nasty smile, "but with your help—and your wife's—I think I can do well enough." He signaled, and one of the soldiers stepped forward.

Whitney gasped when she saw Cutter's knife in the man's hand, the blade wicked and sharp. What were they going to do? Then she heard, with a sickening lurch of her stomach, West explaining to Cutter that though he did not *want* to harm a woman, he knew that Whitney was not as strong as her husband, and would surrender quickly under threats. Her backbone stiffened.

"You're wrong, Captain! You can threaten me with any kind of torture you like and I won't betray my husband!"

West stared with amusement at Whitney's flashing eyes and defiant face. "My dear Mrs. Coleman, I had no intention of actually threatening *you*—it is your husband whom I am threatening. Do you think my superiors would like it if I so much as put one small bruise on you? No, but I don't think they'll care if I slice this renegade to pieces with his own knife. . . ."

Whitney heard her scream as if from a distance, saw, with disbelieving eyes, the soldier step between her and Cutter, and knew from the very slight narrowing of his eyes what West intended.

"No! Don't hurt him!" she heard herself pleading, and if not for the man beside her, holding her firmly in his grasp, she would have flung herself between Cutter and the knife.

Cutter did not betray by so much as a flicker of an eyelash that he cared—or even noticed—what the sergeant was doing with the knife. He came from a hard school, and did not view pain in the same way as these soldiers did. It was all a matter of concentration, of focusing the mind on something else, ignoring the urgent demands of the body. He simply chose not to notice.

It wasn't that easy for Whitney, who felt a blinding pain as seeing blood flow over Cutter's chest. The soldier who held her grimaced, and muttered under his breath that she was much stronger than she looked as she fought him to get to Cutter. It was only when West managed to exact a grim measure of satisfaction—not from Cutter's stubborn silence but from her wild pleas—that he gave the signal to stop. Turning to Whitney, he lifted one light brow questioningly.

"I shall repeat some of my earlier questions, Mrs. Coleman, and if you will consider that it will greatly lessen the chances of your husband being gutted in front of your eyes, you may find it agreeable to answer them."

Panting, weak from the racking sobs that tore at her, Whitney choked out, "I'll answer anything, only don't . . . oh, don't hurt him anymore. . . ."

"Whitney!" It was Cutter, and his eyes were fixed on her so coldly, she quailed. "Don't answer *anything*! Do you hear me!"

West was smiling, and his voice was soft. "Of course he's going to say that, but you and I know that if you do not answer my questions . . ." He let his voice trail into silence, and she shuddered.

When, at West's signal, the sergeant with the knife stepped toward Cutter again, Whitney immediately capitulated, her eyes begging Cutter to forgive her, her heart aching.

"Very good, Mrs. Coleman." West sounded pleased, and he was almost gentle when he asked her the questions again, some of which she knew the answers to, others not. She told him about the camp in the valley between two ridges, described it as best she could remember, and told him it was mainly women and children:

"No warriors, just a few men to do the hunting, mostly old," she said, unable to look at Cutter. She wasn't able to look at him when she told West about the gold either, and how it had been exchanged with the Mexicans for rifles, food, and supplies. Cutter hadn't known she understood the details, hadn't known until then she could speak Spanish, and she wondered if he would forgive her. She gave names, places, every detail she could recall, until she was exhausted.

Then West asked her about the man known as Téjas, and she gave a start. "Téjas? What . . . what about him?"

"Do you know his real name, or where he lives? Or how involved with the renegades he is?"

Biting her lower lip, Whitney gave a shake of her head. She couldn't betray Téjas, she just couldn't. And besides, she didn't know where he lived, just the general area. It was hard not looking toward Cutter, for after his first angry objection to her answers, he had retreated into a stiff, furious silence. He would find it hard to forgive her weakness, but she knew that if she betrayed Téjas, he would never be able to forgive her.

Yet when West gave her a narrow smile and said he did not believe she was telling the complete truth, and lifted his arm to signal to the sergeant again, Whitney gasped out the information that he lived near the border, and that his name was Vega. "And that's all I know. I swear it!" she said, hot tears streaking her face. Her imploring eyes begged Cutter to forgive her, but his face was taut, his gaze condemning.

The cold contempt in his face haunted her later, when West returned her to the small, stuffy room and locked her in again, and she was left alone with her thoughts. West had promised he would not continue the "interrogation" of the prisoner, that he'd found out all he needed to know from her, yet Whitney was still afraid for Cutter. And she was afraid for herself.

Would he ever forgive her? She'd not been able to bear seeing him hurt, watching the knife slice at him as he'd stood with a stoic expression, stubbornly silent. Surely he would understand that! Wouldn't he?

Hours passed, agonizingly slowly, turning into two days, then three, crawling in a haze of filtered sunlight and whirling doubts, until Whitney thought she would go mad with it. She didn't know anything about what was happening outside her locked room, what was happening to Cutter, or what West had decided, or where her father and Daniel were . . . dear God how could she go on much longer without resorting to demands for answers?

The Mexican woman who brought her food and picked up the untouched tray she'd left earlier had no answers for her beyond a shy shrugging of her shoulders and the information that "the señora should not worry so much." No, she did not know what had been done with the prisoner they had brought in, but she did know that he had not been executed yet.

Yet. The word held frightening implications for Whitney. Did that mean he *would* be executed? But the woman would say no more, leaving the room with rapid shakes of her head.

Pacing, Whitney literally wrung her hands with worry. She heard the tinny notes of a bugle, and the rushing sound of feet and hooves on the hard-packed soil outside mingling with shots and deep shouts, but when she stood on tiptoe to try to see out the window, she was met by nothing but an adobe wall, and flat desert beyond that. There were whoops and screams, the shrill cries of what sounded like Apaches, and the barrage of gunfire was deafening. It seemed to last for hours, and at one point she crawled under her cot and waited for the end to come. When, finally, silence fell, no one came to tell her what had happened, and the sun slid slowly out of sight, leaving the room in total darkness.

By the time she heard a key in the lock of her door, Whitney was exhausted from her emotional struggle. She sat on the edge of the cot, gazing blankly at the door swinging open. Dark shadows filled the tiny room, so that the person entering was momentarily halted. She heard West say, "Hand me that lamp," and then a glowing ball of light entered with him. Still Whitney sat, straight and stiff, her eyes fixed on a spot past the captain, as if he did not exist.

"Here she is, sir," she heard West say then, and her face turned a fraction, only a faint glint of interest in her eyes. That interest leapt when she recognized the man with West, and she stood slowly, her voice disbelieving.

"Papa?"

Morgan Bradford rushed forward, folding her in his embrace, his sturdy frame shaking in spite of his efforts to remain calm. "Whitney! Daughter . . . you're so thin . . . by God, I'll have heads for this!" He ended on a more familiar note of anger, and Whitney smiled.

Touching his cheek with a light finger, she looked past him to West, who stood still holding the lamp, his face tight. "Am I free to go?" When West gave a curt nod, she asked, "And Cutter? Is he free?"

West only laughed harshly, and she felt Morgan Bradford's arms tighten around her. "Daniel is with me," he said then. "He got to Fremont and did some speedy talking, so you're free now. It took us longer to get here than we'd thought, and as West"—he threw a harsh glance toward the officer—"still a captain as of this moment—chose not to acknowledge the wire he sent ahead, we had to ride hell for leather to get here. I was so worried about you, and now that—"

"Papa. Cutter. Where is he?"

Morgan's arms tightened again, and this time Whitney gently disengaged herself from his embrace and took a step back. Her eyes held her father's, demanding a reply, and he looked down at the floor. It was West who answered.

"Dead, if you must know," he snapped out, and his eyes glittered with malice in the lamplight. "Some of his friends tried to help him escape, and in the fighting that followed—perhaps you heard it?—your renegade husband was killed. . . ."

That was the last Whitney heard for a while. The room whirled faster and faster, and in the shadows the burning lamp grew first brighter, then dimmer, until finally it disappeared in a pinpoint of light, leaving only the utter black shadows of despair.

Nineteen

"Whitney . . ." David Coleman's face was young and miserable, and for a moment drew her out of her daze. "It's late, and Ma thought . . . thought you might want to come in now. Nights are kinda cool. . . ." He let his voice drift into silence as Whitney just gazed at him, and in the rosy light from the lantern, he could see a faint smile curling one corner of her mouth.

"That's what Cutter said the last time he came to me on the patio." Her voice was bereft of any emotion. "It was September then, and the nights had barely a hint of chill in them, no more so than usual, but he said . . . we talked about flowers too." Looking down, her fingers smoothed over the cover of the illustrated book on flowers, the book Cutter had bought her.

"Flowers?" David cocked his head to one side. He sounded frankly skeptical. "I never would have thought Cutter to be interested in flowers."

"His interest, I assure you, was hardly of a botanical nature." Whitney allowed a hint of mockery in her tone, an amused, affectionate mockery, but it was better than the flat, lifeless tone David was so accustomed to hearing, so he came to sit down in a cane chair beside her, his gaze fixed on her steadily.

Wrapping adolescent arms around his gangly legs as he drew them up with his feet tucked under him, David said, "I think Cutter was wrong."

Whitney looked at him in surprise. "Wrong? About what?" *Why did it still hurt so badly, as if a knife were piercing her heart, constantly turning and twisting each time his name was mentioned, each time she closed her eyes and saw his face in her memory?*

"Wrong about wolves," the boy said, further confusing her.

"I don't know . . ."

"He told me that you can't make a wolf into a pet, but he was really talking about you when I was talking about him." He grinned suddenly, and Whitney had the thought that there was a certain family resemblance between Cutter and his young half brother.

"I suppose," Whitney said faintly, her voice trembling with a mixture of sadness and amusement, "that you were both right. About making pets out of wolves, I mean."

Shrugging, David looked down at the stone floor of the patio. "Aw, I don't know about that. I mean, I wouldn't give anything for having had some time with Silvertail—that was my she-wolf—but it was her nature to be a wolf. Maybe I didn't have long, but it was better than not having any time at all."

A pang struck Whitney, and for a moment she couldn't speak, couldn't breathe. Was the short time better than none at all? She didn't know. It hurt so terribly that, at the moment, all she wanted was an end to the pain, even if it meant not ever having had Cutter. But did she really? Could she ever give up her memories of him, of his lazy smile and green eyes glittering with amusement at something she'd said to him?

She let her head fall back against the curved cushion of the cane chair, and her voice was cool and distant. "Do you think they'll ever find out . . . exactly what happened to him?" she asked into the gathering silence.

She could feel David's pained shrug. "I don't know. Maybe they will. Apaches take their dead with them, and after the attack on Fort Grant, and the confusion later, it was hard to tell what happened. At least, that's what Pa said, and he should know."

Another silence fell before Whitney asked, "Did they hang West for his defiance of orders? I never did follow the reports of his court-martial in the papers. There was so much else going on, and . . . and somehow, vengeance is not as satisfying as I'd thought it would be."

"No, there was no hanging. After all, it *is* war between the renegades and the army, and both sides are doing terrible things. . . ." He let his voice drop off suddenly, seeing Whitney's sudden wince. It was too bad that she'd had to find out about the massacre at Red Shirt's camp. She blamed herself for the death of all the inhabitants. Not one had survived the soldiers' brutal attack in retaliation for the assault on Fort Grant. When Geronimo and his warriors had not been found, the soldiers had reacted with frustrated fury. Even Elisa, the young Mexican girl Whitney had befriended, had been killed along with her infant. The news had shattered Whitney.

"Cutter didn't want me to talk, and I did, and now he's dead and so are all those innocent people!" she'd wept into Deborah's comforting arms, and no one could console her. But at Deborah's urging, she'd agreed to go back east to her father. The reminders of Cutter here were just too painful.

"You're leaving early in the morning," David said, and she nodded quietly, still not opening her eyes. "Pa said I could ride to Benson with you to catch the train, and that maybe he'd take me to Tombstone later." His voice lifted. "Did you hear about the gunfight at Tombstone? Marshal Earp and his brothers had a pip of a fight with some ranchers. I hear there was the Clantons and McLaurys, and one of Wyatt Earp's friends, a fast gun by the name of Holliday. By the time it was over, three of them were dead and three wounded, and two of them got off without a scratch!" He shrugged. "Of course, Marshal Earp's going to end up losing his position as city marshal because of the fight at O.K. Corral, Pa says."

Remembering her long-ago conversation with Andrew West about the conflicting factions in Tombstone, Whitney was hardly surprised. Only a thin veneer of respectability had shielded Virgil Earp from the men he professed to fight against. But she would no longer have to think about gunmen or renegades. She was going home. After six months in Arizona Territory, she was going back home. Odd, that she should feel so suddenly bereft at the thought. . . .

"Brandy, Whitney?" Morgan asked, lifting a cut-crystal decanter, but she shook her head.

"No. I don't think so. Thank you."

A frown creased Morgan's brow, and he set the decanter down on the rosewood table. "You aren't depressed about the critics' reviews of your book, are you?"

A faint smile curved her mouth, and she turned away from the window, where she'd been watching the wind send March leaves skittering across the park. "No, not really. Actually, I hadn't thought a great deal about it. I wrote what had to be written, not what people want to hear."

"Well, you must admit, criticizing the government for its treatment of the Indians on reservations is hardly a popular view at this time. Especially in light of Geronimo's continued depredations. Of course, I realize that the army is hardly blameless. . . ."

" 'To do injustice is more disgraceful than to suffer it,' " she quoted softly, and added at the lift of her father's brow, "Plato."

"Dear Lord, the girl is quoting philosophers at me now! You've changed a lot, child."

"I suppose I have." Whitney thought of the letter she'd received from Téjas, a long missive telling her not to worry about giving his name to the army, that she had done only what she had to do, and he didn't blame her for telling West about him.

It did no harm, anyway, he'd written, *because Daniel Coleman managed to get to Fremont in time. Pardons were passed around like piña nuts, and I just stood in line for mine.*

There had been more, mainly conversation about the dull life on the hacienda and his sister's wedding, then he'd ended the letter with an odd quote from Shakespeare, "Sweet are the uses of adversity," adding, *You've used it well and to your advantage, and I pray that you will appreciate its rewards.*

Looking up at her father, as he obviously expected more from her, she added, "I think I've become rather good at disposing of husbands. This last one took only two months instead of years, or so says one wit in your rival's paper. Of course, he couldn't know that—"

"Blast it all, Whitney!" Morgan exploded. "Are you going to grieve forever? All these months—since October!—and you have hardly smiled at all. And when anyone speaks to you, you mouth enough cynicism to fill every empty cup in Manhattan! And you won't leave the house or office, you just sit staring out that damned window like a soulless puppet!"

"A very good analogy of the way I feel, Papa." A light frown touched her brows, and she repeated softly, "A soulless puppet—yes, that's very much how I feel. Not only did I lose a husband, I lost a part of me."

Morgan came to her and clumsily pressed a kiss on her cold, pale cheek. "Whatever you need to do, I'll do what I can to help you," he said heavily. "Only"—his voice was tight with frustration—"only please tell me what I can do."

Whitney smiled. "If I knew that, I'd do it myself. But I'll be all right, Papa, really. It just takes time, I suppose."

Morgan tried to give her a reassuring smile as she turned away and wandered across her office floor to the window. It had begun to rain now, rivulets streaking the glass panes like tears, and he thought, angrily, that he was becoming just as morose as his daughter.

"Well," he said abruptly, his voice loud where the only noise was a faint ticking from the clock on the mantel and the hiss of coals in the grate, "I think I'll go over to the newsroom and see what's going on. Why don't you come with me? You may get an idea for another book." When she shook her head, Morgan persisted, "There isn't anything else to do on a day like this, and it would do you good to get out for a while."

"I like the quiet," Whitney said without turning around, and Morgan made a noise in the back of his throat that sounded like "Pah!" before shutting her office door. She almost smiled. She did like the quiet. It made much more sense for it to be quiet than it did for the world to go on so noisily around her.

Standing at the window, watching rain patter down outside and the streets grow wet, carriages rumbling past and pedestrians dashing for cover, it was difficult for Whitney to remember those days in Arizona beneath the hot, searing sun, where nothing moved for miles and miles except for the hawks soaring above.

And if she closed her eyes and let her mind drift, she could almost feel the heat, could almost smell the soft, sweet fragrance of moonflowers in the night, could almost hear Cutter's drawling voice. . . .

"Daydreaming, tiger-eyes? I thought you were going to wait for me."

Whitney froze, not daring to turn around. Her breath caught, and she thought for a moment she must have gone mad, must be hallucinating. Then she heard slight scuffling sounds, a frightened squeak, and the fall of footsteps, and she turned slowly.

Cutter stood outlined in the doorway, looking very much as if he had just stepped out of the pages of the catalog of a Manhattan haberdashery—until she saw the suspicious bulge of a pistol on his hip beneath the long blue coat. He wore a red vest, starched white shirt with a highpoint collar, and slim-legged trousers, and his hair was trimmed neatly.

Behind him, with eyes staring wildly and his Adam's apple bobbing like a turkey's neck, Whitney's secretary Augustus Frye, was making incoherent noises. Cutter slanted him an impatient glance, then slung his gaze back to Whitney.

"If this man works for you," he said, "fire him. He hasn't made an intelligible sound since I first walked in the door."

"It's the gun," Whitney said calmly, wondering if she was in another dream. "Most men in New York don't wear guns on their hips."

"Really? How dangerous." Cutter looked again at the little man at his elbow, and shook his head.

Then he crossed the room to Whitney, his stride as lazy and casual as she remembered it, the same reckless light in his green eyes, the same half-mocking smile curling his mouth. And she was suddenly—inexplicably—furious. He must have seen the glint of anger in her eye, for as he reached her, instead of being swept into his embrace, she found her arms pinned behind her back.

"How dare you let me think you were dead all these months!" she blazed, trying to squirm away from his viselike hold.

"You're not going to throw me over your shoulder again," he warned. "So forget it. Calm down, and I'll explain."

"Explain!" Tears stung her eyes, tears of anger, tears of joy, tears she didn't understand. "It's been six months! Six months since you were supposedly killed, and you just now happen to remember me?" She stamped her foot, barely missing one of his. "I've gone through hell, and now you waltz in here as if I just saw you yesterday— Cutter!"

Swinging her from her feet into his arms, Cutter pushed her down to the thick Aubusson carpet on the floor and slanted his body across her squirming curves. His face was only inches from hers, his eyes dancing with wicked green lights.

"Hold still, tiger-eyes."

"Cutter! You let me up this instant! Cutter! What do you think you're doing?"

"Cutter?" shrieked a voice from the doorway. Augustus Frye hopped about like a frenzied toad. "Did you say *Cutter*? The renegade? The . . . the gunman?"

"Get out," Cutter ordered calmly, his gaze narrowing on the secretary. "And close the door behind you."

Frye squealed with alarm, and it wasn't until he heard Whitney's voice, muffled but clear, say, "Get out, Frye. And close the door behind you," that he did so.

"He's afraid," said Whitney, her eyes fastening on Cutter's face as the worst of her anger eased, "that I might hurt you."

He laughed, and his grip tightened on her wrists as he dragged her arms up and over her head. "So am I," he said, bending his head to kiss her. "You're the fiercest tiger I know." His lips lingered on her mouth, teasing and seductive and promising, and Whitney gave a soft moan of satisfaction.

"I'm still angry at you, you know," she said between kisses, her head reeling, her heart lurching with joy that he was alive and there with her.

"We can talk about that later—what now?" Cutter ended with a snap, turning his head as the door to her office swung open again.

Morgan Bradford stood outlined in the doorway, his first rush of alarm fading quickly away. "Oh. It's you. Frye didn't make any sense. But he never does." Morgan scanned his daughter, lying under Cutter's lean frame, and his brow lifted. "I guess I'll get an explanation later."

"*Much* later, Papa," Whitney said, and Bradford grinned, then left.

Inside the elegant office overlooking the park, Whitney smiled against Cutter's hot lips, her head tilting back and her eyes closing as he peeled away her layers of clothing. She was flushed with heat, not from the fire in the grate, but with the flames of love and desire.

The blood surged through her veins in a sluggish rhapsody that made her feel languorous and fevered, and she felt the slap of passion carry her up in a graceful rise to meet Cutter's body. His hands on her were tormenting, his mouth moving urgently from her ear to her lips to linger as his body swept them both in a heated rush.

Whitney's hands smoothed over the flexing muscles of his shoulders and down to his slim hips, and she matched his pounding rhythm with a fierceness that made Cutter catch his breath. Her legs twined around him, holding him, enclosing him between the satiny thighs as if she'd never let him go, and she thought—hazily—that she wouldn't. Who knew when he might disappear again?

The abrasive rub of carpet beneath her was almost sensual, and the sweltering touch of his skin against her stomach, breasts, and thighs was a steamy enticement. With her arms hard around him, her body as close to him as a woman could get to a man, Whitney heard her voice, sounding drugged and lazy, whispering in his ear, "I love you, I love you. . . ."

And then, making her heart soar, she heard him say the words she'd thought she'd never hear, roughly muttering, "I think I've loved you since you demanded that I kiss you again, tiger-eyes." His kiss was long and deep, and her heart was roaring in her ears like ocean surf when he repeated, "I've always loved you. . . ."

Twenty

It was dark, and the rain was still spattering on the windowpanes, but they were in her bed now, the covers piled high and a low fire burning in the grate. Replete with satisfaction, Whitney curled into the hard angle of Cutter's stomach and thighs, letting her hand drift up the ridged surface of his chest.

"So," she murmured softly, "you were telling me how Daniel got you another pardon from Governor Fremont."

"Mmm," Cutter said, his drowsy lids barely lifting. "Oh, yeah, when West left with you, Daniel left for Prescott. He wired your father first, knowing it would take him a while to get there, then rode like a bat out of hell. He had to rout Fremont from bed, and he was rather grouchy and reluctant, I take it, to sign anything until he'd heard the full story from Daniel. Then he had to check and double-check, and you know how that takes time."

"What were you doing while West was questioning me?" She almost shuddered at the memory. It had been so horrible and frightening, and she still had nightmares about being helpless.

"I was on my way to meet Geronimo in Mexico. I will say this for West, he had a good idea when he hired Apache scouts. That's probably what it'll take to end this thing once and for all."

Silky curls of her hair tickled his jaw when she tilted back her head to look up at him in the rosy firelight. "What do you mean?" "Just that—it's going to take an Apache to catch an Apache. Geronimo's too wily, too used to the rocks and desert, where those fresh-faced soldiers aren't."

Cutter stretched lazily, reminding Whitney of a great cat, and settled an arm around her shoulders again, pulling her back into the curve. His gaze slid over her, pausing on her breasts before drifting back up to her face.

When Whitney said softly, "You came to give yourself up for me," he nodded, his eyes narrowing slightly.

"I wasn't too sure about West's motives. I knew how he felt about you . . . anyway, even after he found out what he wanted to know, he wasn't about to let me get away again." His mouth curled into a faintly mocking smile. "Someone should have told West that for an Apache escaping a staking out is as easy as it would be for West to play poker with marked cards."

Whitney's eyes grew wide and indignant. "He staked you out?"

"Not too well, unfortunately for him. Leather stretches when it gets wet, and I managed to work loose enough to be able to escape when Téjas got there with help."

"It was Téjas who helped you escape?" she said in surprise. "No one told me!"

"No one was supposed to know."

"So why—*why* didn't someone tell me you were still alive all this time? And why did West think you were dead?"

Cutter's hand moved to the gentle swell of her stomach and lay there. "One question at a time, tiger-eyes." He bent to press a kiss on her nose, then her brow, drawing back to say, "West thought I was dead because I did get wounded, and several soldiers saw me fall. I got loose, but I didn't quite make it out of there without catching a bullet."

Her fingers sought and lingered on the puckered scar on his right shoulder, then her lips touched it lightly. In a shaky voice, she said, "You lead quite a dangerous life!"

"Much more dangerous since I met you," he said, laughter edging his words.

She gave an ironic snort but persisted. "You haven't answered my main question—why did no one tell me you were still alive? Cutter, I wanted to die . . . I've never been so miserable . . . *why*?"

He held her close, his chin grazing the top of her head as he said, "You break too easy, tiger-eyes. All they'd have had to do is threaten someone you care about, and you would have told them anything they wanted to know." His voice was husky when he added, "You can endure anything if it's you, but if I'd been captured again, you would have crumbled like wet cake."

Painfully, Whitney said in a choking whisper, "I never meant to hurt Red Shirt and the others. . . ."

"Hush." He squeezed her tightly. "I know. It wasn't your fault. Fortunes of war. Somebody always gets caught in the middle, and it's usually the innocent." There was a brief silence, then he said, "I'm going back, you know."

There. It was out. What she'd been dreading to hear since he'd sauntered into her office—she tilted back her head again, and her gilt eyes were wet. "When?"

"Soon. I just came to get you."

For an instant the world reeled, then righted itself. "Get me?" she repeated slowly, hardly able to believe what he was saying. "But . . . but what if I crumble again?"

"It won't be the same." He sighed heavily. "Look, I tried to make things better by reasoning with Geronimo, but he's too full of hate and won't listen. So I had to make a decision. My motives were to help all the people, not just one stubborn chief, so . . . so, I joined the army."

Whitney bolted upright, her eyes wide with disbelief. *"What?"* A tremor racked her. "After what they did to Red Shirt, and . . . you joined the army?"

"As a scout." His green eyes were amused, and then, as his gaze dropped from her startled face lower, they began to gleam with another emotion. "It's really," he said, his lips moving to graze her half-open mouth, "the best solution. Geronimo can't"—his mouth found the velvet skin beneath her ear, then drifted downward—"keep running forever, and if the Apache people are going to survive as a nation . . ." Nuzzling between her breasts, his voice was muffled. ". . . surrender is inevitable."

"S-s-surrender?" she echoed shakily, shuddering as his mouth found and teased the peak of her breast.

"Mmm-hmm. You know, to relinquish possession or control of to another because of demand or compulsion . . . at least, that was the definition the last time I heard it." His lips returned to nurture hers in a lingering kiss, until she forgot the thread of the conversation, forgot everything but Cutter.

Outside the brownstone apartment in Manhattan, it was rainy and windy, but inside, it was as hot as the Arizona desert. Whitney had the thought—her last coherent one for some time—that she had never dreamed surrender could be so sweet.

Coming next month . . .

THE MATCHMAKER
by Kay Hooper

Kay Hooper is indisputably one of the top romance writers today. Known for her wit and cleverness, Kay is beloved by readers and critics alike. For months, Kay Hooper's fans have been following her Once Upon a Time Series with great delight, propelling this series within a series to the top of romance best seller lists. THE MATCH-MAKER is the story everyone has been waiting for! Cyrus Fortune, the mysterious figure who has guided the destinies of many lovers, gets his own unforgettable love story in this novel of sheer magic set at the turn of the century. Cyrus, who has always been something of a womanizer, has fallen passionately in love with Julia Drummond. Julia is unhappily married—but promises never to break her vows. In the following excerpt Cyrus trails Julia to the library.

"Hello."

Julia stiffened, recognizing the voice even though she'd never heard it, because it matched the nakedly sensual warmth of his black eyes. Slowly, she turned her head, recapturing her aloof mask with the ease of long and constant practice. She watched him stroll across the room, the size and lazy grace of him making her feel a panicky, threatened sensation. He sat down in the chair on the other side of the table and looked at her with that bold stare, and she felt suddenly exposed. Vulnerable.

With all the coldness she could muster, she said, "I don't believe we've been introduced."

His well-shaped mouth curved in a smile. "No, but then, we know who we are, don't we? I'm Cyrus Fortune, and you're Julia Drummond." The words were terse to the point of rudeness, his manner was definitely arrogant—but the voice was elegant black velvet.

Julia began to understand Anne's warning about the need for a chastity belt. She would have sworn she was the last woman in Richmond who could have felt any temptation to break her marriage vows, but that voice affected her like nothing ever had. In her mind was a strangely vivid image of the way a cat arched its back when it was stroked, in an instinctive ripple of unthinking pleasure, and she wondered dimly if the sound of her racing heart was anything like a purr.

"I've been watching you tonight," he said. "But you know that. Do you know I've been watching you for days?"

That was a shock, but one she endured silently. She had to stop this before . . . before it was too late. Her own thoughts were scattered, panicked, and she didn't know why or how he could affect her like this. She drew a deep breath; it felt as if she hadn't breathed at all until then. "Mr. Fortune—"

"Cyrus." It was less a request than a command.

Julia ignored it. "Mr. Fortune, I'm a married woman—"

"Drummond must have robbed the cradle to get you," Fortune said abruptly, cutting her off without civility. "Somebody said you'd been married for two years, but you can't be a day over eighteen."

Oddly enough, Julia knew she couldn't accuse him of trying to flatter her; she had a strong conviction that Fortune was too blunt a man to waste time with insincere compliments—even to get a woman into his bed. He wouldn't need to resort to such tricks, she admitted to herself silently, and was appalled at the realization.

Holding her voice even, she said, "I'm twenty-one, Mr. Fortune. And I am *very* married."

His mouth quirked again in that mocking smile. "Not tempted to stray? Drummond can't be such a good lover; the man's heavy-handed with his horses."

The sheer effrontery of that remark made Julia gasp. Her own nature was toward frankness—or it had been, before her marriage—and she was hardly a prude, but for any man to speak to a woman in such a way went beyond the bounds of good taste *and* decency. But before she could gather her wits, he was going on, and if she'd thought he had gone as far as possible already, she was in for another shock.

"Drummond isn't making you happy and we both know it, Julia. You're frozen inside; I can see it. You were never meant to be that way. Red hair is a badge of passion, and yours is like fire. I've never seen hair so red or eyes so wildly green. Or such an erotic mouth, like a lush flower. You have a magnificent body, a body made for pleasure. Even those dull colors and fabrics you wear can't hide your wonderful form. And you move with such grace, as if you hear music."

"Don't—" she got out in a strangled gasp, but he went on in his black velvet voice that made even the reprehensible words a sensual caress.

"Drummond wouldn't know what to do with a woman like you. I'm sure of it. He can't appreciate the fire in you. He probably takes you in the dark with your nightgown pulled up and thinks of nothing but his own pleasure. Does he apologize when he turns to you with his carnal appetites, Julia? Does he make it a hurried, shameful act instead of something joyful?" Fortune uttered a low laugh that was derisive. "Gentlemen like Drummond believe there are only two kinds of women: ladies and whores—and only whores enjoy bedding men. So the gentlemen marry ladies and fumble in the dark to breed. Is that all you want? To be a brood mare and never feel the hot pleasure of real passion?"

He laughed again, his eyes blacker than anything she'd ever seen and filled with a heat that burned her. "I'm no gentleman, Julia. I don't want a lady or a whore in my bed—just a woman. A beautiful woman. I won't apologize for wanting her and I'll look at her naked in the light because God meant for a woman to be seen by a man. And touched by a man."

She wasn't conscious of moving until she was halfway across the room, her heart thudding, the smothering sensation of panic overwhelming her. She didn't go to the door that led back to the ballroom but another one, and she had no idea where it would take her. It didn't matter. Anywhere. Anywhere as long as she could escape him.

"Julia."

That voice. It tugged at her—and the realization she could scarcely resist terrified her. Her hand on the door handle, she half turned to stare at him. He had risen to his feet, but didn't move toward her. He was smiling almost gently.

"I want you. I want you in my bed."

"No." It didn't come from morals or consciousness of her marriage vows, or anything else of which society would have approved. It didn't come from a lack of attraction, shocking though that was to her; she felt the attraction, the strange, irresistible pulling at all her senses. The denial came from deep inside her, without thought, spurred by instinct.

"I can make you happy," he said.

"You can destroy me," she heard herself whisper.